SPECTRA

EBONY OLSON

EBANDMUSE
PUBLICATIONS

Published 2020

Published by

EbandMuse Publications

Sydney, Australia

http://ebonyolson.com/

Hierarch Series
(Radish Fiction Exclusive)

Succumb

Numinous

Masked (Coming 2020)

Exodus (Coming 2020/21)

Raven's Wing Trilogy
(Radish Fiction Exclusive)

Phased

Standalones

Of Shadow and Light

Boundary

Halos (Coming 2020)

Silver Rogue (Coming 2020)

To Gracie and Kate for listening, reading, and supporting my passion.

To my very patient husband who not only endures my staying up all night to write, but encourages me to keep going when I doubt.

To the Pxy, without whom I would never have started writing.

To all my readers who made publishing Spectra a possibility.

Thank you.

CHAPTER 1

Spectra

STEPPING down the stairs was effortless. The boots I wore were more practical than fashionable. That was the appeal of the Goth club. Wearing practical clothing, I still fit in as long as it was black. With naturally pale skin and long black hair, by adding a black dress, black tights, boots, and a military jacket, I automatically appeared Goth. Add black eye makeup that made my pale blue eyes pop, and I was right to go.

When I reached the basement level of the club, I moved through the crowd and slid into an empty space at the bar.

"Evening, Spectra, the usual?" Tommy, the British bartender and owner of the club, acknowledged my arrival. He didn't smile; I don't think I'd ever seen him smile in the years I'd been frequenting this bar. He was your typical punk

Goth, hair that should have been blond dyed shock black, makeup, and piercings to go with it.

Compared to the other club patrons, I was definitely the most conservative. My ears were pierced, I bore a couple of tattoos - nothing big and flashy, and I steered away from the studded cuffs that adorned several necks and wrists throughout the crowd.

I nodded at Tommy and pulled my purse out to pay. Tommy put the still-sealed bottle of water on the bar and waited while I cracked the seal myself and handed him the lid. It was an understanding between the staff that served me that I needed to open my own drinks, and if my drink ever left my sight, even just for a second, it was trash.

I handed Tommy cash to pay, and he shook his head, "I'll put it on your client's tab like usual when you're working."

I frowned, wondering if I'd missed an email from a client. "I'm not working tonight."

Tommy raised a heavily pierced brow, and I wondered how much more attractive he'd be without the steel. "Well, the guy asked for you specifically. He's been waiting an hour."

Tommy's eyes drifted down the bar to an attractive man in a suit. He stood out like a sore thumb for more than just the outfit. He was obviously uncomfortable in his surroundings, but was making the most of it and enjoying what looked to be a scotch. He was watching Tommy and I talk, his eyes casual. Despite the noise in the club, I held no delusion he hadn't heard my name when I arrived and had been listening to the exchange.

My eyes grew angry as I looked down at my water. I shook my head and handed Tommy the money. "Not my client. I don't work with his kind."

Tommy nodded understandingly and took the money as he

moved to serve someone else. I picked up my water and drank most of it down in one hit, intending to leave straight away. I didn't like a stranger asking for me by name. Usually, if a client recommended my services to someone new, they would arrange the meeting with me via email. Not since the early days had anybody simply turned up at a club I frequented and asked for me.

Tommy approached as I finished the bottle. "Thanks, Tommy, I'm out of here."

"Spectra, he wants to meet you." Tommy slid a business card across the bar to me and continued on.

I picked up the card. It was blank except for a phone number. I flipped it over and lifted my brows. In beautiful cursive writing, it said *I'll pay whatever price.* I flipped the card again and looked at the number, still not looking down the bar to the suit.

I sighed. I looked to Tommy and gave a small nod before turning as if leaving for the door. Cutting through the writhing bodies on the dance floor, I made a sharp turn towards the back corner of the club where the crowd was minimal.

When I got to what Tommy had affectionately nicknamed as my office, I put my back to the wall and waited. The suit emerged from the crowd a few meters away, though he was tall enough that I'd been able to track his naturally dark hair through the crowd. He was pale enough that if he ditched the suit and slipped into some black jeans and a heavy metal shirt, he could have blended right in. He looked to be in his late twenties, early thirties at the most, but that meant nothing when it came to his kind.

"Thank you for agreeing to meet me," his accent was aged, Welsh. "I'm sorry I wasn't aware there was a standard protocol to engaging your services. I've heard you're the best."

"You should have also heard I don't work for your kind."

"I did, but I need someone good, and quick, and you come highly recommended."

"By who?" I lifted a brow, wondering who was whispering my name in the wrong circles.

His ice blue eyes focused in on me a moment, weighing his response options. "I'll pay whatever price you ask."

"Your firstborn." I didn't smile with the sarcasm.

"Died centuries ago." His face stayed emotionally blank.

"Then I guess you're out of luck." I held his business card out in front and ripped it in half before dropping it on the floor. "Forget my name, forget we met, and whoever is using my name in your circles needs their neck broken. I don't work for predators."

I took two steps towards the crowded dance floor. He grabbed my arm firmly but not aggressively. I met his eyes and noticed the strain around the edges. "Miss..." he looked puzzled for a second.

"Michaels," I answered for him. "Spectra Michaels. And you are?"

"Mr. Bay Ryder. I need a full set of documents in two days."

I closed my eyes in annoyance. "Damn it!"

I took the two steps back to the wall, grabbing Mr. Ryder by his expensive-looking suit jacket and pulling him hard against the front of me. He was surprised, but his eyes nearly left his head when I started pulling his shirt out of his waistband. He opened his mouth to object, and I gave him my best death stare.

"Shut it. You come here asking for me by name, with no formal introduction, and then proceed to state your business openly, even after I politely turned you down. You're not a cop, so I'd say you're NSIO." The Nachtwelt Security and Intelligence Office is the law in the Nachtwelt. It keeps the supernatural hidden from humans. Forging identification documents definitely impinged on human Federal law, but for obvious reasons, was a service the Nachtwelt utilized regularly. However, helping citizens of the Nachtwelt change their identity and disappear entirely may just infringe on Nachtwelt law enough to get me in trouble. I had no intention of being busted by them.

I slid my hands in against his bare abdomen, caressing up with splayed hands to his upper torso, before circling around and searching his back. As I brought my arms back to the front, I started unbuckling his belt. Mr. Ryder grasped my wrists, his eyes fierce on me. While the search of his upper body seemed to bore him, this more invasive search angered him.

"I don't believe this is the place for a strip search, Miss Michaels."

I smiled. "See that girl over there." I tilted my head and watched as he turned to look. He found the man with his back to the room, his hips moving back and forth. I saw his pupils dilating when he realized there was a girl kneeling in front of the man, her face hidden by his body. "I don't think she's searching for a wire, so trust me, no one is going to think for a second what we're about."

I unzipped his fly as his angry eyes met mine. I maintained eye contact as I slipped my hand in smoothing down to the base of his flaccid member, circling around, feeling around his sacs, and down his inner thighs. I was impressed when the most he reacted was a slight pulse against my forearm. I slipped my hands around to check for anything at the back. When I was sure he was clean of any listening device, I withdrew my hands from his pants. He stepped back a small step to right his clothing. I took out the small bottle of hand sanitizer I kept in my bag and cleaned my hands till I could access the bathroom.

"You look disappointed I didn't get hard for you." Even his voice was tight.

"Relieved actually," I responded honestly. "Admittedly though, you are the first of your kind who I've let get this close to me. So, I'm not sure if that's just a physiological thing for you, that you prefer men, or that you're so old you need pharmaceutical intervention."

"If you are satisfied that I'm not setting you up?" He stepped closer, and this time his height made him very imposing as he pressed his hands to the wall on either side of my head and put his mouth to my ear. I only came up to his shoulder, so it forced him to move his lower body away from me. "I require a full set of documents that could pass the most rigorous scrutiny within two days. You will take me on as a client and once you provide what I'm after, I will happily forget your name and where to find you. The only option you have in completing this service, now that we are so intimately acquainted, is how much you are going to charge."

Wow! I'd really pissed him off doing the wire search. I met his eyes with the same fierceness and pulled my own business card out of my bag. It was a black card with just an email address on it in silver print. On the flip side, I quickly wrote a figure using a silver pen. It was a ridiculous amount to ask for. Nearly four times my usual fee for a rush job. I added the name of a church and tomorrow morning's Mass time.

"I need passport photos and clear copies of your current documentation. If you are going to change any details other than age, I need that listed as well. Mass is at six in the morning. I'm gathering holy ground isn't an issue for you?" Because I'd run across enough of his kind in daylight to know sunlight wasn't. He shook his head, his face back to a mask of emotion-free patience as he took the card. "Good. I expect a quarter of the fee as a deposit, the rest upon delivery of the goods. I'll give you a pickup point tomorrow."

"Here is my most recent birth certificate." He pulled out two folded pieces of paper, one that looked old. "I just need the birth year to change, and my parents' names. The rest I will get to you tomorrow. I will email you the address of a party I am attending on Sunday night. That is where you will deliver it to me." His voice was matter-of-fact.

I shook my head, taking the folded papers and putting them in my pocket. "I'm not going near any party of yours."

Mr. Ryder slipped my business card into his pocket, bored already. "The party is not mine; I'm merely a guest. The majority of attendees will be your kind, Miss Michaels; you will be perfectly safe. I will see you at church tomorrow."

He turned on his heel and walked towards the exit, the crowd of bodies parting easily as if repelled by him as he moved through. I swallowed hard. Never in the past five years was I ever out of control of a situation as I was just then. I avoided predators of any kind. I could have been very rich very fast if I took their business, but I'd kept well away. I didn't like that my name was even mentioned in their circles, and I especially didn't like how easily Mr. Bay Ryder just took away the one thing I worked very hard to keep.

I blew out a breath in frustration and made for the exit. If I was going to deliver a full set of forged documents in two days, I was going to need to start tonight.

Bay

I waited in the dark outside the club for her to leave. There was something about her that made me more curious than I'd been in centuries, starting with the way she looked at me. I didn't have to wait long. She made her way out of the club and immediately crossed the road, dodging traffic. I waited for her to be quite a distance away before I stepped out of the darkness and into her drift. A person's drift was like a smoky trail of their aura.

Hers was fainter than most other humans, making me even more curious as I casually followed the fading color channel of her aura. Most humans ignored the predators amongst them, but even those who were aware didn't know that they could be hunted by more than scent, and Miss Michaels was obviously very aware of what lurked amongst her own kind.

When I'd started looking for a master forger, her name came with a warning. Apparently, predators who tried to deal with this master forger had a tendency to disappear altogether. There was only a couple, and no one could say for certain they approached the forger or that she was involved in any way. Her name just came automatically with that warning.

With the whispered warning that came with her name, I'd expected something different when I finally found her, and it took quite an effort to track this human to one location. Lots of effort and a lot of bribes to people who wouldn't normally deal with my kind. She was beautiful, not in the model way, but in that old world natural beauty that let you know she put no effort into her appearance, and in fact tried to detract from it. So when the bartender called her name, I'd looked past her and at the woman nearly twice her age. It took a moment to realize the young girl, who barely looked old enough to vote, was my forger.

Her age was the first thing to surprise me. That she recognized me immediately for what I was, floored me. But when she watched me approach her, and touched me, without an ounce of attraction, her fingers sparking electricity under my skin, I was speechless. I couldn't remember the last time I'd been surprised by anyone, but it was all nothing compared to the moment she made my cock twitch. Two hundred years since I grew tired of women for anything except sustenance, and this young human caused me to react.

I followed her drift through the many twists and turns of the city streets. It took me fifteen minutes to notice I'd completed a full loop of the city area the club was based in. I realized she'd taken evasive maneuvers to ensure she wasn't followed. To cover her tracks, Spectra walked past fast food outlets and the backs of clubs where the stench of beer hung in the air to cover her scent. She turned enough close corners that anyone following by sight would quickly lose her.

Her aura led me to the government business area of town before it disappeared into the back door of a building. The aura was quite faint as I approached the building, as if it was already hours old instead of minutes. In fact, the aura was faint enough that had I been a younger predator, I would have lost her trail several blocks ago. I took note of the "Employees Only" sign on the door and the number pad entry before making my way around the block to find the front of the building.

I stood across the road from the births registry office and felt the strange sensation of smiling for what must have been the first time in decades. I made my way down the side street and located a dark niche to hide myself in, which allowed me to see the back of the building, but also if anyone walked down the main street. An hour later, a well-dressed woman walked out of the building next door with a man. They kissed, and he hopped into his car to drive away while she walked quickly in my direction. As she passed by my hiding spot, I moved quickly to pull her into the darkness, hand covering her mouth before my mouth found the pulse in her neck.

Her neck was heavily perfumed in a horrible floral concoction and the man's scent. Her blood, however, was full of endorphins and feel-good hormones produced from recent sexual satisfaction. I closed my eyes as I took enough to sate my thirst and enjoyed the taste of pleasure. I released her gently and set her aside so she could sleep off her blood loss. When she woke, she would wonder why she had collapsed here, but nothing would remind her of me. The bite on her neck would appear merely as a bruise and would be mistaken as the work of her lover.

Three hours later, I started to think I had missed Miss Michaels leaving while I was distracted by dinner. Then I noticed her faint drift leading away down the street even though I'd never seen her physically leave the building. I checked on the woman who was sleeping off my feed at my feet and stepped out to follow the forger.

The aura became stronger again a few blocks later. Another few turns bought her raven hair and fit body back into view. She stood at a late-night food vendor making a purchase with a few teenagers as she chatted with them. I watched her pay for the food and distribute it to her companions before waving goodbye and continuing on.

I was starting to think Miss Michaels was a night owl when she finally entered a swanky apartment building. This building I knew all too well, and if Miss Michaels were visiting one particular occupant, I would not be happy.

The building next door was too quiet to be a nightclub but possessed enough foot traffic at this time of night to tell me it was a business dedicated to pleasure. Another predator like myself made their way up the street and into the business, sparing a look in my direction as they entered. It was annoying that predators of the same age could sense each other nearby.

I heard a familiar male voice as a door to a balcony slid open on the third floor of the apartment building and Miss Michaels stepped out with a male in his mid-twenties. I felt my anger ignite at his proximity to this girl. For his age, Alexander Williams made a very quick name for himself among the Nachtwelt as someone not to be messed with. That Miss Michaels knew such a powerful sorcerer well enough to come to him at this early hour told me she was a lot more deeply embedded in the Nachtwelt than I'd expected.

Alexander's brown hair was disheveled, as if he'd been asleep when she arrived, and his athletic upper body was bare, with just dark jeans pulled on. He lit up a cigarette and leaned back on the railing, watching Miss Michaels with interest.

"I don't know what you think I can do. You get good at what you do, of course, the unsavory clients are going to come knocking. You should just take the money. You'd be raking it in if you dealt with both sides of the coin."

"I don't want or need their money, and I want to make sure tonight doesn't happen again." Spectra's voice sounded annoyed.

Alexander shrugged. "So handle him. You've handled other predators before."

Spectra shook her head. "This one is too old, and I really pissed him off when I searched him for a wire."

I felt my hands clench at the memory of her hands on me. Not because I'd hated it. It was, in fact, the opposite, which was the problem. For centuries, every woman looked at me with lust, and I couldn't stand them anymore. But this one, she looked at me with loathing, but her touch was full of curiosity and wonder, which fascinated me.

"You did what?" Alexander coughed, choking on his cigarette. "You not only let one get close enough to touch, you actually searched him? You thought he was a cop?"

Spectra shrugged and leaned against the wall opposite. "He pissed me off. I was really looking forward to just chilling out tonight."

Alexander stood straight, putting his cigarette out. "How did the exams go?"

"All done. Graduation ahoy. Now I can get a legitimate job and earn an honest living."

I frowned at the sadness in her voice. Alexander stepped towards her and bent his face to hers, capturing her mouth in a slow, careful kiss. I felt the ball of anger that was building within slam into my chest as it tried to escape. I knew that my outward appearance was still and calm, but inside, as his mouth caressed hers in the most tender of kisses, I wanted to grab the next person to walk near me and rip them limb from limb.

Spectra put her hand on Alexander's chest and gave a gentle nudge. Alexander pulled back to look down at her. "Stay with me tonight. I'll celebrate your graduation with you."

Spectra smiled shyly. "If I stayed, I'd miss morning Mass,

and I have an angry client to meet." She stepped towards the door. "I should get some sleep."

Alexander dropped his head in disappointment but didn't try to convince her to stay. "What's the name of your predator? Maybe I can find out more about him."

"Bay Ryder," Spectra replied easily.

Alexander's shoulders squared, and his body went rigid at the mention of my name, and I understood that reaction. Spectra didn't miss it either. She waited patiently for Alexander to explain his reaction. Alexander lit another cigarette. "Stay the night."

"I just explained..."

"I'll come with you to the meeting in the morning, make sure he doesn't try anything."

"He won't. I don't think he's into women."

Alexander laughed. "He's not into anything and hasn't been for centuries. But he is a predator, Spectra, and I don't want him near you."

"Why would he be in such a rush for this stuff?" Spectra folded her arms across her body, still halfway inside the balcony door.

Alexander took a long drag before he spoke. "He runs a business that has been awarded a government contract. They are due to sign this week, and he'll need to prove who he is for the deal to go through. Stay with me."

Spectra gave Alexander a sad smile. "If you were still that guy I knew in high school, the answer would be yes. But you're the popular guy now that all the girls want, and I'm the quiet nerd without a chance at more than being a drunken party hookup."

Alexander caressed a hand down her cheek. "You were the

popular girl in high school, and you dated the most popular boy, but you always gave me the time of day, Spec. Everything changed out in the real world, but even flipped around, I will always give you the time of day. You will never be a drunken party hookup."

He kissed her again and this time the kiss was more insistent, but Spectra ended it quickly. She stepped back, and I saw she was crying.

"Dating the popular boy got me killed, remember? I'd rather not repeat that experience." She turned and moved back into the darkened apartment.

Alexander took a deep breath, pulled out another cigarette, and lit it before turning to look down at the front door of his building. I stayed still amongst the shadows. Miss Michaels emerged from the building and made her way down the street. Alexander watched her till she rounded the corner a block away then stubbed out his cigarette. I'd met Alexander on several occasions and never once seen him smoke, and several times we'd been in each other's company for hours. His behavior around Miss Michaels suggested he was a chain smoker, but I'd never caught even a whiff of smoke around him.

Alexander stood to his full height, and his power swirled his aura around him like a kaleidoscope in a tornado. I smiled again as understanding dawned on me. The cigarettes were guilt. Her presence caused him pain for some reason. Alexander's head tilted, and his eyes turned angry as they fell upon the place I waited. I knew the moment he'd recognized my presence.

I stepped out of the shadows and gave a small nod before following Miss Michaels's drift. I saw the anger set into

Alexander Williams's features and suddenly understood what would make such a powerful young man feel guilty. Love. Alexander Williams loved Spectra Michaels so much it hurt.

My phone rang a few minutes later. I answered, already knowing who it was. "Mr. Williams, I trust you are enjoying this beautiful evening."

"Leave her alone, Ryder."

"She spiked my curiosity; that's all. I just like to know who I am doing business with. My interest goes no further." I continued following the trail of her aura.

"She's been through enough, Ryder. We are not friends, but she doesn't deserve to be brought into this."

I paused to assess his words. "A lesser man would exploit a weakness like Miss Michaels in his adversary. I have no such intentions. I learned a very long time ago that love will make a man stronger, not weaker."

Alexander didn't deny his feelings, which impressed me further. "Thank you."

"Mr. Williams, if I may offer some advice?" When Alexander stayed quiet, I took that as approval. "You do yourself no favors hiding who you really are from her. If she is to love you, she should love you for who you are."

Alexander chuckled. "Only someone who has never truly been in love would think it is that easy."

I rounded the corner in time to watch Miss Michaels walk into church grounds and cross the gardens to the convent. "She lives in a convent?"

Alexander audibly swallowed. "As I said, she's been through enough."

The phone disconnected, and I slipped my mobile into my pocket, curiosity taking seed as I thought through all the reasons a young civilian girl might live in a convent. Her interaction with Alexander suggested they were lovers at some point in the past, if not on occasion now, so she didn't intend to take vows. I watched for a light to switch on, telling me where I could find her should I want to, before I turned and went in search of supper.

CHAPTER 2

Spectra

THE CHURCH WAS NEVER full for the early service. Only the devout attended. So when Bay Ryder walked in, enough people took note of the new face. He stayed in the back pew during the service; I was with the sisters from the convent, and he didn't dare approach. After I had taken communion, I continued down the aisle past my usual pew and slipped into the bench beside him. The others paid no heed. I'd met clients here enough in the past years that it didn't surprise anyone anymore.

Not that they knew what I did for a living, but Mother Superior commented a few years back that a new face at Saturday morning mass was usually a result of murder or my side business. She just hoped the two were not connected. It was a joke on her part. Mother Superior was one of my first clients years ago when she needed false documents for an abused woman and her children needing to escape her husband. That job opened the door for my side business in helping victims and survivors escape their pasts.

As I sat back from praying after taking the sacrament, Ryder slipped his hand in his pocket and began to withdraw an envelope. Shaking my head as Father Mathew started the final prayer, Mr. Ryder left it alone, standing beside me to sing the last hymn with gusto in a perfectly pitched tenor. As Father Mathew came alongside, he gave my client a stern look before taking my hand, stealthily slipping a piece of paper into it before continuing outside the church.

The rest of the congregation followed after him except for those who knelt and continued their prayers. Opening the slip of paper, I read the request before pocketing it and turning to face my client. Ryder raised a brow at me, having seen the priest's communication.

"Even the Rectory employ your services, Miss Michaels?" Bay sat back down, slightly slanted to face me while I stayed standing.

"Everyone has their needs, Mr. Ryder, and sometimes those needs can only be met at a cost."

Slipping past where he was sitting, I headed for the side door out of the church. Outside, the sun was already up and promising to be a beautiful autumn day. Walking to Mary's Grotto, I took the seat a few meters back from where I usually kneel to pray. Ryder followed casually, taking in the gardens before sitting next to me.

"It's quite beautiful and peaceful here. I never knew a place like this existed in the city. I should feel privileged that you would bring me here." His eyes glanced over me. "I much prefer that dress on you than last night's casual attire."

The flowing black velvet maxi dress with long lace sleeves, cinching under the bust, was a favorite of Alexander's too. "Mr. Ryder..."

"Call me Bay."

"I'd rather not be on a first name basis with you."

"You've fondled my genitals, Miss Michaels."

"I'd prefer we not use the word fondled either."

"Would you prefer caressed?"

"Definitely, not!"

"Then, since you have fondled my genitals, I believe you can call me by my Christian name, and I shall call you Spectra."

"As long as by midnight tomorrow you stop calling me at all, I can live with that. Shall we do business?"

Giving me a quick nod, Bay handed me the envelope from his pocket. "My license, passport, recent passport photos, and fifteen thousand dollars cash. The agreed deposit for your services. I would suggest not depositing it all in one hit with the way governments monitor cash withdrawals and deposits these days."

"Thanks for the advice." Reaching into my sleeve, I withdrew a piece of paper rolled around my arm under the sleeve and handed it to him. "Your birth certificate stamped and authenticated." Standing up, I took a step away. "While I can get a license fairly easy, passports are difficult to forge these days. I'll do my best to make it back for your deadline. If I'm running late for the drop, I'll call and reschedule the meet before sunrise."

Bay stood. "You got my email with the location and time?"

"Yes. Do you have other plans that may cause an issue if I run late?"

"Just dinner." Swallowing hard, I closed my eyes on the

mental image. Bay's voice dropped an octave, "I do not kill my food like humans do, Spectra. I am old and have a lot more self-control than younger predators."

"And yet I feel no more comfortable in your presence than I did two minutes ago." Turning on my heel, I headed towards the convent to grab my bags and take the morning train to our country's capital.

WITH ALL THE SECURITY PROCEDURES IN PLACE THESE DAYS, IT was near impossible to forge a passport in our country. So, I didn't. Three hours of train travel and two different bus rides later, I was sitting in an office cubicle of the passport office creating Bay Ryder's tamper-proof passport based on his most recent birth certificate. Honestly, I thought it would take me longer to access their files, but one of the staff responsible for issuing new ones went off on a long lunch break without logging out of their computer.

The system still prompted for her password during the steps in the process, but I'd already watched her process two passports before she left, so I was good to go. After I finished processing the passport, I just needed to wait for it to generate and authentication. The bonus of doing this on a Saturday was that the place ran on skeleton staff who tended to take long lunches. The downside was that generating and authenticating took longer. By the time I held Bay's passport in my hand, I'd missed the train home.

Booking a cheap hotel, I opened my laptop to check my emails. My business account only held one new entry, a request from a longstanding client at a woman's refuge. It wasn't an urgent request, so I flagged it to follow up next week and closed the browser. Setting the laptop aside, I lay back, closing my eyes.

The dream floated in like always. Snippets of scenes like a mangled videotape. My vision was foggy, I felt sick, and Jeff, my high school boyfriend's smile, swam through that fog.

❧

Come on; it'll be fun.

I don't want to. I don't feel well. I want to go home.

Just chill, babe. I really want to try it. His hands were pulling my knickers off as I lay face down on his college room bed. *Everyone's doing it.*

I'm not everyone. I really feel sick, Jeff. I think I need a doctor.

You'll be fine.

Did you give me something? My eyes were struggling to focus on the can of Coke on his bedside table.

Chill, babe, I just wanted you to relax. I've wanted to try this for so long.

I don't remember going into cardiac arrest from the allergic reaction. Just gasping with a shock, my lungs burning, body freezing cold, everything hurting, and then Alexander's face, tears streaking his cheeks.

I thought I was too late. I'm sorry, Spec; I couldn't lose you.

❧

Returning to the waking world, my eyes opening slowly in the gloom of the room, I turned my head and looked at the window. It was light outside. Groaning, I sat up and looked at the clock beside the bed. Swearing a string of profanities, I quickly gathered my stuff together and bolted for the door.

Another four hours and a rushed taxi ride later, I disembarked the train to find Alexander standing on the platform.

"You look like you just crawled out of your grave, Spec." His face was serious.

"Thanks for coming. This place crawls with predators after dark."

Yawning, I let Alexander pull me in close to his body as we left Central Station for the walk to his apartment just ten minutes away. We continued walking with his arm around me till we entered his building, then I let him lead the way up the stairs to his apartment.

"I'm still down the license. I'll have to get it on the way to the meet."

Checking the watch on his wrist, Alexander opened his door. "You'll be hard pressed to make the meet then."

"I have a contingency set up if I miss it." Walking into his bathroom, I freshened up, since I was still wearing my clothes from yesterday.

"Take the time to shower, and I'll leave you a dress on the bed." Alexander's dark eyes were alight with mischief. "Pity we are both pressed for time, or I'd join you in the shower."

Rolling my eyes, I headed for the bathroom. I didn't question Alexander having clothes ready for me. He probably arranged them the minute I called from the train station and told him the time I'd be getting in.

"I have to get going, Spec. You right to let yourself out?"

"Of course, have a good night."

The click of the front door closing and locking sounded as I stepped into the shower and washed away two days' worth of travel grime. In the bedroom, a short-sleeved black cocktail dress, stockings, underwear, heels, and an ankle-length jacket all in my size were waiting for me. I wouldn't spend this sort of money on myself, and Alexander knew it. He knew my sizes because he'd bought me clothes when I first went off the radar. He took care of me. Hiding me out in a hotel room while I learned to deal with what happened to me.

Getting dressed, I slipped Bay's passport into the pocket of the elegant but practical jacket, along with my smartphone in its wallet case, which I only used for checking emails and emergency calls. Cursing Alexander's choice of shoes halfway to the licensing office, I continued regardless. As I approached the building, I breathed out entirely and slipped through the employees' only entry.

Licenses were an easy ten minutes. Calling up Ryder's last license, I changed the date of birth and reprinted it. While I was waiting, I updated his details to reflect the most up-to-date birth certificate information. Alexander was right, except for passports, I could make easy money working for the Nachtwelt, but my morals cringed at the very idea. Committing federal felonies to help abused women and children escape their tormentors didn't give me the 'burn in hell for all eternity' feel that assisting predators did.

With the license safely tucked into the passport protector pouch, I walked the twenty minutes to the meet.

The rooftop party was in full swing when I exited the elevator. My name was at the door like Bay promised. Slipping out of my jacket at the coat check, I kept his passport wallet in hand and made my way into the thick of the party. People were dancing to jazz music while others socialized by the bar. The area by the pool was relatively quiet, so I made my way there and waited for Bay to find me. I checked my watch; the window for the meet closed in five minutes.

Closing my eyes, I reopened them and focused on recognizing predators. When I first learned to do this, it would instantly alert all of them to my presence, but with Alexander's training, I'd learned to do it without most of them even knowing. There were several predators here, a handful of them Bay's kind, which was precisely the reason I avoided the modern nightclubs. The crowd parted as Bay approached me from the bar direction, his lips pulling slightly up in a smile. His expensive suit fit in a lot better at this party.

"I was starting to think you wouldn't make it." When he held out his hand, I placed the passport wallet in it. His eyebrows lifted as if that's not what he expected, but he opened the fold, checked the license and passport, then pocketed them before once again putting his hand out to me.

Raising a brow, I kept my hands to myself. "I believe this is where you hand me my payment, and we bid each other farewell, Bay."

Bay nodded but moved no further. When I failed to do more than look at him, Ryder exhaled in frustration and scooped my hand up in his, leading me to the dance floor. Tugging me into him, Bay started dancing. My body was instantly rigid, firstly from being held so firmly against him, and because I'd also never danced with a guy like this before.

"Relax, I'll lead. I promise not to tread on your pretty shoes." Bay smiled. It hit me how good looking he was. Letting my eyelids fall shut, I growled at myself as my skin itched against his. "I've angered you?"

"You're trying to charm me." I kept my voice low and bitter. "I don't understand, considering how angry it made you when I touched you only two days ago."

Smile dead, Bay's face returned to his emotionless mask. "We are at a party, Miss Michaels. Your money is in my coat. When we have finished this dance, you will escort me out, and

I will give you your payment in the elevator on the way to the lobby."

Tensing in his hands at the idea of being alone in an elevator with him, I shook my head and stepped back. "Screw the money."

Bay's eyes focused on mine with curiosity. Stepping away from him, I turned to find the exit. Nothing was worth the risk of being alone with him. I'd never done this for the money anyway. The presence that Bay exuded followed me through the crowd. Examining all my options for escape, I was distracted when a tipsy brunette stepped into my path, a predator smiling charmingly at her side as he led her to the exit.

"God, I'm so sorry." She laughed as she turned to apologize for running into me.

I had a split second to recognize Heather, my best friend from school before her eyes fell on me. Heather's eyes went wide with fear. "Spec?"

Concerned about the predator next to her, I kept my face controlled and serene. Luckily, he was focused elsewhere and missed Heather's reaction. "He's a predator, Heather. Leave with him, and you may never make it home again." With Bay at my back stopping my retreat, I breathed out entirely, becoming incorporeal. I fled through the crowd for the exit.

"Spec?" I heard Heather's voice call again weakly.

Bay

Spectra chose to refuse payment rather than enter a confined space with me. I shouldn't have been shocked. It may have been centuries since I'd bedded a woman, but I used my charm on humans daily, so I should have known when my mesmerization failed to work on her that she would run. All my confusion went out the window when I saw the brunette's big brown eyes widen in horror, the blood draining from her face enough to look shock-pale despite her fake tan and heavy makeup.

Spectra warned her about the predator before she turned and vanished into the crowd, and I lost her amongst the milling bodies, her aura already very faint. The eyes of the alarmed brunette locked with mine in the absence of Spectra.

"Are you well? You look like you've seen a ghost." My eyes searching for Spectra moving through the crowd.

"I did," she whispered, tears starting to run down her cheeks. That response got my attention. "She warned me..." She looked over her shoulder at the man she was with, busy talking to another of his kind and a drunk blond human. The scared brunette quickly moved into the crowd away from the danger. Holding her elbow, I stopped her tripping in her hasty retreat.

"Possibly you've drunk too much." Spectra was real. I'd touched her, so she definitely wasn't a ghost. Yet, this woman's reaction was fascinating. "You obviously haven't seen your friend in some time..."

"Seven years," the brunette sobbed. "Spec died seven years ago. We used to be so close; it tore our whole circle of friends apart when it happened. Her boyfriend, Jeff, he didn't mean to hurt her, he couldn't have known she'd react badly to what he gave her. After what happened to her sister and her mother, it almost seemed as if the family was cursed, and Spec was fated to die young too."

Gaining a little insight into why Spectra resided at a convent, I swallowed my instinct to taste this woman's blood and see her truth with my own eyes. "How long was she dead for?" This explained why Spectra could identify predators, why she stood with one foot in the Nachtwelt. She'd crossed the veils.

The brunette looked at me, exasperated. "We buried her seven years ago."

Standing straight, hearing the honesty in this woman's words, I turned and looked towards the exit. Spectra was there, waiting for her jacket to be given to her. Striding away from the distressed woman, I focused on my prey. There are very few ways someone comes back from the dead and stays human. If her friends buried someone, it wasn't this woman. There was no way Spectra ever went into a grave. Which meant Spectra never died entirely and went into hiding for a reason. Or, and this is what stirred his hunger, Spectra Michaels was something new.

Grabbing her elbow to stop her retreat, I handed over the ticket to collect my own jacket. Turning her pale eyes toward me, whatever she saw in mine caused Spectra to swallow hard. Closing her eyes, Spectra looked away as I took my jacket and led her to the elevator.

We waited quietly for the elevator to arrive. When it did, I stepped us both inside, hit the button for the basement, and turned to block her view of the control panel. Removing the envelope containing the rest of her payment, I held it out to her. "Your payment. Thank you for your professionalism, Miss Michaels."

Taking the envelope hesitantly, Spectra slipped it into her jacket pocket without checking it. Her anxiety was filling the elevator. Moving a step towards her, I touched her cheek. Blue eyes flashed up to mine, surprise swimming like a torrent behind them.

"I want you to stay the night with me." I intended to take her with me the moment I saw her. No one had stirred my desire in centuries, and suddenly there was this woman. No situation on earth would make me pass up the opportunity.

Pale eyes hardened and flashed fiercely towards me. "I'm not food."

"I've already eaten tonight. I want you in the biblical sense. Stay with me tonight, and tomorrow morning you can walk away from me. I'll never seek you out again."

The answer was in her eyes before Spectra even opened her mouth. She was not the sort to be ruled by desire. Taking her face in my hands, seeing my chance at knowing pleasure again quickly disappearing, I kissed her passionately. Excitement flooded my system. My cock stirred the moment I saw her upstairs, but now, it swelled full and hard and pulsed with the ache of centuries of disuse. There was no letting this precious thing escape.

Running my tongue over my teeth, I sliced my tongue open before thrusting it into her mouth. Surprisingly, Spectra wasn't pushing me away, the temptation radiating off her as the elevator stopped and the doors slid open. When I pulled back to look in her eyes, the fear within her overcame her curious nature. Shaking her head, Spectra stepped away to alight the elevator but paused when she saw we were in the car park.

Moving forward to stop the doors from shutting, I put a hand on her lower back to encourage her onward.

"What about the word 'no' do you not understand?" Giving me a look full of rage, Spectra refused to budge.

Keeping my face neutral, I put enough of my strength behind my hand to let her know getting off the elevator was not an option. Because it wasn't now. I couldn't leave her defenseless in a place like this. Stepping out of the lift, Spectra turned, putting her back to the wall immediately outside.

"No, I'm not staying with you. No, I'm not having sex with you. No, I'm not feeding you. No, I will not ever see you again. Our business is done, Mr. Ryder. We agreed that you would forget my name, forget me..."

Swaying a little, Spectra put a hand to her head. Waiting patiently, guilt gnawed at my consciousness as she put her hand on the wall and her knees started to weaken beneath her.

"What?" Tilting heavily to one side, Spectra stumbled.

Catching her, I lifted Spectra into my arms effortlessly. Her head rolled into my chest, unconscious, as I started walking to my car.

CHAPTER 3

Spectra

My eyes fluttered open, and I cringed internally, waiting for the pain of breathing to hit, but it didn't. I relaxed and sat up to take in my surroundings. I lay on a big timber bed in a luxuriously designed bedroom, all but my jacket and shoes still in place. There were four doors leaving the room and two large windows with the heavy drapes closed. Moving to the windows, I pulled the curtain back enough to peer outside. It was still dark, too dark to still be in the city though, and I was at least two to three stories off the ground.

I looked back around the room for my jacket. My shoes were placed neatly in front of a chair. My jacket was laid neatly across the back of it. I felt inside the pockets, the envelope with the money still bulging on one side; the other held my phone. I pulled it out, unlocked it, and called Alexander. The phone beeped at me and the call dropped.

"No, no, no!" I whispered as I realized there was no signal. Moving around the room, I tried to find a spot with enough signal strength to call. Eventually, I gave up and sent Alexander a message, hoping if the signal picked up that he would get it.

I don't know what happened. I drank nothing. I passed out. I don't know where I am. I can't call anyone, so hoping this message will get out as soon as I find a signal.

Once I pressed send, I closed the phone and started looking for a way out. Considering sneaking around the house, I decided that I would just hold my head high and walk out. Slipping into my shoes and jacket, I opened the first door. Wardrobe. Closing that door, I went to the next one. Bathroom. Moving to the two doors on the opposite side of the room, the first led out to a landing and stairs leading down two flights. Stepping out, I started across the timber floor to the stairs, walking on my toes to stop the heel from clacking. From the door directly at the top of the stairs was a deep voice talking inside. Audible, but not discernable. Not wanting to risk being caught from behind, I started the descent.

Halfway to the first-floor landing when a woman's ear-piercing scream froze me where I stood. Seconds later, a man's malicious laugh echoed up from the room at the foot of the stairs where the door was open. A second man's sympathetic voice filtered through.

"Scream all you want, honey."

The woman sobbed loudly before a ripping sound reached me and she screamed a bone-chilling scream this time. Slipping out of my shoes, leaving them behind on the stairs, I breathed out entirely, and descended to the first-floor landing.

Passing by the door slowly, I dared to look in. I was relieved to see Bay wasn't one of the men in the room. One was one of his kind, but the other was another sort of predator. The woman screaming was on all fours on the floor, and I understood the noises I'd heard now. She was halfway through her first change.

Her animal eyes locked on me and she opened her mouth to alert those with her, but her body chose that moment to take the next step. Her scream pierced my ears, and I moved quickly to the stairs and floated down to the ground floor and out the front door. Running across the front lawn to the driveway, I just made the tree line when the front door flew open and Bay rushed out, looking around. He peered across the lawn and seemed to know exactly where I was, despite me being incorporeal.

A huff of beasstly breath behind me alerted me to Bay's security. Turning slowly, terrified of what I would find, I was relieved to see two lionesses approaching me cautiously. While most beings couldn't see me when incorporeal, animals were different. So, when a Changeur de Corps, a predator of flesh who could change into animal form, saw me with their animal eyes, they saw through me but knew I was there.

"Spectra, stay still!" Bay yelled from where he stood on the front porch.

Glancing back to where Bay was watching the lionesses stalk towards the tree I stood behind, I resisted taking a deep breath and ran for the road. The Changeurs turned their heads to follow my escape but didn't follow.

Most animals didn't bother with ghosts, and that's what they would have taken me for. When I made it to the road, my phone started ringing. Inhaling deeply, I returned to corporeal substance, and pulled my phone out to answer it.

"Spectra, where are you?" Alexander's panicked voice came across the line.

"I don't know. Bay Ryder's place I think. He's a predator master." I looked up the road and wondered where the closest town was.

"Yes, amongst other things. Are you away from him?"

"I just made it to the road, but he was close behind me."

"I'll be there in a minute." When Alexander hung up, I stared at my phone, wondering how he was getting here that quickly.

A moment later, Alexander stepped out of nowhere to stand in front of me. He was just like the other night, with only his jeans on, and I knew my message woke him. He stood taller than usual, and his power swirled around him like a tornado as he came towards me.

As Alexander reached me, his eyes went over my head and filled with rage. "We had an agreement." Wrapping his arm around me caused Alexander's power to burn across my skin and for me to grit my teeth to prevent crying out.

Bay stood just a few meters from me on the road. "She is unharmed. I didn't take her to rouse your anger."

"Then what is she doing here?" Moving me behind him, Alexander swilred his power around him angrily.

"I kissed her, I'm attracted to her. It has been centuries since I kissed someone, so I accidentally cut myself. Spectra ingested my blood. I couldn't leave her there to the mercy of other predators."

Alexander looked shocked as his eyes turned to me for confirmation. I looked away, not willing to meet his eyes. "Oh, Spec! You must have been terrified." Alexander turned his eyes towards Bay. "You should have brought her to me. Your business is done with her now, so stay away from her." Holding me tight to him, I felt Alexander's power sear along my skin. Closing my eyes, I resisted screaming at the feel of being stretched apart before I snapped back together like an elastic band.

Standing pressed to Alexander's bare chest in his lounge room, he didn't release me for a long moment. Which was good because my legs weren't holding me up. When he finally did, it seemed to require all his effort.

"You're in trouble, Spec. Bay Ryder hasn't met a woman who roused his interest in centuries. He's attracted to you. My telling him to stay away isn't going to have much effect."

"My telling him to stay away didn't work either." The reminents of his power making me cringe as I shrugged out of the jacket. "I'm sorry, Alexander. I didn't mean for this to happen."

Alexander took my hand in his and led me to his bedroom. "It's late, Spec. Let's get some sleep. Unless you'd rather stay up and watch that porn movie in your bag?"

"It's for a client."

Droping his jeans, Alexander climbed into his bed while I unzipped my dress and stripped. From his chest of drawers I collected one of his t-shirts and tugged it over my head. "Plus, I don't think nuns in habits are your thing."

When I climbed into bed, he pulled me against him. "Sex with you is my thing, Spec." His lips dropped a kiss across my collarbone.

"As I hear it, sex, in general, is your thing, Alex."

Alex rolled to reach the light switch, but it put him on top of me at the same time. He used his knee to nudge my thighs apart as he turned off the light. In the dark, his face came back to mine. "Say yes, Spec. It's been months."

Grabbing the hem of the shirt I'd just put on, I pulled it up my body and over my head, Alexander lifting his body enough to let the material pass before pressing against me. His kiss was gentle, kissing me thoroughly till I was gasping for breath. His mouth ventured down my throat, across my collarbones, and further to seize my nipple. I gasped at the feel of his tongue flicking across my sensitive areola. I missed Alexander. I loved him, but he'd been the one to put the brakes on, and now I kept the distance to protect my heart.

My fingers twined in Alexander's thick head of hair as he kissed over my stomach and disappeared between my legs. My back bowed, and I bit my lip at the way he made butterflies take flight in my stomach. As he kissed his way back up my abdomen, I caught a glimpse of lightening sky through the highlight window above his bed. He kissed up my exposed throat and gently used his hand to tilt my face back to his, eyes searching mine before he smiled and captured my mouth.

He slid into me with the same gentleness he kissed me. I broke from his mouth and moaned as he pushed deeper, his teeth nipping at my throat while he waited for me to recover from that first penetration, because it truly was that amazing every time he pushed into me. When I didn't bring my mouth back willingly, he turned my face to his and kissed me as he started moving inside of me. I could tell straight away we were racing the sunrise. He was angry and trying very hard not to take it out on me. I'd seen this side of him plenty of times.

Touching his face gently, I pulled back from the kiss. "It's okay, Alexander. Take what you need from me."

His pupils dilated as he pulled away from me and flipped me onto my stomach. Tugging my hips off the bed, Alexander shoved into me with a little more force. Possession. He felt like he'd nearly lost me tonight and needed for me to submit to his need.

My nails clawed the sheets as he pounded into me and I bit the pillow to keep my moans to a minimum as my body rose to meet his need. I wanted to be his; I wanted Alexander to own me so much that I would give him anything he asked of me if he promised to make me his entirely. And that's what scared me most.

Alexander slowed his movements as my body tightened around his engorgement. He laid his body over my back and used his fingers in my hair to turn my face to that awkward angle and kissed me hard. "I want to cum inside you."

I wanted him to, but I shook my head. "You'd have to marry me."

"I want to do that too, Spec. As soon as you're strong enough to be my wife, I will make you mine. Please Spec, I need this tonight."

His eyes begged for me to let him take it to that next level. Biting my lip, I touched his face gently, willing him to understand. "I'm already breaking my rules letting you be inside me without protection, Alex. Until you marry me, you can't put your seed in my womb."

He knew I always used condoms when we finally started having sex. After Alexander began sleeping around, he promised he'd use protection with everyone else and pull out if he could have this level of intimacy with me.

His eyes looked pained by my answer, and I was so tempted to give in, to try and make up for the mess I'd made with Bay Ryder by letting Alexander have this. I kissed him gently, and he pulled out of me, his hand pulling my hip so that I rolled beneath him, and then he slid into me again. I tried to break from his mouth, but Alexander held me there and forced me to kiss him through it. He kissed me as he brought me to orgasm and when my body contracting around his sent him over the edge, Alexander kept kissing me as he pulled out and released his pleasure over the smooth skin of my stomach.

He kissed me for several minutes afterwards, until his phone rang. Alexander looked over at his bedside table before he stood, pulling me off the bed and taking me into the shower with him. The sun was rising as we washed each other clean.

Alexander hugged my back to his chest and kissed across my shoulder. "Are you any closer in your practice?" I lowered my head and shook it. Alexander didn't push it, "You'll get there, Spec. My mother was thirty before she could prove herself worthy of my father, and he met and started teaching her when she was fourteen."

I smiled, considering. "We met when we were in primary school, Alexander."

He smirked against my shoulder. "Yes, but I didn't realize you were a potential candidate until you turned sixteen. Once I did, I started teaching you the basics without you even realizing."

Frowning, I thought back. "The meditation you made me do before we studied together each week?"

Alexander nuzzled the back of my neck. "Remember that massage course I told you I was taking and asked you to let me practice on you?" I nodded, remembering how good he'd been with his hands. "There was no course. Mom suggested I take that approach to introduce our bodies to each other slowly, to let you get used to my power as it grew, rather than hurting you if I didn't take you till I was at full power."

Alexander ran his hands up my body to caress my breast. I sighed, hanging my head back as his power sent sparks of electricity through me in a pleasurable way.

"I thought for sure you were done with Jeff after we spent

the summer break mostly holed up in my bedroom after graduation. Did you ever tell him about us? That I was your first?" Alexander's other hand slipped between my legs. I gasped as his body grew hard against my back again.

"He didn't know it was you, though he probably suspected. He knew I gave my virginity to someone else while he was backpacking around the world with his mates. He was screwing around, so he couldn't complain."

Alexander turned me and pushed me against the wall, his eyes filled with sadness. "Why did you go back to him?"

"Our friends expected it, and you went to the capital for university. I didn't love him, but you ignited a fire in me, and then you left me."

"You got accepted, you could have come with me."

"Even with the scholarship, I couldn't afford to go to an elite university. You know that. Mum squirrelled away every penny of my college fund and all her savings searching for Danika."

"My parents would have paid for you..."

"I will not be indebted to anyone, Alexander, especially to the parents of the man I love. I made my decision."

"Your decision got you killed, Spec!" Alexander raged. "Just like last night could have gotten you killed. Why the fuck would you allow Bay Ryder to kiss you?"

I knew it was coming after last night. He'd been holding this in for six years. Meeting his angry, dark angry eyes, I kept my voice peaceful. "Remember the first time we were together? It was Christmas Eve. I was staying with your family for Christmas, like I did every year after Mom..." Swallowing the painful memories, I got back on topic.

"You came into your bathroom after I showered and told me I looked tense. You got me to lie on your bed still naked with just a towel to cover me while you massaged my back. You waited till I went to get up, and you took my face in your hands and kissed me with everything you felt. You kissed me till I lay back and gave you all I owned to give you." Alexander's eyes softened as I spoke.

"He surprised me. He kissed me so intently I was blown away, Alexander. I didn't want to, trust me, the idea of being with one of his kind sickens me, but there's something about him. When I touch him, I'm not sickened, I'm curious about the way he makes me feel." I dropped my eyes, ashamed, and Alexander took a deep breath.

"He's going to seek you out, Spec, because he feels that curiosity too. The same genetics that makes you a candidate to be my wife makes you a candidate for him as well."

I looked at Alexander, shocked, my mouth moving to ask if I'd understood right, but my voice failed me.

Alexander smoothed a strand of hair back from my face as he took it in his hands. "He was what I am before he was taken. When he realizes what you are, he's going to go to war with me for you."

"But I love you. Shouldn't that matter?"

Alexander's eyes darkened. "Until we are married, nothing will matter. He will work to capture your heart just as hard as I have, but, where I have tried to coax you into your power gently, he will force you into it painfully if it means he can claim you."

"Could you do that?" I remembered the woman screaming in agony as she went through her first change last night. Not that I would turn into an animal, but the suffering she must have felt.

Alexander gave me a wicked smile and kissed me deeply. His power came alive around me, at first like a warm wind, then it picked up ferocity till I felt like I was standing in the middle of a forest fire. I tried to pull back from the kiss, but Alexander held me to him, his mouth muting my whimpers. A spark of something started in my chest, and my eyes popped open.

Alexander's eyes were open, watching me. His eyes silently asking me permission to push further. Closing my eyes, I kissed him harder.

He pushed more of his power against me. I was being burned alive, my flesh melting away from me, falling off my bones. I screamed, and Alexander clamped his hand over my mouth. That spark yawned open a little further, a soothing coolness in the centre of my chest when everything else burnt with such intensity, but it wasn't enough to soothe the burn. My lungs burned inside me, and I struggled against the suffocation.

All of a sudden, the firestorm disappeared leaving me hyperventilating into Alexander's shoulder as the pain still coursed through my body. That soothing coolness stayed, it didn't recede

"That's what he will do to you, Spec, except he won't stop when you use your safe word."

I wanted to ask how the hell he knew about safe words, but I couldn't get my breathing under control. The world grew narrow in my vision, and eventually, it all disappeared as I fell into the oblivion of unconsciousness.

Bay

I walked back to the house, furious I'd lost her. There was something about Spectra Michaels that allowed my guards to let her pass freely from the property. Calin was standing on the front steps, watching his newest wife roll on the grass, finally having finished her first change. Calin's brown eyes met mine, and he ran a hand through his shoulder-length blond hair.

"I'm sorry, boss. She must have passed by during one of Serena's screams. As soon as Gina and Cynthia return, I'll find out why they let her pass too."

"You'll bring them to me. I want to hear it straight from their mouths. In the meantime, I want to speak to Bronwyn. She recommended Miss Michaels in the first place. I want to know everything she knows about her."

"Yes, boss." Calin bowed his head, stepping aside while I passed and then following me into the house to go to the wing that he shared with his wives.

I climbed the stairs, Luke joining me on the landing and following me up to my study. I collected Spectra's shoes from the stairs where she'd abandoned them. It was stupid of me to leave the room to deal with business while I waited for her to wake.

"She couldn't have gotten far?" Luke looked amazed that I came back empty-handed.

"She would be here now, but I underestimated her, and I'm not dealing solely with her. She has high connections within the Nachtwelt that are not happy with my interest."

Luke's eyes widened a little as I opened my study door and stepped inside. "Did you want me to look into these connections?"

I shook my head. Calin came into the office with Bronwyn in tow. The petite blonde woman held her head high in my presence. Calin was only attracted to strong women. "Is there something wrong, boss?" she queried confidently.

"You recommended the girl named Spectra to me for the documentation. What do you know about her?"

Bronwyn paled a little. "Did she not deliver?"

"Answer the questions, don't ask them," Calin suggested gently.

Bronwyn swallowed and nodded. "I only met her twice. My sister was in a bad marriage, and when I asked around for extraction options, her email address was passed to me by the people who would help my sister disappear. She was good, really good, and fast. She suggested we just get a license and birth certificate to start, and that a passport would be easier to apply for later using the other documents. She hacked my sister's bank accounts and changed the details so that she was money ready at the other end."

I tilted my head with curiosity. "You failed to mention she could access banks as well."

Bronwyn's eyes widened a little. "I figured she'd suggest it to you like she did me. I did warn you she didn't work for our kind. She only agreed to help me because my sister was human. I wasn't meant to circulate her name, but you were obviously in a bind, time-wise."

I nodded my head, accepting that made sense. Her anger at me showing up was evident across the bar. "You know nothing about her as a person?"

Bronwyn shook her head. "I'm sorry, boss. Our interaction was rather short and to the point."

"Did you know she frequented Ténèbres?"

Bronwyn shrugged. "When you contact her, she organizes

a meet there, and she'll suss you out first. I think she's pretty tight with the bartender. He watches her pretty closely."

Luke frowned. "Are you talking about Tommy Donald? He has the Goth bar down the wharf district." Bronwyn nodded, and Luke met my eyes. "Tommy is a watcher. That's why she's using his bar as the office. If her gig is usually to help female victims, Tommy will watch over her and even protect her if someone tried something. It's why so few predators go to that bar."

"That explains the welcome I got, especially when I asked for her."

"She can't be straight human if she's able to spot watchers as well as our kind." Calin considered. "A witch maybe?"

"Not likely. How many of the Nachtwelt can even recognize a watcher, let alone still conduct themselves in a manner that would have a watcher protecting them? I can't even think of anything. Maybe it's just exposure that's led to her being able to identify us." Luke argued.

I shook my head. "Not straight human. Her aura fades in and out at times, like she's struggling to stay with the living."

Bronwyn stood straighter, and I realized she gave off heavy military vibes. "Boss, the sun is coming up. I'll go fetch Gina and Cynthia to report if you like?"

I nodded. Calin smiled at her with pride, and Bronwyn blushed before leaving the room. Calin possessed a remarkable knack with his women. He could be stern but still sympathetic and gentle so that they never felt slighted. Yet they knew not to cross him and tried hard to please him.

"I could have used your ability with women last night, Calin," I grumbled.

"I'm sorry, boss. It was Selena's first change, and it's important I lead them through it with kindness." Calin was very subtly telling me his wives came before my personal pleasure, and I could understand that.

Cynthia and Gina entered my study. The two women were polar opposites in appearance and personality except for their long blonde hair and that inner strength all Calin's women possessed. "You requested our presence, boss?"

"You let a human walk off the property last night. Why?" Calin questioned instead. He asked it gently, but both women immediately cringed.

"No human crossed our paths. Just the ghost, boss." Gina quickly answered. "She was scared but determined. We thought she was just reliving her past."

"Ghost?" Calin queried, stepping closer. "She was incorporeal?" Both women nodded. Calin turned confused eyes to me. "Explains why I didn't see her come down the stairs, but she can't both be a ghost and a human, boss. I don't know what your girl is."

I looked to Luke. He shook his head. "I'll do some research, but if you could find out more about her, it could help."

I nodded and moved towards my room. "I'm due at that meeting at ten o'clock. She went to school with Alexander Williams. Try looking up his senior yearbook as a starting place to identify her."

CHAPTER 4

Spectra

A PHONE RINGING REPEATEDLY WOKE me from the darkness of my unconsciousness. I blinked and saw Alexander run into his bedroom and collect the phone from the bedside table before he answered. He wore his usual jeans and nothing else and as he sat facing away from me on the other side of the bed, I cringed at the fresh claw marks gouging in his back. I sat up slowly, testing for any residual pain. My nerves felt overly sensitive, but nothing I couldn't handle.

"I can do that. I'll meet you in thirty minutes." Alexander hung up the phone and swiveled to face me. He looked guarded. "How are you feeling?"

"I'm fine. You?" I let my eyes linger on his back.

Alexander looked over his shoulder and smirked. "I've suffered worse, and it was nothing compared to what you did."

He stood and moved to the wardrobe, pulling out a suit and throwing it on the bed. "I've got a big meeting today and need to meet someone else before that. You barely slept last night. Why don't you stay here the day and tonight as well?" He didn't look at me, focusing on changing.

I stood up and kissed his cheek before I raided his wardrobe for the few items of clothing I left here for when I spent the night. "I have something I want to do today, and since it requires travel, an early start works in my favor."

Alexander stopped buttoning up his shirt and turned me to face him, touching my cheek gently. "If you get back after dark, you call me. I'll drop everything to meet you."

I smiled and nodded before stepping away to pull the long black dress over my head. I collected my boots and put them on before standing and smiling as Alexander finished his tie and pulled on the suit jacket. Alexander looked at me with his own smile. "What's that look for?"

"You look good in a suit. I rarely see you in one, so I'm enjoying the view."

Alexander reached out and pulled me into a deep kiss. When his phone rang again, I slipped away and grabbed my messenger bag to leave. Alexander caught my hand. "Come back to me tonight?"

I felt the smile die on my face. "You know I can't, Alexander."

Alexander's dark eyes met mine and he let me see the pain in them. "How long will you make me wait this time?"

"It's not about punishing you," I answered softly, confused by his pain. "You know what today is and that I keep vigil for Danika."

Alexander's eyes folded back in his head. "I'm sorry, Spec. I knew today was important for another reason but couldn't remember why." The phone stopped ringing for a minute and then started again. "Tomorrow night?"

I blinked. "We agreed on random for a reason, Alexander. You made the rules so you could be free to do what you needed and so I wasn't targeted." I wanted to be with him, but it took so long to get used to him not being there after he decided we needed to put distance between us.

"I meant for you not to stay every night, not for you to disappear for months on end." Alexander lifted my hand to his chest, placing it over his heart. "I stopped bringing women back here years ago. That's why you stopped coming so regularly, isn't it? You came over and saw me with someone?"

"Yes," I answered honestly. "I know there are other women, that you need to look like a free agent and keep the possibility open of meeting another balance who might work for you, but I need to protect myself too, just in case that possibility turns into a reality." The chance was too high that I would never be worthy of him, that he could meet someone in the meantime who would become his balance, and what would be left for me then?

I stepped away, our hands falling away from each other before I walked out his apartment door. I caught the train an hour south of the city to the town we grew up in and caught the bus to the graveyard where my mother was buried. Twelve years ago, my older sister Danika went to college with my mother's pride of raising a daughter successfully all by herself. Six months later on this date, my sister went missing, her blood found splashed over the wall of her dorm room. Her body was never found.

My mother fell into a deep depression, and ten years ago, on this same day, I came home from school to find her exsanguinated in the bath tub. I was sixteen when my mother died, and I went to live with the nuns in the city, catching the train forty-five minutes every day so I could keep attending the same school. Despite already dating Jeff, Alexander had been my rock with each loss.

I placed two pots of flowers on my mother's grave. Yellow roses for my mother, yellow lilies for Danika. I took out my notebook and wrote up the last few days of excitement in my life, then ripped out the pages containing the last year of my life, folded them together, dug a shallow hole, and buried them. It wasn't a detailed account, but whenever something of interest occurred that I would want to tell them, or something funny, or special, or maybe just when I thought of one of them. I would write it down for them. Each year for the past nine years, I buried those pages and details with my family.

I sat quietly for a while and then picked myself up and caught the bus to Alexander's family home. I rang the doorbell, trying so hard to hold back the tears of all the emotions bottled up inside me. When Phillipa Williams opened the door, her green eyes widened slightly before they softened in her pretty heart-shaped face and she pulled me into the biggest hug. "Spectra, I'm glad you came."

I breathed in the scent of her conditioner in her auburn hair and felt instantly calmer at the familiarity of it. She held me till I relaxed and then moved me inside to shut the door. She took me into the kitchen, sat me at the table, and made us both tea before she sat down opposite me.

"You've been to see your mother?" I nodded. Phillipa smiled, "I was going to go past this afternoon and put some flowers down." She pointed to a bunch of beautiful fresh-cut roses sitting in a vase on the table. "Do you still keep vigil each year?"

"I do." I sipped my tea, and we sat quietly with each other for several minutes.

"Alexander told us he finally told you everything." Phillipa started gently. "I thought you would have come before now."

"I wanted to come. I have so many questions, and I didn't even know where to start asking. But Alexander told me I needed to find my own way to him for this to work, and I didn't want to ruin my chances. So I kept visiting Mom each year and resisted coming here. It's been hard, though."

"But you've come now?" I nodded. Phillipa leaned forward. "What happened?"

I swallowed. "There's another sorcerer," I lifted my eyes to Phillipa's, "and he's found me."

Phillipa closed her eyes. "What's his name?"

I got the feeling she already knew. "Bay Ryder."

Phillipa took a deep breath and stood abruptly from the table, turning her back to me, her hand going to her mouth where she started biting her nails, something I'd never seen Phillipa do in all the years I'd known her.

"I need you to explain it to me, Phillipa. Alexander told me, but I think he's only told me the easy bits. I need you to explain it to me properly, and then, if you can, I need you to teach me."

Phillipa took a breath and composed herself before she returned to the table. She folded her hands, squared her shoulders, and met my eyes. "The really powerful sorcerers need their power to be earthed. They need someone who can draw the power from them when it gets too much, who can bear to have that power pressed against them and not flinch. This person takes the form of a balance. A balance can't just be anyone. You have to be born of the right stuff, for your genetics to be right. And not every balance will be strong enough to endure the most powerful sorcerer.

"Your genetics makes you a balance, Spectra, and Alexander is one of the most powerful sorcerers to walk the earth in centuries, just like his father before him. What would you like to know?" Phillipa lifted her tea to her lips and sipped.

"What's the point of the testing? If I can be with him physically now, why do I need to prove I'm worthy?"

Phillipa smiled. "He holds his power back from you to protect you, Spectra. That takes a lot of effort. When he unleashes it, if you can't shield yourself or absorb it, you will feel like you are on fire."

I nodded, having a better understanding of how much Alexander was protecting me after our shower this morning.

"Then there is the need to carry on the line. If you conceive my grandchild, you will develop minor powers during your pregnancy. If you are strong enough, you will keep those powers as your own after the child is born. If you are not, Alexander would lose you and his child to what I've heard is a very tragic and painful end."

I took a deep breath. This was all new. "How did Alexander know I was a balance?"

Phillipa smiled softly as if in memory. "A boy started a fight with him at school one day. Alexander was trying so hard not to lose his temper and hurt the boy. Apparently, you got between them and shamed the other kid to back down, and then you took Alexander's hand in yours to walk him home. He should have been too hot to touch, but he said as you walked, he felt his anger seeping out of him, and he realized you were taking his anger without even realizing that's what you were doing. Do you remember?"

I nodded, eyes wide slightly with shock. "My hand was so

itchy that I kept rubbing it against his to try and scratch it. I didn't want to let go of his hand, so I just made myself endure it. He'd always been there for me, and I wanted to be there for him."

Phillipa nodded. "After Alexander told me, I looked into your family line. Your mother was lovely and courageous raising two headstrong daughters on her own, but she was very human. Your father was a bit of a mystery. What do you know about him?"

I shrugged. "He was a one-night stand. I never met him."

"I didn't really know my father either. He cared for my mother and set us up financially, but I only remember snippets of him coming to visit. It stopped well before I was old enough to question his absence." Phillipa gave me a sad smile. "It is our father's genetics that makes us a balance, Spectra. Not just for sorcerers either. In essence, we are just as much a child of the Nachtwelt, if not more so. But we are something not spoken about or remembered by many."

I gave Phillipa a doubtful look. I had held no power before I died, there was nothing special about me then, and really, I didn't believe there was anything special about me now. The ability to become invisible and pass through solid walls was great, yes, but it took ages to learn control over it.

Phillipa smiled and held her hand out towards the kitchen. She wiggled her fingers for a second, as if they were cramping, and closed her eyes, clearly focusing. A moment later, the pen sitting on the counter flashed across the room and landed in Phillipa's outstretched hand. She opened her eyes and smiled.

"I thought I was extremely ordinary growing up. I stood out in no way really. I wasn't a stunning beauty and as a teenager, yuck!" Phillipa screwed up her face, "I was gangly and clumsy, and all I wanted was for my breasts to actually form. I was flat chested till I went to college, and even then, what I developed I didn't require a bra for."

Spectra looked down at Phillipa's voluptuous chest and raised a brow. Phillipa held what I considered to be the epitome of a feminine figure. She was curvy in all the right places and absolutely beautiful. Phillipa blushed. "These boobs didn't arrive till I was pregnant with Alexander. Thankfully, they stuck around after he was born. The telekinetics developed during my pregnancy too."

She reached across the table and took my left hand in hers before she placed it palm down on the table and started drawing with the pen on it. "Being a balance is a combination of two things, Spectra. The first is the shield." Phillipa finished drawing, and Spectra could see the old-fashioned shield symbol along with a few symbols on it. "We feel the others. We don't have to see them because their power calls to us and we can sense them near us. With the Nachtwelt who can wield power to harm, rather than just to transform, we need to be able to shield, because that power burns in them and will feel like it is burning us.

"The benefit is that each power burns a different way or at a different frequency, which makes their power like a finger-print. If you learn to sense those frequencies, you could work for the government to identify Nachtwelt criminals. I still free-lance occasionally, but there are very few balances in the world so they will always welcome another.

"In the case of sorcerers, they burn over several frequencies, and we need to learn to shield ourselves on all those frequencies. They learn at a young age to shield others, but there are times when they will lose control and drop those shields. The more powerful the sorcerer, the more frequencies we need to be able to shield. The test to be worthy to be a wife of a sorcerer is that you can shield against them at their full power."

I touched my chest where I remember feeling that soothing coolness, like a stone against my chest, and wondered. "Alexander tried to force my power this morning. Is that what he was doing, trying to force my body to shield?"

Phillipa's eyes widened with fury. "Yes." She gritted her teeth and took a deep breath. "Sorcerers can force a balance to shield by exposing them to their power, but if they go past the balance's threshold, they can kill you. Alexander knows better than to do something like that."

"He was letting me know what Bay Ryder would do to me if he worked out what I was." I tried to soothe.

Phillipa shook her head. "Alexander really hates Bay, but I can't believe even he would do that. I've known Bay Ryder for many years now. Henry, Alexander's father, and Bay dealt with a lot of issues in the Nachtwelt together. Maybe it's the difference in their jobs that put Alexander on edge around Bay."

"When Alexander stepped in as L'Ordre in the city, he made a name for himself very quickly and pissed off a lot of the predator upper echelon." I murmured before sipping my tea.

Phillipa nodded. "Alexander detests the predators for his own personal reasons. Though I would have thought Bay would support the new proposed law about not killing to feed."

I threw up my hands. "Stuffed if I know what the hell happens on that side of the Nachtwelt, Phillipa. I only met Bay Ryder on Friday night, and so far, all I know about him is he wants to sleep with me." I cringed the moment it left my mouth. I'd never discussed sex with Phillipa before and worried that was too much information.

Phillipa dropped her eyes to the counter. "I'm surprised. Bay has a reputation for his lack of interest in women."

It was my turn to look at the counter top. "Apparently, he reacts to me."

Phillipa frowned. "Do you react to him?" I bit my lip. Phillipa threw her chair back, standing over me furiously. "How the hell did he get close enough to you for you to even know?"

I turned my head away, ashamed. Phillipa didn't know about the business I'd set up for myself while I completed college. Phillipa rubbed the back of her neck, walking away to look out the window.

"What happened between you and Alexander? You were basically living together when he told you how important you were to him. What changed?"

I swallowed. "When he became L'Ordre, he decided it was for the best the Nachtwelt not know I exist, and for him to be able to see other women." I felt the tear escape and swiped it away. "We still see each other, but it's not as often anymore."

Phillipa kept her back to me. "Are you seeing anyone else?"

The silence stretched out between us. I cleared my throat. "You said there was a secondary thing?"

Phillipa nodded, wiped her face, and composed herself before she came back to the table. She picked up the pen and started drawing on the back of my other hand. This drawing I didn't recognize immediately.

"You need to be a shield and a sponge." She clicked the lid back on her pen. "Just like the first time you took Alexander's anger and morphed it into something else. You need to be able to take the fire of their power and morph it into whatever they need at the time, or, at times, whatever you need."

"It's sounds so easy, but it's not," I murmured.

Phillipa nodded. "Usually we are more gifted at one than the other. You automatically siphoned Alexander's anger from him with no training, Spectra. I would say that is your strength. So, focus on controlling when you do that, exert your energy on shielding." Phillipa sighed and used her finger to tilt my chin up so I would meet her eyes. "In order to learn, you need to be exposed more regularly, Spectra. If you stay away, you will never become what he needs."

"Alexander fears Bay will come after me if he knows what I am, that he will try to claim me."

Phillipa took her hand back. "You are the first woman in centuries to get Bay Ryder's attention, Spectra. Balance or no, he's coming for you, and from the sounds of it, you're not going to be able to resist him any more than you did Alexander."

CHAPTER 5

Bay

I MET LUKE AT THE BUILDING where the contracts were being signed. He was waiting out the front with his briefcase and his tablet, which he was currently frowning at.

"Luke, we all set?"

Luke looked up, "Yes, boss. I also have that information for you." He handed over the tablet device as we walked into the building. I started scanning through his notes and the photos and newspaper articles he'd attached.

"You were right that she went to school with Mr. Williams. I used his graduation book to find her. Surname was Bailey back then. Her sister went missing at age eighteen and was determined to have met foul play. The mother couldn't cope and committed suicide two years later, leaving sixteen-year-old Spectra alone.

"There wasn't anything else on her until six months into her first year of college. Her boyfriend drugged and raped her. She reacted badly to the date rape drug he used, and she died. He was charged with manslaughter but was brutally murdered before he even went to trial. By the looks of the newspaper report, it was a predator that killed him, most likely one of ours."

I raised my eyebrows at that. "So, she's definitely a walking corpse?"

"There's a grave with her name on it in Wolfenden. She's not a predator, and she's too substantial to be a ghost. I have no idea what she is." Luke grumbled.

I looked at Luke in understanding. He was a scholar before he was taken and prided himself on knowing as much as he could about everything.

"Wolfenden is only an hour away. Have Calin drive down there and look at the grave." I flipped the cover on the tablet and handed it back to Luke as the elevator opened and we stepped out onto the fortieth floor of the Government Security Vetting Agency.

A man in his thirties with a buzz cut and cheap suit was waiting in the lobby. "Mr. Ryder, if you'll follow me." He about-faced and marched up to a glass door where he placed his hand on the palm pad, waiting for it to scan and the door to unlock. There were no signs here, no business names or agency area identification markers.

The man held the door for them before leading the way farther into the maze of glass-walled offices that made up the government's local Nachtwelt Security and Intelligence Office. Average citizens may be oblivious to the Nachtwelt, but the government was well aware and even had its own entity where Nachtwelt citizens were employed for their specific skills.

Buzzcut opened a glass door and held it open for us. Once we were safely deposited in the meeting room, Buzzcut closed the door and waited outside, stepping sideways into an at ease posture.

Alexander Williams stood leaning over the table at one end of the room, reading over a stack of papers in front of him. Two men on either side of him were having a quiet discussion over his head. One I knew as Gary Pearce, the Changeur de Corps who pretended to be human, a government representative who negotiated with me for the renewal of my contract. The second man was more a boy, old enough to be in college, but still a boy and no doubt a sorcerer and Alexander's assistant. They looked up as Luke placed his briefcase on the table and unlocked it to pull out his pile of papers.

"Mr. Ryder." Alexander stood straight, closing the pile of papers. This was his show until the contracts were signed, then Mr. Pearce would take over again.

"Mr. Williams. You look tired. Did you have a late night?"

Alexander glared, but under the burning in his dark eyes, his lips curled upwards with pleasure. "That I did, but she was worth it, and she made sure I knew how much she appreciated me staying up for her."

I glared right back at Alexander's lack of subtlety at taking what should have been mine last night. "Shall we do business? I have other business I'd like to tend to this afternoon."

Alexander indicated we should take a seat. I sat, Luke stayed standing.

"Do you have your original identity and business documents?" Alexander requested, a glint in his eye as he picked up his file and moved to place it on the table next to Luke's briefcase.

Luke took out the various documents and handed them to

Alexander. Alexander took them, quickly looking through them before handing them to his assistant. He kept hold of the passport, flicking it open and looking over it as he casually walked behind me and sat down on my other side.

"She does beautiful work, doesn't she? Who suggested her to you?" Alexander spoke quietly, closing the passport and skimming it across the table to his assistant with the checklist.

"I was very impressed. What is she?" I met Alexander's eyes, casually letting him know I wouldn't be answering his other question.

His eyes darkened, but he smiled just the same. "An MIT graduate. She's extremely good with computers. She's also off limits."

"Does she have free will, Mr. Williams?" I watched his eyes grow darker still. "Then she is free to make up her own mind, isn't she? Or is her signature on a contract in your vault?"

Alexander's eyebrows rose in humor. "Now there's an idea. I don't have to bind her to me, just have to bind her from ever letting you touch her again."

I couldn't help the growl that vibrated up my throat.

Alexander clicked his fingers, and the file he'd left next to Luke floated open. "You have some reading to do before you sign, Mr. Ryder. Please sign the bottom of each page as you go to save time." Alexander held out his pen.

I took the pen, wondering why Alexander was determined to let me think Spectra was human, but decided it was wiser not to let him know I knew otherwise, at least until I knew what she actually was. Luke took the first page of the contract and started reading before handing it to me with a nod. I quickly read and poised the pen to sign. I felt a sharp stab to the pad of my index finger. I frowned at Alexander.

"What good is a binding signature if it's not signed in your blood, Mr. Ryder?" Alexander smirked, watching my blood flow into the barrel of the pen and mix with the ink solution. Once the pen was full, the needle retracted. I signed while Luke checked the next page.

After a few pages, Alexander stood and walked to the opposite end of the meeting room, pulling out his phone. "Hi, have I caught you at a bad time? Are you going to see her tonight? No, I just want to know someone will be there till I can get there. She shouldn't be alone right now, that's all." Alexander hung up the phone and moved back to the far end of the table, where he opened his laptop and sat down to work quietly.

I took the next page from Luke and kept signing. After half an hour of reading and signing, Luke handed me the last page. Alexander's assistant cleared his throat, and Alexander closed his laptop and returned to my end of the table to watch me sign my full name on the final page.

"Thank you, Mr. Ryder. My assistant and I will leave you with Mr. Pearce to discuss your payment. Enjoy your day." Alexander collected the signed contract while his assistant collected his laptop and papers from the end of the table and headed for the door.

"Mr. Williams," I called, turning to look at him, pocketing his pen, which still retained some of my blood. I'd be burning it when I got home. "I apologize."

Alexander frowned. "For last night?"

I shook my head. "I want her, Mr. Williams, only for one night, but I will not step away until I get what I want. So, I apologize in advance if that is going put us at loggerheads."

"Who are you talking about?" Mr. Pearce queried, annoyed about his time being wasted.

Alexander turned to face me completely. "Don't. I could

give you many reasons to leave her alone. The first you already know, the second I think would be obvious, the third, she is not the sort of woman you spend one night with and walk away from. You may think you can do that, but she seeps into your bones, and you'll want her again, and then again, and again until it stops being a want and becomes a need."

I could see Alexander meant what he said. "Mr. Williams, please do not take this as an insult. You are young, and despite your reputation with women, still somewhat inexperienced. I've been around a lot longer."

Alexander gave me a cocky smile. "She's extraordinary, Mr. Ryder. That she got your interest should tell you everything." He had a point. Alexander stepped towards me again. "If you succeed, and you hurt her in any way, shape, or form, be warned, I'm not the only person in the Nachtwelt that will come for your head."

I stepped down into the gothic club and made my way to the bar. As soon as I sat down, Tommy shook his head and casually made his way towards me. A man in his late twenties, a tattoo curling up around his neck from under his black shirt, stepped up to the bar next to me and looked over my suit. He was of the Nachtwelt, not a predator, not a watcher like Tommy, though of the same genus. He developed a mischievous smile before looking back to Tommy.

"Hey Tommy, when Spectra gets here, tell her I'm looking for her. I have a bone to pick with her." He winked.

Tommy looked disgusted. "Do those pathetic lines really work on her?"

The man rolled his lapis eyes and combed a hand through

his dark brown hair, embarrassed. "God no! It's a joke. I have to put in the hard yards to get into her. Entirely worth it though. I just wanted her to know I was here."

I studied the man, trying to recognize why he was familiar, and finally placed him as one of the attendants at the church service on Saturday. An altar server. I wasn't surprised by his presence at the church; his kind are usually drawn to temples or places of worship.

"Sorry to disappoint both of you, but Spectra will not be anywhere near this place tonight. She's keeping vigil all night." Tommy answered, but his eyes were all for me.

"Is it that date already?" The man looked at me, his eyes defying the age of his flesh. "She must be dropping by if her client is here."

Tommy shook his head. "Sorry Mercury, I have no idea what the suit is doing here, but Spectra won't be in tonight."

Mercury frowned. "Damn, I've finally got some nights off, and my girl is holding vigil. Guess I'll just have to wait till tomorrow." Tommy raised a heavily pierced eyebrow at Mercury, who gave that naughty smile again. "She grieves today. Tomorrow she'll want to get shit-faced and forget again. I'll be the person she'll want to hide away and get sloshed with."

Tommy shook his head, but the side of his mouth turned up in a hint of a smile. A young woman with dyed blue hair, pierced everything, including tongue, and brown eyes blood-shot from intoxication shimmied in and pressed up against Mercury's side, running her hands over his broad chest and fit body before blatantly rubbing him through the front of his jeans. "Hey, Merc. Been awhile. If your girlfriend isn't here, I'll take care of you."

Mercury smiled down at her, shrugged, and stuck his

tongue in her mouth. A minute later, he was dragging her off to the darker area of the club. Despite it being a dark corner, I could clearly see when Mercury pushed the girl against the wall, put his hands on her shoulders, and pushed her down before thrusting something else into her mouth. I turned a raised brow back to Tommy, who was also watching.

"That's what Spectra is into?" I couldn't help but ask.

Tommy frowned. "If Mercury even thought of treating Spectra like that, she'd rip his cock off and shove it down his throat, and he knows it. They've been seeing each other for years and worked out their own system for seeing others as well. He's an Angelis, a doctor, and dominant. The Nachtwelt and human girls alike are happy just to be the catch of the day."

An Angelis, not a Nephilim. That meant he was the half-breed son of an archangel, not one of their Nephilim grand-children. I was starting to think Spectra was highly attracted to very powerful men.

Tommy's eyes drifted back to the dark corner, and I realized he could see into that darkness as easily as I could. We both watched Mercury wrap a fist in the girl's blue hair and use it to drag her up his body where he kissed her hard while lifting her legs to his waist. A few seconds later, he was banging her up against the wall.

"I'm guessing she's the catch of the day kind for a lot of men, with the lack of obstacles he's found getting to those orifices."

Tommy chuckled. "Definitely!" Tommy's eyes came back to me. "My bar is a safe place."

"I was looking for Spectra, nothing else. No offense, I like my food upper class." I stood to leave, understanding this was a dead end tonight. "Though I can't believe you let his kind in here. They may not be predators, but his kind can pull some nasty shit to get their way."

"He's Raphael's son. He does not manipulate humans, he heals them. By giving of himself, that girl will walk out of here healthier than when she walked in. I have no issue with him."

"Is he the one who bought Spectra back?"

Tommy studied me a moment then shook his head. "Dead is dead. You're thinking of the wrong Angelis to bypass that dilemma."

I nodded, understanding Mercury could only heal the living or near-dead.

"You're not her type," Tommy warned.

"Maybe if I ditch the suit and get a tattoo?" I lifted a brow in jest. "What night does she frequent?"

Tommy shook his head and gave me that shadow of a smirk. "She comes and goes. Friday night is her only set night. She likes to wind down at the end of the week."

I studied Tommy for a moment. "I didn't expect you to tell me when to find her."

Tommy gave me a hard look. "I know who you are and your reputation. Any other predator came in here looking for her, the answer would have been different, but I'm interested in the way she reacted to you last Friday."

"Reacted how?" I knew her hands were full of curiosity when she touched me, despite her anger.

"You made her fingers itch. She reached out to touch you, and normally she hates touching or being touched by strangers." Tommy cocked his head towards the dark corner. "You just met the one guy here who can get away with putting his hands on her."

"You want to watch us together?" I asked, intrigued.

Tommy smirked and quirked a brow. "They don't call us

watchers because we turn our backs when things get interesting." To prove his point, Tommy's eyes drifted back to the dark
corner where Mercury was bringing it home.

I nodded acknowledgment and made a path for the exit,
having a good idea where to find a religious girl holding vigil,
especially if the altar server knew about it. As I climbed the
stairs to street level, the corner of my mouth pulled up. I made
Spectra Michaels's fingers itch. She was tempted. Tempted I
could work with.

Spectra

I MADE IT BACK TO THE CHURCH BEFORE SUNSET. A bone-chilling wind was starting to pick up as I slipped into the church from the side door and made my way to the Lady's chapel in the apse. I lit three votive candles, one for each of my family members, and placed them into the prayer stand before kneeling. Taking out my rosary, I began the prayers for the dead Father Mathew taught me when I came to live here ten years ago.

I heard the hushed whispers of others' prayers out in the nave but quickly tuned them out, focusing my thoughts on my loved ones. As the light through the LED-light windows faded to darkness, so the side chapel was only lit by the candles in front of me, the mellifluous voices of the men's choir echoed through the church and added to the atmosphere. Another hour later, the singing faded, and Father Mathew lit a candle of his own as he knelt down beside me to pray, speaking his words in unison with mine.

Lord our Father,
Your power brings us to birth,
Your providence guides our lives,
and by Your command, we return to dust.
Lord, those who die still live in Your presence,
their lives change but do not end.
I pray in hope for my family,
relatives, and friends,
and for all the dead known to you.
In company of our lady,
Who bore Your son,
may they rejoice in Your kingdom,

where all our tears are wiped away.
Unite us together again in one family,
to sing Your praise forever and ever.
Eternal rest, grant unto them, O Lord,
and let perpetual light shine upon them.
May the souls of the faithful departed through
Your mercy rest in peace.
Amen.

As the candles burned down, Mathew crossed himself, stood, kissed the top of my head, and left. When the three candles I'd lit burned down and started to flicker their last light, I collected three more and lit them off the dying flames. I sensed a predator and looked over my shoulder, noting the familiar figure seated out in the nave deep in their own prayers, the usual black hoodie covering their head and shadowing their downcast face. Predators in the church weren't unusual. Some were religious in life and prayed for their souls. For years, this same predator would turn up during the night of my vigil, stay outside in the nave, and leave hours later. They weren't a threat to me. They came here for their own pain.

I knelt down and began the rosary. Images of my loss flashed behind my eyes. My sister's dorm room, her bed messed up, her blood splattering her rumpled white sheets. My mother's ashen face in the bathtub, floating in the bloody water, her veins open, but her eyes, happy, as if she finally found peace in death.

I let the tears fall; they would flow plenty as the night wore on. It was the only night of the year I acknowledged my grief. Admittedly, I cried nowhere near as hard or long as I did when Mathew first suggested this ritual the year I came to live here.

I finished the rosary and returned to the prayer for the

dead. I felt a new predator enter the nave and caught my breath, recognizing Bay Ryder's presence. My eyes flashed open as I waited to see if he would approach. Moments passed, nothing happened. I closed my eyes, now slightly on edge, and returned to my prayers.

I jumped slightly when a blanket fell around my shoulders. "Easy, child. It's very cold tonight. You need not catch your death," Mother Superior murmured reassuringly. She knelt, lighting her own candle, and prayed with me a short time before crossing herself and retreating to her bed.

It was after midnight when I next lit fresh candles from the dying flames, pulling the blanket tighter around me before starting the rosary again. By the time I started the second round, Alexander was lighting four candles and kneeling down beside me. He held his hand out to the side. I placed mine in his, and we bowed our heads and continued praying together until the first rays of dawn broke through the stained glass windows of the chapel.

I sat back on my ankles and shed the last of my tears for another year. Alexander stood, drawing me up to my feet gently and cuddling me to him, still wrapped in the blanket. He walked me back to my attic room. He closed the door behind us, pulled the curtains across the two gable windows between which my desk sat, and unwrapped the blanket. I held my hands in the air as he lifted my dress over my head before dropping to his knees to unzip my lace-up boots and lifting my knees to step me out of them.

When I stood only in my underwear, he undressed and tucked us both into my king bed. It was my bed. All the furniture in this room was mine. It was a storeroom when I first came here, and I negotiated with Mother Superior to make it mine since it was a little larger than the normal rooms and gave me a bit more privacy. I performed chores just like the sisters, helping with cleaning and cooking, but this room was my own little space well away from the sisters.

"I can only stay a few hours, Spec." He kissed my shoulder as he cuddled me into his chest and laid us back on the bed. When he was still in college, he'd stay and sleep the day away with me, but since he started his job, it depended on how busy work was. He touched the back of my hand that rested on his bicep. "What's with the ink?"

"Just doodling," I sighed. I didn't know if Phillipa would tell him I visited, but unless she did, I wouldn't either. I snuggled into him and was torn between crying and smiling. I missed going to sleep in his arms.

This part of the vigil ritual started the year after I died. The first time Alexander bought me back and cuddled into bed with me, Mother Superior had a few strong words. Alexander simply glared at her, never once opening his mouth, but Mother Superior backed down very quickly and left. She'd not objected his presence ever again. The fact that I knew about her and Father Mathew's relationship probably helped.

Not that we ever had sex here. It was simply physical comfort, Alexander's way of making sure I knew I wasn't alone, that there was still someone who loved me walking this earth. I think Mother Superior understood why he was here, and that's why she let me have this. I fell fast asleep in his arms, his heartbeat lulling me into the darkness. I barely woke when he rolled away from me, got dressed, and left. I cuddled into the warm space his body left and let exhaustion wash over me.

CHAPTER 6

Spectra

WHEN I WOKE UP, Alexander was gone, and it was late afternoon. I climbed out of bed and headed straight for the shower, my knees protesting the entire way. The warm water soothed my aching muscles from twelve hours in genuflection.

After getting dressed, I walked back to my room and found Mercury sitting on my bed in slacks and black button down, his lapis blues alight.

"What are you doing in here? Mother Superior will skin you alive." I quickly shut my door.

Mercury totally ignored my worry and looked my outfit over. "Nope, that outfit isn't going to work."

I frowned, looking down. "For sitting around your room getting drunk, it's perfect."

"Except..." He picked up some material off the bed and

threw it at me, "we aren't going to my place. There's a party on tonight, a very sophisticated party, which offers plenty of free booze, and that is where we are going."

I held up the little black dress that left very little to the imagination. "Which bimbo did you steal this off?"

Mercury looked offended. "I bought it for you, snob! Now put it on. I dragged my sorry arse out of bed before lunch on my first day off in weeks to get you that dress. So you will wear it."

I held it up. "If you can afford to buy this shit off-handed, why the hell are you still living in the caretaker's cottage? You should go get your own place and be free to bring your loose women home."

Mercury stood, raising his eyebrows. "May I remind you, that for all intents and purposes, you are my woman. And maybe I like having a reason not to bring other women to my place. Maybe I consider that my sanctuary and only allow the most special of people into that space with me. Now get changed."

I pouted and pulled the light jumper I'd thrown straight over my bra off and dropped the knee length skirt to the floor.

Mercury let out a low whistle. "Nice lingerie. When did you start buying the good stuff?"

I smirked. "I didn't."

"Williams?" Mercury quirked a brow.

"Don't be like that."

"What? I was just asking if he bought it for you."

"You know he did. How many other people even know I exist, let alone buy me clothes?"

"Exactly why I asked if it was Williams." Mercury grabbed the dress and held it up, holding it above my head for me to raise my arms and lowered it down over my body. "I'm not jealous. You and he have your arrangement, we have ours. We do what works for us."

I turned to look in the mirror and didn't mind the way the dress looked on me. Its skirt was slightly flared and fell to mid-thigh. With my knee-high lace ups, I sort of looked awesome, but if this place was sophisticated, I was going to look a little trashy. I sighed and unzipped the boots, kicking them under the bed, pulling out a pair of four-inch heels.

"Wow! Putting in the effort. Nice." Mercury wrapped an arm around my waist and kissed my neck. "Let's get going."

I grabbed my jacket, slipping into it, and let Mercury pull me towards the door. Normally I would have asked where we were going, who would be there, all the important questions, but tonight was about getting trashed and forgetting.

Twenty minutes later, we were pulling up out the front of a very nice townhouse in the hip part of town. As Mercury paid the taxi driver, I recognized a predator walking into the building with a human on his arm.

"You didn't mention this was a predator party, Merc." I scowled.

Mercury placed his hand on my back. "I'm with you, I won't let anyone near you or anything happen to you. The host works at the hospital, and while she is a predator, I've really got no excuse not to come, and she knows it. I think she was hoping to score with me, and that's why you are coming to protect me while I'm protecting you."

I chuckled, and Mercury kissed my cheek, his own smile falling into place. "Let's go drink the place dry, shall we?"

Inside an attendant took my jacket, and a waiter offered us a glass of champagne. We accepted, and I tipped the flute up as Mercury led us into the large foyer with vaulted ceilings and a grand staircase that led up to a sweeping balcony. A beautiful chandelier hung suspended by wires over the foyer, and the color scheme was classic black and white.

People milled around the foyer, some of them giving us the once over as we walked in, a male predator de Sang, what the Nachtwelt called predators who drank their prey's blood, giving me a smile and a wink as I emptied my glass.

I turned to Mercury. "You better not have bought me to a smorgasbord party, Merc."

A waiter approached us with a tray full of champagne flutes. Mercury placed our empty glasses on the tray and took two more, handing one to me. "I was told it was a housewarming." His voice low as his eyes glanced around the room warily. He was getting the same feel for the place I was. "I'll say hello to Gladys so she knows I was here, and then we'll get out of here. Shouldn't get too out of hand in that time."

I nodded and took a sip of my champagne this time, deciding this wasn't the place to get wasted as we moved through the room. Mercury stopped at a waiter serving hors d'oeuvres. "Where's the host?" he asked with a smile as he took one of the appetizers. The waiter pointed up the stairs and continued circulating. Mercury sniffed the appetizer and threw it into a potted plant before he grabbed the one I was about to eat. "You don't want to eat that."

I balked as he disposed of mine as well. "Oh, that's gross! Who caters for changelings?"

Mercury shrugged, took my hand, and started up the stairs. I hesitated moving deeper into this place but trusted Mercury to keep me safe so I stepped lightly up the steps with him. Several shut doors curved around the balcony that circled the void, and one set of double doors stood open opposite another set of stairs leading up to the next level. There were a few people scattered along the balcony talking or flirting, some a little more than, but nothing like what happens at the club.

Mercury led us through the open doors into a parlor room with comfy lounges, a few backless vintage style settees, and one large ottoman placed dead center of the room. Oh yeah, it was a smorgasbord party, and this is where the main action would be happening.

Mercury squeezed my hand as if sensing my sudden anxiety and spun me in to face him. "Keep breathing, Spec. You do not want to disappear in front of this lot." He kissed me gently, lips pinching mine, his tongue darting across my lips to taste the champagne I'd just swallowed. It was a quick kiss, just enough to relieve my anxiety for a moment.

He spotted someone over my shoulder and stuck a false smile on his face as he started to cross the room, pulling me along with him again. A woman in her mid-thirties caught sight of Mercury over the shoulder of a male she was speaking to. Her heavily made up face cracked in her own smile as she waved Mercury over. She flipped her lustrous-rust colored curls and batted her false lashes at Mercury before he even reached her.

I rolled my eyes as we came close, but almost froze as the man talking to her turned to see who approached. Bay Ryder turned his pale blue eyes to Mercury first, blinking his disinterest, but when they slipped to me, his eyebrows raised slightly. Not enough that it was noticeable to those around us, but I was watching him closely. My heart jumped into overdrive as soon as I recognized him, and in that moment my desire to be invisible was overwhelming.

Mercury instantly turned to look at me when he spotted Bay, worry etching his features, his eyes flicking back to the exit as he calculated the distance to get out of here before he turned back to the host. He squeezed my hand hard. The pain made me suck in a breath, and I looked to Mercury, surprised. He glanced at me quickly, and I realized I'd actually started exhaling entirely when I'd seen Bay. I took a sip of champagne and concentrated on breathing in and out.

"Merc, you made it!" Gladys grinned, pulling Mercury in to kiss his cheek and rub her body against him.

"Of course, I can't stay long though, my girlfriend and I have plans tonight." Mercury stepped back, creating a buffer zone between him and the de Sang.

Gladys finally looked at me, and I could see her scrutinizing my appearance as she looked me over. "And here I thought you'd brought a nice wine as a housewarming gift."

I clenched my jaw, but Bay responded for me. "Miss Michaels is not food, Gladys, and Mr. Williams would have your head if you dared to serve her up as such."

Gladys frowned. "Why would L'Ordre worry his gorgeous head about this human?"

"Because his job is to keep order between the Nachtwelt and humans, and a human must be willing or unaware, that is the law. Spectra would not be willing and is very much aware of us." Mercury replied lightly, tucking me into his side. "Nice place, Gladys. Heritage listed?" He changed the subject.

Gladys smiled. "Yes. It required a bit of work, but I think I've restored it to its former glory." Gladys's eyes returned to me, "So how long have you two been seeing each other?"

"Over four years now." Mercury smiled.

Gladys's eyebrows jumped off her face. "But she's so young!"

Mercury smirked. "She's just finished her college degree, Gladys. She's older than she looks."

Gladys looked to Bay. "You've met Miss Michaels previously, I gather?"

Bay's eyes were intent on mine. "Yes, Miss Michaels and I are business associates."

"Former associates." I added, "I don't work for your kind." I took a larger sip of the champagne.

Gladys looked intrigued. "And what sort of work do you usually perform, Miss Michaels?"

"Spectra helps victims of violence," Mercury answered casually, "It's how we met. We both attend the same church."

Gladys's brows connected in her confusion. She tried to puzzle through the tidbits she'd been fed but gave up, obviously not the brightest de Sang to stalk the night. She beamed at Mercury, slipping in to take his free arm. "Let me give you a tour. Bay will keep Miss Michaels company for you."

Mercury smiled but unwound his arm from hers. "Maybe another time, Gladys. If my guess is right, you are about to serve dinner, and Spectra and I do have plans for this evening."

"Dinner is still twenty minutes away..." Gladys frowned.

"I'll keep Miss Michaels safe while you have your tour." Bay stepped up to my other side, slipping his arm through mine.

I bit my lip as his hand slid along my exposed forearm, tingles shooting up my arm. I gripped Mercury's hand harder, and he stepped us back from the circling de Sang, relief and disappointment flooding my system as I lost contact with Bay.

"I really will have to take a raincheck, Gladys. Maybe next time." Mercury took two more steps backward with me, smiled, then turned and walked us out of the parlor.

As we reached the double doors and I looked back over my

shoulder, my eyes met Bay's. His eyes filled with interest, and I knew I was in really big trouble.

"You're amazing, Spectra." Mercury grumbled as we descended the stairs. "You're the only woman I've seen on a regular basis, so trust me, I know how amazing you are. But to bring Bay Ryder out of a two-century dry spell is a whole new level of amazing."

I frowned at Mercury as we collected our jackets. "How did you pick that up just now?"

Mercury gave me an unhappy look when he realized this wasn't news, took my hand, and led me out to the curb where he hailed a cab. "I didn't. He turned up at the club looking for you last night. I thought he was still as a client until I heard what you said tonight. Then I recognized the way he was looking at you. It was subtle, everything about Bay Ryder is understated, but that was the look of a man ready to devour a woman in a very non-food way."

I sighed as the taxi pulled up and Mercury opened the back door. "I know." I slipped into the back seat and sagged.

Mercury sat down next to me and took my hand. "Saint Benedict's Church please." The taxi started moving, and Mercury touched my cheek, bringing my face to his. "Be careful with him, Spectra, for all the same reasons you need to be careful of Williams."

I nodded and closed the distance between our lips. Today wasn't for this stuff. Today was about forgetting. So I would put my issues with Bay Ryder aside for now and focus on nothing but Mercury's mouth and hands on me. Mercury hesitated for a moment till I took his hand and pushed it up under my skirt. He smiled against my mouth and threw himself into helping me forget.

When the taxi pulled up at the church, we made our way

to the caretaker's cottage that Mercury shared with the actual caretaker. Mercury opened the door, dragging me inside and pinning me against the door, hands gripping my hips, body pushing hard against mine as our tongues thrust and volleyed for the upper position in each other's mouths.

A loud clearing of the throat came from just behind Mercury. He pulled back and turned to see the caretaker, Robert Mulley, standing at the hallway to the bedrooms at the back.

"Oh, hey Robert, thought you were going out tonight?" Mercury smiled.

Robert blushed. "I am. Was just about to head out when you came back." He rubbed at the back of his balding head, and his blush deepened as his eyes scanned over my body.

Poor Robert was a widower in his late sixties now. When Mercury started bringing me back to their cottage four years ago, Robert decided that was motivation as any to get out and start having a social life. He'd taken up ballroom dancing first, but it wasn't on every night of the week, and with Mercury's work roster, Robert slowly added bingo and bowling to his social calendar so he effectively had something on every night of the week that I might visit.

I felt bad at first scaring the poor guy out of his home, but Mercury explained it was overdue, and his getting out and socializing was a healthy change for the aging man, and in truth, Robert seemed to be a lot happier now. Just not on the occasions we started early, or worse, when we didn't quite make it back to the bedroom, and he walked in to find us on the lounge room floor.

Mercury smiled devilishly and tugged me away from the door so Robert could get out. "Have a good night, Robert." Mercury pulled me into the lounge room. I smiled shyly and waved goodbye, which made Robert blush even harder as he made a quick escape out the door.

Mercury walked to the cabinet, grabbing two shot glasses and a bottle of vodka. He poured two shots and handed me one. I threw it back, cringed at the burn, but put my glass back out for a refill. Mercury complied, still not drinking his own.

I threw back the next shot as I sank onto the lounge and held the empty glass out again. Mercury refilled it another two times before he put the bottle on the table and emptied his own glass. He took my empty glass, placing it on the table, and casually pushed me to lie back on his lounge, laying his body over the top of mine. He smiled down at me then ducked his head to my collarbone. Mercury didn't mind me getting plastered when I was with him, but he controlled how drunk I got.

We'd started hooking up at the club several months after Alexander and I broke up. Then when the anniversary of my family's death rolled around, I'd got so drunk the next day that I couldn't even hold my head up. Mercury just held me that night. He told me the next morning that while he didn't mind me getting wasted on his watch when I needed it, he didn't like seeing me that gone.

Over the years, he'd worked out the exact amount of alcohol required to get me buzzed but still within my senses. It was one of the reasons I trusted Mercury. He truly did care about me and took care of me when he was around. I loved Alexander, but I cared deeply for Mercury. I reacted differently to his touch, it wasn't so much an itch caused by flames running under my skin. Mercury was more like floating in a pool of cool water on a hot day. Relieving, comforting, soothing.

As his mouth kissed down my chest, his hand pulled the strap of the dress from both shoulders. He licked and kissed along the edge of my cleavage, and I moaned as his thumb brushed over my nipple through the material. Mercury's mouth kissed back up to my ear, he licked and bit my earlobe, and I squirmed under him.

"There's something I've always wanted to do with you. Can I?" he murmured, his thumb brushing over my breast again, sending thrills to lower areas.

"Yes," I gasped.

Mercury pulled back, grinning at me. He grabbed the top of the dress with one hand and pulled back harshly, ripping the front of it away.

"Jesus, Merc!" I looked at the dress, wide-eyed. "That was silk, it must have cost a fortune!"

Mercury gave me his devilish smile. "It was worth it to see you in it, and now even more so to get you out of it." His index finger hooked under the front of my bra. "How attached are you to this underwear?"

I gaped wide-eyed as he pulled hard and ripped the bra from me. He smiled and fell upon my breasts, licking and sucking, his hands kneading the firm softness. My head fell to the lounge, back automatically arching to give him better access to me. I wrapped his head in my arms, fingers threading into his hair as my body responded to him.

His hand slid down my front and beneath my underwear to find my clit. His finger added pressure just above my hood and circled to start a slow tease. I gripped his hair in my fingers and pulled his smiling mouth up to mine. "Not here. Robert hasn't recovered from the last time he found us on the lounge. I don't want to be responsible for giving him a heart attack."

Mercury rolled his eyes and wrapped my legs around his waist. He slipped one arm around me and lifted me easily with him as he stood. He picked up the bottle of vodka in his free hand and walked to the back of the cottage to find his room. It was a small room, just big enough to fit the double bed he slept in, a wardrobe, and the two bookshelves containing his few possessions in it.

Kneeling on the bed, he dropped me back onto the mattress and tipped the bottle up to his mouth, taking a mouthful. He smiled down at me and held the bottle above my face. "Open up."

I closed my eyes and opened my mouth. The cold liquid poured into my mouth and, as I swallowed, burned down my throat. Heat flooded through me. Mercury dripped the vodka down the center of my body and dropped his mouth to lick and suck it from my skin where it was running off in rivulets.

His tongue found my ticklish spot just under my ribs, and I twisted as I laughed loudly. Mercury slid one hand under my back, his body causing a barrier as he found that spot again and held me to his mouth. I screamed and squirmed, pushing on his shoulders to try and escape. "Merc, stop, please, I can't breathe." We both knew what happened if I stopped breathing.

Mercury smiled sinisterly and took another swig of the vodka before putting it to my lips, letting me take one mouthful before he put it aside on the floor. "Let's see how these panties rip…"

"Merc! I've got nothing left to wear home tomorrow."

He ignored my protest and grabbed one side of the panties with both hands before pulling quickly in opposite directions. And just like that, hundreds of dollars in underwear and clothing was destroyed. If I'd paid for it, I would have been pissed. If I'd been sober, I'd still be pissed. I loved that underwear set. Grabbing the other side of the panties, Mercury gave another quick tug, and the material gave easily to his strength.

Folding the material back, Mercury ducked his head between my thighs. I gasped, my back arching as his first lick opened my labia to his probing tongue. His finger trailed through the wetness of my lips and then slid into me roughly. I bit my lip, fingers twining in his hair, the other hand grasping the quilt under me. With a smile that could make a nun go weak at the knees, Mercury dropped his mouth and nuzzled my clit while his finger gently caressed inside me.

He licked, sucked, and stroked gently, teasing me till I was twisting across the bed, trying to escape. Mercury put one restraining hand on my hip, holding me in place as he lifted above me, the other finger still teasing inside me.

"Your turn, Spec."

I bit my lip, trying to focus. I caressed my hands up his front to the collar of his shirt. "Are you sure?"

Mercury raised one brow and gave me that smile. I gripped the shirt and pulled as hard as I could. A few buttons popped off, but I wasn't as strong as him. I pushed over, throwing him on his back, forcing him to relinquish his hold on me. I straddled him and felt his hardness through his slacks. I positioned myself over that hardness and started rubbing back and forth. I moaned at the feel of that rough material against my delicate flesh. Mercury groaned, gripping my hips with strong fingers.

I grabbed his shirt and gave a really good pull this time, the rest of the buttons popping free. I dropped my mouth to his stomach and licked a line to his nipple, swirled my tongue around the nib, and then bit it. Mercury hissed and fisted my hair, pulling my laughing mouth to his. I continued to rub over him, bringing myself closer to the edge. Mercury moaned and threw me off him.

"Fuck! I can't wait."

He stood up, dropping his slacks before stepping to the bookshelf and opening the wooden box to retrieve a condom, which he threw at me. I was ready and waiting when he turned to face me. I took his huge cock in my hand and stroked it lovingly before licking over the tip. I started to slip my mouth over him, but he gripped my hair and pulled my face away.

"What about can't wait didn't you understand, woman?"

He snatched the condom from my hand, frustrated, and put it on himself. I smiled wickedly as I crawled back on the bed away from him. "I'm starting," I informed him as he went to grab me.

With a sigh, he fell onto the bed and waited as I straddled him. Positioning myself, I slid back and forth along his shaft, bringing myself back to that point again. Mercury gripped my hips, teeth gritted as I slid his thick shaft between my labia. I bent and took his nipple in my mouth again, licking and flicking it, hearing his breathing pick up as I held out on him.

"Spec!" He warned.

I smiled and lifted my mouth to his. I kissed him heatedly then leaned to the side and retrieved the vodka from the floor. I sat up and took a large mouthful, closing my eyes and enjoying that rush of heat as the alcohol flooded my system. I put the bottle back on the floor, lifted myself, and slid down over his already throbbing cock.

Mercury threw his head back, and I mimicked him as he slid home inside me. He was too big for me like this, it normally would take rough sex off the table, no pun intended. We usually had to be sleeping together regularly for a few days before he could go hard on me, because our first couple of days together he was too turned on and too large for my body to handle. But tonight, I was wet and loose, if you forgive the wording, but that's what alcohol does. Inhibitions be damned.

Mercury grabbed my hips and thrust up to meet my next down stroke. I cried out, dragging my nails down his chest. Mercury moaned deep and moved my hips up before forcing me down hard again. I placed a restraining hand on his chest, knocking his hands away, and started moving at my pace, short, shallow strokes followed by one hard deep one. Within a very short time, Mercury was ready for more.

Sitting up, he pushed me off him, twisting in behind me and pulling my hips back as he thrust into me quickly. He let go on me, thrusting hard, fast, and deep. I felt the burn of friction inside me, his cock too big, and with the condom, that natural silk slide of skin on skin was lost. I gritted my teeth and moaned through the burn, Mercury pounding into me till I felt him bruising my cervix.

I heard a noise, and Mercury moaned, picking up speed for a moment before he pushed me away, frustrated.

"Fuck!" He stepped off the bed, pulling the broken condom off and throwing it on the floor before he retrieved another. I blinked, annoyed that he'd stopped his onslaught but sort of glad for the reprieve as I fell to the bed and rolled onto my back. When Mercury returned, he smiled down at me, "That'll work."

He lifted one knee to his shoulder and slid home again. I hooked my other leg around his waist as he thrust back into me. He kissed me hard, and I sighed into his mouth as the change in position instantly returned the stimulation to my clitoris. Mercury's mouth drifted down, arching his body as his hand cupped my breast and lifted it so he could assail my nipple while he stroked inside of me. I threw my head back, nails digging into his shoulders as he took me to the edge. His face came back to mine, his body pausing as I grew too tight around him.

He kissed me heatedly, my body squirming under him, pulling him into me until I could feel the head of his cock rubbing against my cervix, and that deeper orgasm started to build. Mercury pulled back with a smile, his eyes bright. "Oh, we're there tonight, are we?"

He circled his hips, building that deeper orgasm faster, the smile on his face massive. It was harder for me to have these ones so if he felt my body trying for it, he'd coax it all the way. I arched my back, hands gripping the headboard as my body clamped down around him. I bit my lip, Mercury keeping those perfect circles going until my body spasmed and I cried out my pleasure. It flooded through my whole body, and when it was over, I dropped limp to the mattress, breathing ragged, a huge smile on my face.

Mercury withdrew, and I frowned. "Wait," he instructed as I went to object.

He rolled me onto my side and lay down behind me, sliding straight back in. I gasped and let my head fall back on his shoulder. He propped his head up on the one hand, looking down at me, his other hand guiding my hips back and forth on him. As I started to add to the rhythm, his hand smoothed over my skin and pinched my nipple.

The pressure started to build again, this time on the front wall. Mercury closed his eyes and took a deep breath. His hand slid down, my body now keeping the rhythm for him as his fingers found my clit and he drew circles over the sensitive bud. I gasped and bit my lip, Mercury groaned, and I knew he was moments away from finishing this, but he wanted me to come again first. He was going for the trifecta tonight.

He swelled inside of me, and I struggled to move, putting all my strength into thrusting back. Mercury breathed out harsh and pinched my clit between his fingers. That did it, a wave of pleasure crashed through my body with little warning. Mercury put his hand back to my hip and thrust deep, finding his own release. He dropped his head to the bed, body still spasming with his release behind me. He bit my shoulder, and I moaned again and started to squirm.

Mercury grabbed my hip to stop me. "I'm pretty sure I just filled that condom to bursting. You start that shit, and you'll break it." I groaned unhappily, and Mercury carefully removed himself from me. "Don't bitch at me. You're the one who insists. You know I can't give you anything..."

"You can get me pregnant." I sighed, not really caring in this moment.

"Except that, of course." He kissed my shoulder, dropping his voice. "Would that be so bad?"

I shook my head. "I'm not getting pregnant out of wedlock."

"So marry me," he murmured, his hand caressing my body tenderly. "I'll buy us a place, we can marry, move in together, fuck like bunnies and breed."

"I'm drunk. Stop talking shit to me." I sighed and snuggled down to sleep.

Mercury chuckled, kissed my shoulder again, and climbed off the bed. He collected the broken condom from the floor and left the room, going next door to the bathroom. I gathered enough energy to climb beneath the blankets and stayed conscious long enough to feel Mercury climb back in behind me and cuddle me to him.

CHAPTER 7

Bay

Spectra's vigil wasn't what I expected. Her emotional despair rang out like a beacon throughout the church, making it easy to locate her. I spotted the predator immediately upon entry, though it was too young to recognize me or my presence, but I knew Spectra could feel me. I stood back observing her for several minutes, then moved upstairs to the balcony, which housed the organ and choir stands. From here, I took a seat so that I could watch Spectra without interfering with her vigil.

A nun covered Spectra with a blanket as the wind outside turned vicious and the ice it carried penetrated the church walls. Her prayers were interspersed with crying, but she prayed non-stop for hours on end. The young predator sat back on her pew after the nun left and pulled out some dirty papers. Her muffled laughs, while quiet, still reached my ears, along with sounds of disapproval and sighs of sadness, interchanging as she read. After another two hours, the predator folded the papers and slid them away.

Alexander Williams walked in before two. I expected him to go straight to Spectra, but he stopped by the hooded predator first and squeezed her shoulder. The predator stood and put her mouth to William's ear.

"What's happening that you would call me?" she whispered.

"I'm worried about her safety right now."

"You put her aside, you broke her heart so no one would use her to get to you," the predator whispered harshly.

"This danger found her all on its own. It's nothing to do with me."

"Fix it!" she hissed. "She was entrusted to your care. So take care of it."

The predator turned and left the church without a sound. Alexander ran a frustrated hand through his hair, ruining the perfection of its style, then went to join Spectra. I waited till they were both intent in prayer to make a quiet exit. The way they held hands while they prayed seemed intimate and not something anyone else should be watching.

Friday night, I walked down the stairs into Ténèbres and made my way to the bar. Tonight I didn't get the curious stares or the looks of contempt of having an outsider in their world. The black jeans and black band shirt I'd borrowed off Calin, along with the way Selena styled my hair, seemed to make me one of their own. Luke, his ever-encouraging self, took a photo, promising to get it blown up to replace the painting above the mantle in my study. It made me miss the days before digital photography when my kind couldn't be photographed.

Tommy was behind the bar as usual and when I first sat down, Tommy glared in my direction. After a moment, Tommy blinked and almost choked on a laugh. He poured me a scotch without me asking and moved to my end of the bar to put it in front of me. "You slide into Goth just like Spectra." I looked at him questioningly, and he smiled. "You just put black clothes on and you're there. Effortless."

"Is she here?" I asked a little louder than I normally liked to talk to get over the melancholy music playing.

Tommy pointed to the dark corner where Spectra first touched me. "In her office doing business." I looked to the corner and saw Spectra talking to a woman. The woman wore a suit, cheap but well-maintained. I decided to wait till her meeting was over to approach her.

Tommy turned and looked at two new arrivals. "Bourbon and Coke, thanks," the taller of the two asked confidently. I smirked into my drink.

"IDs?" Tommy raised a brow.

The two guys looked at each other, their shoulders deflated. "Coke?"

Tommy put two glasses of water on the bar. The kids groaned but handed over their money.

"You should get your bouncer to check IDs," I suggested.

Tommy shrugged. "I don't mind them coming in. Better than getting drunk on the streets, but they won't get served anything but water. Most of them know it."

I shook my head. "With the porn that goes on in here, I still think you should be carding at the door. Some poor guy could end up banging his brains out on jailbait."

"Don't you worry your pretty face about it. I've stopped plenty of that before it happens, or do you think this place is designed so that all the dark corners put them in my line of sight by accident?"

"I'm surprised you let Spectra into the bar. You must have suspected she was underage. I know I did when I first saw her."

Tommy smirked. "It's not the ID's that tell me someone's age, Ryder. Sorcerers' abilities came from the Angels losing themselves in human flesh, remember?"

Blue hair came into my peripheral vision, and I turned to find Mercury's friend from Monday night. "Hi," she smiled, keeping her body pointed towards mine, breasts pushed up and out to gain attention, turning her head to Tommy. "Sambuca please, Tommy." She turned those bloodshot brown eyes back to me and smiled. "I haven't seen you here before. I'm Cassie."

I studied her eyes and realized she was a lot healthier tonight than she was on Monday approaching Mercury. "I'm dangerous. You should find someone else." I turned back to Tommy, who was watching Spectra. I followed his eyes and saw Spectra standing between the woman in the cheap suit and a very tall, angry-looking blond guy who obviously wasn't a patron.

"I like dangerous." Blue hair simpered and moved her body to press against mine.

The man grabbed Spectra by the throat. Instead of becoming fearful, Spectra relaxed and stepped out of his grasp. Literally. She became insubstantial, only barely, a human wouldn't pick it up, and side-stepped before breathing in again. The guy's face showed his confusion as she stepped into him, lifted her knee hard and fast, and the guy bent over with a howl. Not waiting, Spectra grabbed the guy by his belt loop and shirt collar and pushed him head first into the stone wall.

Tommy relaxed as the big guy crumpled. He waved over one of the bouncers and pointed towards Spectra. The body pressing against me nudged me again, and I turned angry eyes to the girl there.

"I said I like dangerous."

"Not my kind, you won't."

"Cassandra!" Tommy scolded. She turned annoyed eyes to the watcher. "Leave that one alone."

The girl pouted, threw back her shot of Sambuca, and walked off to find other prey. I looked back at Spectra, who was consoling the woman in the cheap suit while the bouncer dragged the nearly unconscious guy out of the bar.

"That happen often?" I asked Tommy.

Tommy shook his head. "Not often. It's been a year since the last time. That was a predator demanding Spectra take him on as a client."

"And she handled him?"

Tommy's eyes smiled. "Not the way she handled you. How long has it been since a woman grabbed your balls before Spectra?"

I shrugged. "A week. The difference is that was an attempt at seduction. Spectra did it to piss me off." I stood up as Spectra's client handed her an envelope and left. "I'll go say hello."

Tommy gave me a knowing look. "You do that."

Spectra leaned against the wall with a sigh, closing her eyes for a moment before opening them and looking around her with caution. She spotted me approaching straightaway. She looked me over, face full of surprise, before she swallowed and let annoyance mask her features.

"What are you doing here?" she scowled. "Is it Halloween already?"

I put my hand on the wall beside her head and leaned down to her ear. "Unfinished business." I touched her cheek with my other hand and watched her eyelids flutter as I ran that hand down her neck and across the exposed area of her chest.

"Our business is complete, Bay."

"One night, Spectra." I placed a soft kiss where her jaw ended and felt the shudder go through her body.

"I remember saying no, Bay, several times." She stood straight and put a hand on my chest to push me away. I stayed put and looked deep into her pale blue eyes, so full of confidence moments ago, now filled with confusion, fear, and what I now knew was her curiosity.

"Say it again." I dared moving my mouth to hers. I paused for a heartbeat to give her time to say no, and when it didn't happen, I kissed her.

My body came alive at the feel of her mouth on mine, and when she opened her lips, I took the invitation and slipped my tongue into her hot mouth. I stepped closer to her, pressing my body into hers and the wall behind. I didn't push for anything more, just kissed her till her fingers entwined in my shirt and she pulled her mouth away, gasping.

"I can't." She breathed against my chest. "You're a predator. This would be stupid."

I touched her face, bringing it up to mine again. "Does it feel wrong?"

She stared into my eyes. She didn't need to answer; the truth was swimming in the heat of her gaze. I kissed her again, wrapping my arm around her waist to hold her tight to me this time so her squirming body rubbed against my aching erection. She sighed into my mouth, her hands stretching open on my chest before they slid up, snaking around my shoulders and neck. One weaved its way into the back of my hair, the other hooked her elbow over my shoulder and pulled her up tight against me as her leg lifted and wrapped around my calf.

I let my hand drop to her lifted thigh and ran my hand up her skirt-covered leg till I grasped her hip. I slid my hand under the hem of her top to her lower back and caressed her bare skin. Electricity ran through my fingers, and she pressed into me, her breathing speeding up as the kissing became more passionate and wanton. She gasped as if struggling to breathe and I sobered with worry. She hissed in pain and released me, pushing me away all of a sudden, shock in her eyes.

"You're not shielding! Are you insane? You could kill a girl with that power."

I blinked and realized she was right. The touch of her bare skin made me forget my control for a millisecond, and I'd let my shield drop. Her look softened, and she stepped forward, hands wringing in front of her as if she was struggling to keep them away from me.

"If you can't control your shielding, Bay, I can't be with you, no human can." She walked away, disappearing into the crowd.

I closed my eyes, trying to calm my body while I cursed internally. Spectra was right, I needed to be able to control my shielding, or I could kill her in the heat of the moment. Once my body settled, I took a deep breath and returned to the bar and took my seat again. Tommy placed a scotch on the bar in front of me.

"On the house." His face serious. "I have to give it to you, Ryder, that was hot. Even I had to calm down after that. You're smooth."

"I messed up."

Tommy shrugged. "So you sparked her on your first kiss in centuries, you think Williams's has never lost control while with her?"

I considered him. "I hurt her."

Tommy lifted a brow. "Did you just?" I looked at Tommy, confused. Tommy sighed. "What came before she pushed you away?"

"She hissed at me."

"Before that."

"She gasped."

Tommy gave me an exasperated look. "You're really out of practice." He stood straighter. "Okay, I'll walk you through it. You touched her beneath her clothing, you dropped your shield, you both really started enjoying yourselves, you did what?"

"I pulled my shields back up automatically."

"And that's when she hissed in pain and pushed you away." Tommy cocked that pierced brow at me again then turned away to serve his customers.

I stared at my scotch. "She liked it," I whispered to myself. I looked around the club astounded, wondering where she went. With so many people, her drift was hard to pick up but I didn't really need it. I knew where she'd end her night.

Spectra

I wasn't sure if it was a dream. There was a flash of burning pain and then it was gone. I blinked my eyes open into the darkness, trying to remember my dream. It had taken me forever to fall asleep, tossing and turning as I tried to calm myself down. My thoughts ran rampant as I repeatedly analyzed my behavior with Bay tonight. I'd finally fallen asleep tangled in my sheets. It took several minutes after the pain woke me before I felt his presence in my room.

I sat bolt upright in bed and met Bay Ryder's eyes. The panic started to build inside me but before I could open my mouth to scream, tropical heat bathed my body, relaxation flooded me, and I fell back on bed with a moan of content. Bay stepped around the end of the bed, pulling his shirt over his head and dropping it to the floor. He was good-looking with clothes on, but without he was gorgeous. And he wanted me. All the women in the world meant nothing to him, it was me that he desired. I moved my hands to grip my thighs as they itched to touch him but instead started running them along my own skin, imagining all the ways he could touch me.

"Don't," I panted, and even to my own ears the tone was wrong.

Bay kicked off his boots, socks joining them. "I'm doing nothing. I am casting no magic, nor am I charming you." He unzipped his jeans and dropped them to the ground.

I glanced at his naked beauty and swallowed the sigh edging up my throat. Delicious heat flowed through me, gathering between my legs, and I gasped as my fingers brushed over that area tracing my body's response.

"You're doing something," I gritted my teeth, trying to control myself.

Bay pulled back my bedspread and watched my hands slip over the black satin nightdress I wore, a gorgeous smile spreading across his face. "I really am doing nothing, Spectra. This is all your own reaction." He slid into the bed with me and pulled the covers over us.

I shook my head and swallowed again as the press of his body to the side of mine left me tingling to feel more of him, to explore his body. He reached over and tenderly took my hand from roaming my own body and placed it on his chest. I bit my lip against the sensation that caused in me and tried to pull away, but Bay placed his hand over mine, keeping it there.

"It's not just me reacting to you. You're the first woman to cause this..." he slid my hand to his hard on and I grabbed it, loving the feel of that hardness, the size of it, the throb just from my grasp. Bay moaned, his eyes rolling into his head, "in centuries."

I went to stroke the length of him, but his hand held mine captive. He opened his eyes and met mine, heat burned through his gaze, and I felt my body melt to meet the contours of his.

"But you're reacting to me too, aren't you, Spectra? That's why when I tried to charm you, it didn't work because you don't react to that." He released my hand and slid his between my thighs, cupping my heat in his hand. "You're attracted to powerful men because you react to power."

My head fell back as he rubbed his hand against me and kissed along my jaw.

"Stop, please," I begged.

"I'm being truthful, Spectra. Your reaction is yours. It is up to you to control your power just as it is up to me to control mine." Bay kissed down my throat, mouthing the satin that covered my breasts, sucking my erect nipple through the material.

I threw my head back, reaching for the headboard at the same time. I saw the flash of something on the back of my hand and opened my eyes wider to look closer. The shield Phillipa drew on my hand redrew itself momentarily and then faded again.

I stared at the back of my hand, trying to ignore the heat flooding through me. My reaction. Phillipa explained I naturally absorbed Alexander's power and turned it into what he needed. Was my reaction now to Bay the same thing? Last night it wasn't dropping his shields that hurt, but when he snapped them back up and cut me off from that warmth.

I gasped as his finger slid into me, stroking me, his determination reflected in the pressure he applied and the steady rhythm of his fingers. He'd figured it out. That I'd absorbed his desire and now he was using it against me, dropping his shields just enough to blanket my senses with it.

I swallowed another moan as his teeth gave a gentle tug on my nipple through the material and he started kissing his way back to my mouth as he moved his body to lie between my legs.

I closed my eyes and felt for that shield Alexander activated on Sunday night. I imagined grabbing hold of the cold blackness and tugging hard in both directions. It didn't budge, and when Bay's mouth took mine hostage again, I forgot about trying to shield and lost myself to the heat and passion of his kissing.

Bay positioned himself, and the feel of his naked hardness sliding between my labia nearly undid me. I wanted him so badly, I wanted to feel my desire unleashed again. That thought morphed in my head while he kissed me, I want him to unleash his desire on me.

"Not like this." I murmured, and Bay stopped, pulling away to hear me out. "Please, Bay? You know I'm not in control of myself, that this wouldn't be my choice. It's not right. Not here, not like this."

Bay's eyes were full of the heat I could feel flooding my veins. He swallowed visibly, closed his eyes, and blew out a breath, his voice choked. "How, when?"

"I don't know, I can't think clearly like this."

A tear slid down my cheek and Bay sighed, wiping it away before he rolled to lie beside me and caress my cheek. I felt him slowly pull his power back in, making sure not to hurt me with the whiplash this time. "I hope you respect what I'm giving up here, Spectra."

He slipped out from under the covers, scooped up his clothes from the floor, and the burn of his power flared as he walked across my room. A heat of a different kind, of my true desire, flickered as I watched his muscular physique walk away from me. He took a step into the darkness and disappeared, the same way Alexander appeared on Sunday to save me from this same man.

As the coldness of his absence washed over me, the shield I'd tried to use stretched wide enough to cover my chest and then recoiled back to nothing. I rolled onto my side, Bay's emotions still raw and unchecked inside me, colliding with my own confusion. I cried until I fell asleep from the exhaustion of it.

CHAPTER 8

Bay

I SAT AT MY DESK, trying hard to focus on the report in front of me. Luke sat opposite, his normally patient composure slowly fraying, tapping a pencil against his notepad, the noise of which was driving me up the wall. "That's distracting."

"You've read the same sentence twenty times and counting. You have gone past annoying. Are you ready to talk about it yet?"

"I let her go."

"Why?"

"I discovered her weakness and used it. If I'd continued despite her willingness, it would have been rape." I slammed the report closed and slouched back in my chair. Frustrated didn't begin to explain how I felt.

"There is no law in the Nachtwelt regarding rape." Luke's

face was the perfect mask of indifference, but I knew better. Luke was the only other de Sang in my house, because he was the only one I'd met, so far, who managed to retain his moral fortitude after being taken. He wasn't mine, I'd never taken anyone to this life, and neither did Luke.

"You think the law would matter if I raped the woman L'Ordre loves?"

"He would twist the law to state you took her unwilling."

"Exactly!"

Luke considered me a moment. "Is that the only reason you stopped?"

I sighed. "I have defiled nuns within convent walls, entered their rooms like a messenger of God, seduced and fed from them. None have ever met my eyes and asked me to stop." I stood up and walked to the window. "She was drowning in lust, and she still kept her head enough to ask me not to do that to her."

"I'm surprised you were able to." Luke raised a brow. "You seem pretty intent with her."

"She was siphoning my desire, which took the edge off. She's a siphon, but she hasn't learned to close herself off to it."

Luke frowned. "She's young, so that's possible, but siphons are predators, and the ones who feed on desire feed on humans."

"She feeds on power. That's why she's dating powerful men."

Luke shook his head. "An Angelis would never date a siphon. A watcher would never protect one. You're wrong about this." I raised a brow at Luke, and he shrugged. "I've probably never said that before, but you're definitely wrong on this one."

I sighed. "Then I still don't know what she is, but she can

siphon my power." I watched the sun lowering towards the horizon in the sky.

The door opened, Calin walking in, shrugging out of his jacket before rubbing a hand through his sandy hair. "It's cold enough that my balls may have retracted out there." He moved to the fireplace and put his back to it, sighing with relief. "The things I do for you, boss. Mind you, that girl must be very pious. She spent the entire morning on her knees in Mary's grotto praying for direction. The stone under her knees left her shivering and turning blue, but she stayed there till the priest and a rather scary nun wrapped her in a blanket and dragged her inside the church."

"Probably punishing herself for letting the devil crawl into bed with her," Luke mumbled, shooting me a scathing look.

Calin frowned. "What? What did I miss?"

"Not important," I glared at Luke. "Where is she now?"

Calin took a step away from the fire as he warmed. "Well, she spent an hour sitting in the church talking to the priest, then he walked her back to the convent. That's where she was about the time I started wondering if I'll ever be able to achieve an erection again. Did I mention it's damn cold out there? I reckon it will snow tonight."

Luke sighed, looking at his watch. "We might get dinner early tonight if that's the case. We don't want Calin's balls retracting at a vital moment and you not being able to get your dinner."

I nodded, agreeing. I didn't want to get caught in the city during a snowstorm. Grabbing our jackets, we headed out. I only lived an hour's drive from the city, so by sunset we were safely ensconced in a high-end townhouse at a smorgasbord. They were the best parties for someone like me. I didn't have to be the one dipping my wick to get my food. For the humans, it was a swinger's party. Lots of the wealthy citizens, with more money than sense, usually grew bored and ended up in these promiscuous lifestyles, which enabled predators like myself.

Luke went off to find his own food while Calin and I mingled and picked out my dinner. "That one," Calin pointed to a leggy brunette with pale skin and deep blue eyes. I gave him a suspicious look. "She's the closest to your girl than any other woman here. Maybe if you close your eyes and pretend it's her, you might get a twitch and be able to fix your own meal."

I rolled my eyes but indicated Calin should make his play. I watched Calin approach the woman, the way she smiled at him, and after a few minutes, her body language was very positive. A few more minutes passed and Calin pointed to me. I gave the woman a nod and took a sip of the champagne. She damn near swooned at whatever Calin whispered in her ear next. He took her hand and led her towards the stairs to the rooms set aside for private gatherings upstairs.

I followed them, and at the top of the stairs, they waited for me to catch up. "Private party for three please," I tipped the concierge. He led us down the hall and opened the door, giving the woman a wink as we passed inside and shut the door after us. Calin pulled the woman into his arms and started kissing her immediately as he danced her to the bed. I loosened my tie and slipped it free, throwing it to a chair along with my suit jacket and my shirt.

Calin and the woman were tugging each other's clothes off over by the bed as I stepped towards them. My phone buzzed in my pocket, but I ignored it. By the looks of this woman, this was going to be a quick party.

"Do I get to fuck you both?" She smiled as Calin hovered over her.

"Let's see how you go with me first." He smiled and shoved into her.

I smiled at how in sync Calin and I were. We'd gotten very used to picking the women who would need preparation and persuasion to achieve climax, and those so randy they'd be climbing the curtains as soon as the fucking started. This woman was definitely one of the latter. I knelt at her head, grasping her breasts and squeezing while I kissed her neck. The attention of two men simultaneously was apparently too much, and she screamed her way to her pleasure.

Covering her mouth with my hand, I bit gently into her neck. She moaned anew, and as Calin flooded her with his pleasure, her eyes fluttered, a smile spreading further across her face. I felt her heart rate slow and pulled away, cleaning the bite and sealing it with my saliva.

Calin was already redressing as I stood and pulled the phone from my pocket. Surprised by an email from Spectra.

Eight o'clock. Pick me up from the church. Dinner at Margareta's. You're paying.

Calin raised his eyebrows. "You look surprised."

"That I am." I slipped the phone away and started redressing. "You and Luke right to find your way home?"

"You got somewhere else to be?"

"Apparently, I have a date."

SHE WAS BEAUTIFUL WITHOUT EFFORT. I KNEW THAT THE NIGHT I met her, but with effort... The night the Angelis bought her to Gladys's smorgasbord, I'd been blown away by how stunning she was, and I noted straight away Gladys's jealousy. She walked to the curb where I waited by my car, her long black jacket covering whatever she wore, but by the heels and the minimal makeup, I suspected she'd dressed the part for the high-end restaurant she'd booked.

"You're early?" She looked concerned.

"I was already in the city when I got your email." I opened the passenger side door for her.

She stepped forward but froze before sitting. "You've eaten already tonight?"

"Yes, but I wouldn't mind something solid." She gave me a half-hearted smile and sank into the leather seat, tucking herself in like a trained lady.

As we pulled away from the curb, I examined the set of her shoulders, the way her hand continuously flexed and clenched. She was as nervous as they came, almost to the point of terrified. I reached over and took her hand. Her eyes fluttered, and she entwined her fingers with mine, looking out the window.

"It's become cold very quickly," Spectra sighed.

"Calin suspects it will snow tonight."

"Calin?" She looked at me curiously.

"He's my bodyguard, of sorts."

Spectra looked over her shoulder at the empty back seat. "No offense Bay, but unless he's invisible, he sucks at his job."

I smirked. "I said of sorts. In truth, it's a job title on paper. He takes care of all the training for my company."

"Which company is that?"

I swallowed. I understood she wanted to put herself at ease and possibly get to know me better, but this was something complicated.

"Oh!" She turned away. "This is something to do with that big government contract."

My eyes went wide. "How do you... doesn't matter. While

I'd like to explain the nature of my business to you, I'm actually bound by one of your boyfriend's contracts to not even mention my company name."

Spectra nodded, but her jaw was tense. "Bodyguard it is." She waited for a heartbeat longer. "Alexander isn't my boyfriend. We've never been in a relationship."

"And the Angelis?"

Spectra became fixated on the passing scenery. "Is my boyfriend."

"Does he know where you are tonight?"

She shook her head slowly. "We have a very relaxed relationship."

I pulled up to the front of the restaurant and climbed out while the valet opened Spectra's door. I handed the keys to the valet and walked with Spectra quietly into the restaurant. "The booking is in your name," Spectra mumbled as we approached the maître d'.

"Mr. Ryder." Sophia the maître d' smiled before her eyes turned to Spectra, who was busy scanning the restaurant. Sophia's eyes widened a little in recognition. "Miss Michaels, I haven't seen you in a while."

Spectra gave a false smile and nodded. Sophia stood a little shocked for a moment until I cleared my throat.

"Sorry, your table is ready, Mr. Ryder." Sophia led the way to the back of the restaurant where the private dining rooms were located.

A waiter was waiting and took Spectra's coat. She wore a black velvet dress that clung in all the right places, and flowed enough to still be considered conservative. As she turned to take her seat, I felt my body react to the skin the backless dress exposed.

I waited till we were seated and the waiter drew the sheer

curtain and left with our drink order before raising a brow at Spectra. "I'm guessing this used to be a regular date place for you and Alexander." Spectra avoided eye contact, and I understood she didn't want to discuss her relationships with me. "Can I ask how you managed to get a spur of the moment booking here? Even with my name, it's usually booked out well in advance."

Spectra smirked. "Well, we may want to be gone by nine thirty or the people who did book well in advance are going to have a hissy fit about their booking being moved." I waited, watching her. She eventually met my eyes, "They run their booking system electronically and allow Wifi access so the hostess can use her tablet to access it."

I shook my head. "You hacked it." I smiled at her smile. "What else can you do?" She shrugged. "You've just finished your degree, haven't you?"

"Last week. I graduate in a month."

"Have you started applying for work?" I knew she planned to get rid of her business.

She started fidgeting. "I have onc or two."

"But?" Cause there was definitely a but coming with her tone.

"But Alexander has pretty much arranged a job for me with the NSIO. The money is good for a junior. I'd be insane not to take it."

"And the money is important because you want your own place?"

Spectra frowned and shook her head. "No, the convent is home to me. I'll move out one day, possibly when I get married, but until then."

"Then why is the money important?"

Spectra looked at me. "Isn't money important to you?"

I sighed. "I've gotten used to a way of life."

She nodded understanding. "I grew up in this way of life. While it's not necessary, I miss it and would like the option to have it again if I wanted it."

I wanted to ask more about that, but the waiter entered with the wine I'd ordered and poured me some to approve before filling our glasses to the appropriate amount.

"Can I take your order?"

"I'm going to skip straight to dessert please. I'll have the caramel salted brownie with ice cream and the cinnamon apple pie with double caramel sauce and ice cream."

I smirked at her order, and so did the waiter. "Do you ever eat a decent meal, Spec?" She gave him a wicked grin, and he just laughed. When I raised a brow at how casual he was being with my date, the waiter sobered. "Sorry, we went to college together. What would you like, sir?"

"I've actually never tried dessert here. So I'll think I'll let Miss Michaels pick for me."

Spectra grinned at the waiter. "Give him the chocolate molten volcano with ice cream and whipped cream. Thanks, Brian." The waiter smiled and left.

"Just college friends?"

Spectra smiled and nodded with no recognition of the suspicion in my voice. It was like she didn't acknowledge men would be attracted to her. She lifted her drink, took a sip, and the nerves returned.

"There was a reason I asked for dinner."

"I was hoping so." I took my own drink.

"I have rules. You nearly broke one of them last night, and I would have let you because I was so..." she hesitated, looking away, ashamed. "Not myself."

I wanted to apologize, but I doubted we'd be at dinner

right now if it hadn't happened, so I was struggling to feel guilty this evening.

"You're asking for one night of sex, and I understand that rules wouldn't probably exist for that sort of thing, but I want to make sure if this was to happen, where the limitations are." I met her eyes and nodded. "No unprotected sex..."

"I carry no disease."

"It's not about that for me." She chewed her lip. "My mother was pregnant with my sister at eighteen. She loved the man, but he decided while he was old enough to enjoy sex, he wasn't old enough to be responsible for the outcomes of sex."

"He abandoned your mother."

Spectra nodded. "My mother won a scholarship to college and would have gone far in life. Instead, she ended up working like a dog to raise her daughter by herself. Four years later, she met my father and nine months after one night with him, I was born." She met my eyes. "Despite my mother turning things around for herself and becoming quite successful, I under-stood from a very young age that females really do get the raw end of the deal with regards to sex. I promised myself I would never have children out of wedlock. I won't have unprotected sex until there is a ring on my finger and a man to call my husband."

I placed my drink on the table. "I'm unable to give you a child, Spectra. You know that, right? I understand your fear with your boyfriend and especially so with Williams. But you don't need that fear with me."

Spectra blew out a breath. "Alexander would kill you if he found out I let you come inside of me when I've denied him so long. We have an agreement when it comes to using protection with others."

I laughed. I couldn't help it. "He's going to kill me just for having dinner with you, let alone what he'll do if he found out we had sex." I sobered at the acknowledgment on her face. "He doesn't know about the Angelis, does he?"

"We've never discussed Merc."

"But your boyfriend is very aware of your affair with Williams?"

"I was very heavily involved with Alexander for a number of years. I expected to marry him. Then when he became L'Ordre, he set me aside and started screwing half the Nachtwelt. Merc and I knew each other from church, so he knew my life and recognized I was suddenly around a lot more again."

I felt my jaw tense. "You said Alexander and you were never in a relationship, but what you just described sounded very much like one."

She shook her head. "Alexander isn't available to anyone that way. I thought we were more. He explained to me one night, after I mistakenly introduced him as my boyfriend, that he could only marry a specific type of woman."

"The balance." I nodded. "Daughters of a Nephilim are very rare to find, but to find one at his power level would be an impossible dream. She'd have to be the daughter of one of Lucifer's half-breed bastards to even stand a chance."

"Apparently so." Spectra mourned into her drink. "Which brings us to the next rule. You can't drop your shields with me. It's not fair to do that to me. If I'm going to have sex with you, it should be my choice."

"Yes, it should." I agreed. "Which brings me to my question. What are you?"

Spectra tensed. The curtain pulled back, and the waiter came in with three plates of dessert, setting two in front of Spectra and a rather large chocolate indulgence that was spewing up liquid chocolate, like a volcano would lava, in front of me. Spectra picked up her fork and took a bite of her dessert, so I followed suit, the chocolate cake-like product melted in my mouth, the liquid chocolate smothering my tongue in goo.

Spectra waited till she was sure the waiter went. "We need to agree there are topics we can't discuss with each other. You can't discuss your business. I can't discuss what you just asked me. Alexander would..." She stared at her dessert like it left a bad taste in her mouth. "Let's just say I'm a cross breed and leave it at that."

I watched her eat two more bites of her dessert, pointedly avoiding eye contact. I let what she said soak in as we ate. She was forbidden to discuss it, and it would make Alexander angrier than hell for anyone to find out, but he was sure the watcher knew and no doubt the Angelis did too.

"Have you ever told anyone?" She shook her head. "But Tommy Donald knows what you are, and your boyfriend too?"

Spectra turned glassy eyes to me, her eyes pleading to drop this topic. "The celestials can tell what nearly anyone is, their true age, the weight of someone's soul, even who your heart belongs to. You can't hide from them."

"That's why you'll marry the Angelis, because he knows it all and doesn't need to ask you."

Spectra tensed. "I never said I'd marry Merc. We enjoy each other, and I trust him, but there are reasons that wouldn't work." Spectra met my eyes, "You live with Changeur de Corps's. Can you discuss that?"

I swallowed the last mouthful of my dessert and poured another glass of wine as I sat back, relaxed. "One of my powers is to have an affinity with the beasts. Calin and his wives live in a wing of my residence and guard my property, but I have others in my employ, and that's all I can say on that."

"There was another de Sang."

I nodded. "Luke. He's my friend and my personal assistant. He helps me keep my affairs in order and is very resourceful. He's fascinated with you, but not for the same reason I am. He likes to know everything. You puzzle him, and he hates that."

Spectra smirked then sobered. "So Calin's wives, they are all lions?"

I smiled, seeing that she was trying to discuss my life within the confines of our limitations. "Yes. He has six wives now."

"And they are all happy that way?"

I wanted to laugh. "They are a group of women all sharing the same man, and cats at that. They have their own wing, so I don't have to listen to the carry-on. In saying that, Calin has a unique ability with women and manages to keep them all happy most of the time. He treats them well. I think that makes a big difference."

"Any children?"

"Before I was taken, yes. I had a family, but we are talking centuries ago. My family line is still living. Did you want to meet them? I actually have one of my very great grandsons living close by, and I can introduce you. He and his wife are expecting their first child in a few months."

Spectra's eyes went wide and she shook her head. "I meant the lions."

"Oh. There have been a few." I was really hoping she wouldn't ask the next question.

"And they don't bother you running around the house?"

I picked up my wine and took a long drink. "No. They don't cause me any trouble at all."

Spectra's eyes brightened, and I had a gut feeling this

conversation was going to get bad very quickly. "Can they change at a young age? Are they cubs when they change? Do you play with them? Could I meet one?"

I sighed. "No."

Spectra's face fell at my tone. "Oh, of course. Sorry, I forgot this wasn't an ongoing..." She bit her lip and turned her face. "Sorry, I just got overexcited, that's all." There was a quiet beeping sound and Spectra pulled out her phone, silencing it before looking at the screen and standing. "We should get going."

She walked to the coat rack and retrieved her coat, slipping into it. I rang the bell as I rose to retrieve my coat and the waiter, Brian, stuck his head in. "Bill please, Brian."

Brian nodded and disappeared. He returned by the time we were ready to leave. I signed the authorization to debit my account here, and, placing my hand on Spectra's lower back, escorted her to the front door. The valet pulled my car up as we walked out and I opened the door for Spectra as a car I recognized turned onto the street at the end of the block.

"Bay..."

"In the car. We can discuss anything else as I drive you home." I kept my eyes on the car, hoping Alexander Williams's eyesight wasn't anywhere near as good as mine.

Spectra sank into the car, only slightly startled by the caution in my voice. I slipped into the driver's seat and was pulling out as Williams pulled into the space I was vacating. I pulled up to the lights and watched as Williams exited his car with a very attractive woman.

"Were you expecting Williams to turn up and save you from me again tonight?" I growled.

Spectra startled and looked over her shoulder. She sighed painfully as she turned back to me and let me see the honesty in her eyes. "No. He has a standing booking on Saturday nights but doesn't always use it himself." Her fingers were flexing and clenching again. "I thought he was out of town this weekend. She must be something special to make him miss his father's birthday."

We drove for a few more blocks in silence. When we approached an intersection and I started to pull into the left turning lane, Spectra reached over and touched my leg. "You're in the wrong lane."

I looked at her, weighing the look in her eyes, then pulled off the road into a park. "Are you sure?"

She gave me a shy smile. "That all depends. If it snows tonight, can I still get home from your place tomorrow?"

"Possibly not. Would that be an issue for you?"

Spectra relaxed into the seat and shook her head. "I have nothing to rush back to."

Her answer saddened me. "Spectra, I want you to be sure. I won't walk away from you a second time. If we get to my place and you change your mind, I won't let you leave."

Her eyes were guarded as she reached across and touched my cheek. "Do you know why I insisted we go on a date first, Bay?"

"You wanted to get to know me better."

She smiled kindly. "Partly yes, but the real reason is that a virgin deserves to be wined and dined, to be treated special before they lose their innocence, cause there is no getting that back."

I must have looked shocked because her smile dimmed and her eyes became more guarded.

"You've not been with a woman in centuries. Your first time should be more than a quick seduction in an attic." Her smile disappeared. "And it's my first time too, Bay. I've never been with a predator before and don't believe it's likely I ever will again, so for me, it deserves to be special for both of us."

I caressed her cheek and pulled her mouth to mine, kissing her gently but with enough intensity to let her know this was special. "I won't hurt you, Spectra. Don't fear me."

Her pale blue eyes met mine, strong and determined. "Take me home with you, Bay."

CHAPTER 9

Spectra

THE SNOW WAS JUST STARTING to fall as we drove down the narrow roads between large properties. "I've never been in the country when it snowed." I spoke quietly, watching the white fall through the blackness of night.

"You grew up in Wolfenden?" Bay shook his head, humored.

"It's the suburbs. Estate houses yes, but still the suburbs. This is beautiful. I understand why you've chosen to live out here despite your life being in the city." I turned to look at Bay and found him watching me, an emotion I couldn't pinpoint in his eyes. "What?"

He turned his eyes back to the road. "You've been alone a long time, haven't you?"

I frowned. "Since I was fourteen." I turned my eyes back

to the dark. "My mother didn't die till I was sixteen, but she stopped existing the day my sister died. If it wasn't for Henry and Philippa, I probably would never have made it to college in the first place."

"Henry Williams? L'Paix took you in? That is why you became close with Alexander."

My hands started fidgeting of their own accord. "I've known the family since I was in primary school. They were our neighbors. There were a lot of empty fridge moments in my house after Danika died. My mom went missing for days at a time. She'd come home dirty, covered in bruises from de Sang bites. I don't know if she even knew what was happening to her. Eventually, she lost her prestigious job, and we started eating through her savings and my college fund." I swiped at a lone tear that escaped. "I spent a lot of time next door with Alexander and his family."

"How did you know they were de Sang bites?"

"I heard Philippa arguing with Henry one night about it. I didn't know what they were talking about until..."

"You met one," Bay filled in for me. It must have been in the look on my face.

"He came to the house looking for my mother, except she wasn't there, I was."

Bay's fingers on the steering wheel tightened, knuckles turning white. "He fed on you."

I looked down at my hands. "I screamed. Luckily Alexander was on his way over to bring me home for dinner. After that, they had to reveal it all. A few days later, my mother took her own life."

Bay gritted his teeth. "He did it to punish your mother for not being there. That's why Alexander hates my kind more than any other predator. One of us attacked the girl he loves."

"Don't," I sighed. "Don't ever say that to me. Alexander's feelings are as complex as his power and well above my level of comprehension."

"He only smokes around you."

"I know." I touched the window where a snowflake was stuck to the other side. "I've seen him when he doesn't know I'm there, how he is with others."

I saw Bay glance at me in the reflection of the window then turned the wheel, and we pulled into a driveway surrounded by forest. As we passed by the trees I'd escaped through, I finally recognized the landscape.

"Is there anything else I should know?" Bay queried. I looked at him. "About your preferences with sex."

I shrugged. "I like the plain old boring variety, not the kinky shit everyone's into these days," Bay smirked. "Is that a bad thing?"

"No." Bay kept his eyes on the road. "I was just thinking the last time I had sex with a woman, if she was willing to be naked in front of you, she was considered brazen. Most times they kept their undergarments on at a minimum. I'd been around in the times where nudity was acceptable. Part of my loss of interest was the restrictions and how prim and proper women became."

"What was the other part?" I dared to ask, wondering how anyone lost interest in sex.

"The feeding. You couldn't feed from a woman's neck. The bruising would get questions asked. So things became tricky. It ended up where my head between a woman's thighs achieved my feeding easier. I was able to bring her to pleasure and feed from her femoral as she climaxed, but then she would be unconscious. So I got used to not having the physical benefit myself. One day I just stopped getting turned on."

We pulled into the garage and Bay turned off the ignition. "Until me?"

He turned to look at me, eyes serious. "Until you looked at me with such loathing where any other woman would have looked at me with lust."

I smiled. "So this isn't a special connection, soul mates, or some bullshit. This is you wanting the one woman who didn't want you?"

Bay slipped his hand behind my neck and gently pulled my face to his. "I honestly don't know what this is, Spectra. I just know, from the minute we met, I had to have you."

His lips touched mine, and for a minute we sat there, our lips pressed to each other, and then our mouths started feeding on each other like starving animals. The only sound was my heavy breathing and the wet sound of our mouths kissing.

Bay's hand tangled in my hair and pulled my head back so he could kiss down my neck. I half opened my eyes and saw a man watching us through the window. I screamed before I could stop myself and jumped back to my side of the car, hands over my mouth to stop my heart escaping through it.

Bay turned and was out his car door instantly, ready to face a threat. He immediately relaxed and turned back to the car, bending over to meet my eyes. "It's okay, Spectra. Just breathe deep." He shut his car door. "What the hell, Luke?"

"Sorry, boss. I saw your car return and didn't realize you'd have company. We have a situation you need to deal with personally."

Bay swept a frustrated hand through his hair as he walked around the car and opened my door. "Get one of the wives not on duty." He took my hand, helping me out of the car as the other man walked out of the garage. "I'm sorry, Spectra. Something has come up. I'll need to deal with it first."

"Will it take long? I could go home, and we can try another night."

Bay shook his head, worry creasing his brow. "Stay. Please?"

The man was back with an attractive blonde who was dressed casually. I nodded, and Bay smiled. He pulled me to him and kissed me till my body molded to his, and then we kissed a little longer. Luke cleared his throat. Bay pulled back and looked over his shoulder at him, nodding his head.

"This is Gina, she will keep you company until I get back." Bay took my hand, leading me over.

"And what if you're kept late into the night again, boss?" she asked. No sarcasm intended. Just a factual question requiring a factual answer.

Bay kept his eyes on Gina. "She'll sleep in my bed." Gina gave a singular nod. Bay dropped my hand and followed Luke inside the house. "Tell me?"

Luke lowered his voice so I didn't hear his response. The blonde, however, shook her head before turning her big brown eyes on me. "You were a beautiful ghost, but you're even prettier in the flesh."

I swallowed. "You were one of the lions last week?"

She nodded and turned to walk inside, expecting me to follow. "My husband was very annoyed that you were able to pass by us. We didn't realize you were still alive." I raised a brow, and she shrugged, "He bought you in unconscious. I've never known him to kill a feed, but there is always a first time."

"I wasn't a feed," I grumbled.

"So I hear."

We entered the house from the garage entry and passed by a few rooms on the way in. Gina pointed to the first open door. "That's our gym for working out." She was very fit and strong by the looks of it. A few closed doors later, she entered a small library with what looked to be study desks. "I just have to grab my laptop. I was studying for an exam next week."

"You don't have to stop for me. I know where Bay's bedroom is. I can make my own way upstairs."

She frowned at me. "I don't think the boss would appreciate me letting random women roam his home. No offence."

"None taken, though I'm a far sight away from random, don't you think? Still, I accept I'm a stranger here. Did you want to bring your laptop with you and I'll read or something while you study?" I indicated the walls of books, thinking there must be something I'd want to read here.

Gina smiled. "It's okay, I was getting tired." She collected her laptop and textbook and walked back past me into the corridor. "Here, I'll put your coat in the cloak room."

I slipped out of my jacket, ensuring I kept my phone with me. Gina stopped by a door and stepped inside, hanging the coat up with several others. We turned the corner and emerged into the foyer from the back of the house and started up the stairs. At the first floor, she opened a door and led us into a lounge room, putting her laptop on the side table before plopping down on the lounge.

Gina seemed like such a normal college student it was hard to reconcile she was a predator. I sat at the opposite end of the lounge, unsure what to do next except to take my heels off because they were starting to hurt.

"So you're the woman Bay's coming out of celibacy for?"

I turned and found the blonde's eyes looking me over. "Apparently." I looked down where I was wringing my hands.

"That makes you uncomfortable, that you have that effect on him."

"Psychology major?" I raised a brow.

She smiled. "You'll have to excuse that I'm not very good at girly talk."

"That makes two of us then. I live with a bunch of nuns. We're not exactly up doing shots and braiding each other's hair at night."

Gina frowned. "Wait, are you a nun?"

I laughed. "God no! I just live there." I looked over to where she studied me. "You're in a polygamous relationship, how does that work?"

She shrugged and relaxed a little. "It's not what I expected. It's like having sisters I guess. We don't all get along, but we love Calin, and he manages to make it work." She smiled. "I was never very good at relationships. I always found guys to be either too clingy or assholes. Calin was different. He was up front that there were other women and always treated me well, but at the same time gave me all the space I needed. He was the first guy I ever actually found myself missing."

I swallowed. "How did you end up here?"

She gave me gentle eyes. "You mean how I made the choice to become a beast?" I nodded. "I lived here for a year with them first. It wasn't a choice I made lightly. Calin and I were seeing each other for two years before that. I could have chosen to stay human, and Calin still would have loved me and kept me. The boss doesn't really care one way or the other either. It's always our choice.

"I kept working my job in the city, because that's one thing both men won't tolerate. You have to earn your keep here. You can become one of them and join the company, or you work in the human world. Our choice either way, but there is no sponging allowed."

She tapped her finger on the laptop. "It was this that made up my mind for me. I always wanted to go to college, to get somewhere in life and do something no one else in my family ever dreamed of. I'm trailer trash by birth. I was good at school, but couldn't afford anything past it, so I got a job in a bar. It was a dead-end job, and I was on track to following in my mother's footsteps when I met Calin.

"Along with the benefits of strength and a lack of aging, if you join the company, the boss will pay your way through college. But you have to apply yourself, and you have to study something that will benefit the company. So in the end, I get a family, an education, a good paying job, an amazing place to live..." She looked around the room with a smile and tucked her hair back behind her ear as she did. I spotted a delicate tattoo of a lily behind her ear.

I swallowed. "That's a cute tattoo. Did it hurt?"

Gina's smile disappeared, and she pulled her hair down to cover the tattoo. "Yes, but it was short-lasting. Calin's not really a fan of tattoos, so I try to keep it covered." She turned her face back to mine then met my eyes. "If you could have the life you always dreamed of, would you take the opportunity when it was offered?"

I hesitated. "I couldn't do anything that involved hurting a human."

Gina's eyes flashed with anger. "We eat animals, deer, rabbits, stuff like that. I've never tasted a human ever. The only time we would attack a human is if our work required it."

"I'm sorry. You never know with the Nachtwelt where predators draw the line. It's like the human world, there's good and bad and downright evil. It just seems to be more of the latter two in the Nachtwelt than the first."

"Is he bringing you in?" she asked cautiously.

I looked surprised. "It's just one night." I looked towards

the window and the snow as it fell heavier. "Or until he returns me."

"To the convent?" She smirked. "There's something rather chauvinistic and ancient about that situation, isn't there? Hiding a beautiful woman away in a convent and only taking her out when she's to be used for pleasure."

I felt myself blush, and her smile widened as she laughed. "You've blushed every time I've called you beautiful, but that, that was your liking the idea of being used for the boss's pleasure." Her demeanor sobered. "And yet, last week you ran terrified from him."

I stood up, walking to the window, watching the snow fall over the grounds. "The idea of being with him terrifies me, but last night," I took a breath to steady my heart rate as it suddenly sped up at the memory. "Last night, I felt his intentions, felt why he wanted me. It scared me even more that I could be so heartless to deny him that need."

I watched out the window as one of the lions sprinted across the snow. "You're so graceful when you run, but it must be terrifying for the person you're running toward."

"It took me a while to get used to it." Gina chuckled behind me.

I watched another animal dash across the snow and found myself surprised. "Bay has a panther living here too?"

"What do you mean?" Gina came to the window quickly.

"I just saw one running after one of the lions, like they were playing chase."

"Not one of ours," she said, grabbing my arm as she dragged me towards the door. She opened the door and yelled: "Calin!" She started dragging me up the stairs quickly.

We were at the next landing when a door opened and a

blond-haired man looked over the railing at Gina. "What is it?"

"We've got company."

The blond man's eyes went wide, and all of a sudden there was a cacophony of noises as the front door flew open and claws thundered across the marble entrance and started up the stairs.

I looked down to see a black panther sprinting up the stairs. A second later, a lion caught up and launched itself at the panther's back. A second panther passed the brawl on the stairs.

Gina cursed and threw me back against the wall as she pulled off her top and started transforming. I hit the wall hard and stumbled to my knees as the panther made it to our landing. Gina wasn't through the change yet, and her head snapped up as the panther launched toward her.

"No!" I yelled and threw myself at the panther as I breathed out. I collided, twisted, and passed through the beast in mid-air, concentrating on my siphoning ability. I felt his power and pulled it into me. I passed through the other side and the naked man fell beside Gina, panting heavily, his eyes wide with fear as I continued to fall unseen.

If I'd been corporeal, I would have landed on the stairs and probably broken my neck as I tumbled to the bottom. Instead, I passed through them and kept falling to the ground floor and farther. The string of curse words that passed through my brain, when I stopped falling in the darkened cellar, would have made Father Mathew give me a week's worth of penance.

I concentrated and breathed in, sitting up in the cellar and trying to get my bearings. It was so quiet down here after the noise upstairs that I was tempted to stay put till daylight.

Unfortunately, I'd just taken a predator's power and needed to do something with it. Getting to my feet, I stumbled through the cellar till I found a wall. Stepping carefully, grateful for a cement floor that seemed clean, I followed the wall till a subtle glow came into view and the smell of chlorine hit me.

As the blue light grew brighter, I stepped through the archway into the underground swimming pool area. It was still quiet here, only the whirring of the pool's filtration system preventing dead silence.

"Perfect." I smiled as I walked toward a small garden that grew in the corner of the pool room. I delved my hands into the soil, wiggling my fingers to ensure my hands were buried before earthing some of the power I'd siphoned.

Standing up, I felt heat burning across my back. I turned around and came face to face with a man. His dark eyes watched me intently as I tried to take a step back and found the garden in my way. "Human? How unexpected." He looked down at my dirty hands and smiled. "Are you the gardener?" His eyes assessed my dress. "No, not in that dress. And no bruises, so you're not food. Who are you?"

His narrow mouth pulled up in a smirk when I didn't answer. "What did you bury just now?"

I met the sorcerer's eyes evenly, being very careful to control my breathing as I let it out enough to become insubstantial without it visibly being apparent.

His power cycled around him like a hurricane. He raised a brow when I didn't answer him. "Like that, is it?"

He stepped around me and put his hand out above the garden, smiling at me. The soil shifted, but when nothing came out, his smile disappeared. He went to grab me by the throat and his hand passed through me. It took all my effort to remain non-reactive and just walk off, allowing myself to become fully incorporeal as I did.

The sorcerer shook his head. "Ghost? She seemed so alive." Gathering himself, his eyes became focused again as he stormed towards the darkened cellar.

Closing my eyes, I concentrated on finding Bay. I felt my body lift and float through the ceiling and farther until the noises of the house bombarded me again. I opened my eyes and found Bay standing over a couple of dead naked bodies, his hands covered in blood, anger radiating from him. I breathed in to return to form and Bay turned, grabbing me by the throat before he realized it was me.

"Spectra." He relaxed and exhaled with relief. His hand released and caressed my neck.

"There's a sorcerer in your cellar looking for something."

Bay's eyes went wide. "Stay here," he instructed as he ran out of the room.

I realized I was standing in the kitchen and relaxed. This wasn't my fight. I sat down hard on the floor, eyes staring at nothing, until I focused and saw the bodies in front of me. That's when I pulled myself up, found the door to outside, and started running.

CHAPTER 10

Bay

GINA'S TERRIFIED VOICE GOT OUR ATTENTION very quickly, but none of us reacted as quickly as Calin. By the time I made it to the top of the stairs, Calin was already launching himself over the banister. I looked over in time to see Spectra launch herself at the panther, become incorporeal, and disappear. The panther shivered in midair and transformed back to human in a blink. And when I say human, I mean fully human. Even from this distance, I could tell she'd somehow taken his ability to transform ever again from him.

I would have been fascinated, but more of the enemy was invading our house, Calin's wives battling the intruders. I launched myself over the banister, falling to the first floor alongside Calin while Luke ran down the stairs to Gina's side. A panther growled and launched at me. I grabbed its open jaws and pulled my hands back, dropping my shields as I did. The momentum of the beast's body assisted my strength. I heard a crack and the beast fell dead to the floor, returning to her human form.

Calin, Luke, and I moved around the house, fighting the invaders alongside Calin's wives in their beast form. There were fifteen at least, and I only put a dent in the onslaught, but by the time the sounds of fighting were fading, I stood over my last two kills in the kitchen. I heard someone breathe directly behind me, and, still riding the adrenaline, turned around ready to kill again.

Spectra's eyes bulged as I grabbed her by the throat. "Spectra." I breathed in relief, seeing her safe. I'd hoped she was still upstairs safe, but as I looked at the dirt smudges on her face, I knew something happened to her after she saved Gina. Relaxing my hand, I caressed her neck and opened my mouth to ask what happened.

"There's a sorcerer in your cellar looking for something," she whispered, her voice cracking as if on the verge of tears. I wanted to stay and make sure she was all right, but I understood where the attack was coming from now.

"Stay here," I instructed as I ran out of the room for the cellar.

I walked into the pool room and to the stone arch. The cellar was alight with the flame Falon Lore held aloft. I smiled and leaned on the wall, watching as he tried stone after stone, hoping for a secret passage or room. I waited patiently, well aware his army to distract me was destroyed, but there were other issues I needed to deal with. L'Ordre would need to be called to deal with the carnage, and I was sure Spectra's presence and appearance was not going to endear me to Williams.

While I let Falon satisfy his curiosity, my mind conjured the image of her hands covered in dirt, like she'd had to dig her way out of something. Before I could consider that further, Falon finally turned and saw me watching him.

"We knew the rumor of an antidote would bring you all out of hiding. One by one, you will all die seeking it." I smiled viciously.

Falon Lore hesitated, and that was his downfall. I used my power to launch one of the loose rocks at his head. It struck with a resounding thud, and darkness encompassed the cellar as Falon fell unconscious to the floor.

I walked to Falon and grabbed the collar of his jacket. I lifted and dragged him out to the pool area where I dropped him into the water. I watched him float for a moment before he sank beneath the water. I stood watching, my powers still partially shielded as I felt for the life leaving him. The bubbles stopped coming out of his mouth and nose, and his heart stumbled and stopped. Sorcerer he may be, but human mortality was still theirs.

While I waited those few more minutes to ensure death, my eyes were pulled to the garden that Luke insisted on me planting. I walked over to it and saw the disturbed earth where Spectra had buried her hands. I squatted and placed my hand over those holes. Nothing. Dropping my shields a little more, I waited to see what would happen. Slowly, a small green stem emerged from the soil, leaves bloomed, and in a matter of seconds, a plush catnip bush grew. I shook my head and stood up, wondering what the hell happened here. Taking a deep breath and content that Falon Lore was happily burning in hell, I made my way upstairs to deal with the law.

Calin was the first person I found, squatting above Margaret, her eyes staring blankly into the afterlife. I squatted down next to him, putting an arm around his head. I hugged him to me as he mourned his first wife. He wouldn't mourn her fully tonight, there was still work to be done, but we'd both take this moment until we could farewell her properly.

"How great is your loss?" I enquired carefully. Calin loved his wives, but they were also our employees, and I didn't want him thinking my concern was the loss of guards.

"Margaret dead, and Anna is fighting for her life as we speak. Selena is a wreck. Margaret put herself in harm's way to save her." Calin swiped at his eyes and took a moment to center himself. "L'Ordre and L'Paix are already here. Luke called them immediately." I nodded, understanding this wasn't just a matter of order. Anything that could be considered the beginnings of an interspecies war brought in the peace officer. We both stood, and Calin turned his back on the gruesome loss behind him.

I lowered my voice. "Can you take Spectra out of sight till this is done? She's going to be traumatized, and her presence here will cause us issues."

Calin nodded. "Any idea where she is? She did her vanishing trick again, though I must thank her for saving Gina."

"I left her in the kitchen." I started up the servants' walk to gain access to the kitchen without passing through the main part of the house. I opened the door and moved around the bench where I'd left the bodies. Spectra wasn't there.

Calin tapped my shoulder and pointed to the kitchen door, still ajar. I concentrated and could see her drift leaving through that door, fear and shock strong in that aura. I sighed. "You'll need to track her. She's spooked though, so be careful."

"I'll take Gina. She can use her animal eyes in case your girl has gone ghost again." Calin walked back out the way we came in.

I took a breath, shut my shields, and went out to the main foyer and the chaos that was there.

"What took you so long?" Henry Williams enquired as I joined him, Alexander, and Luke by the main staircase. Seeing them side by side, there was no mistaking they were father and son. Alexander was just a younger version of his father.

"Found a loose end in the cellar," I answered glumly. "Has Luke explained what happened?"

Henry nodded, "Where's Calin?"

Alexander always deferred to his father if present because he was respectful, and as much as he annoyed me for his prejudice, Alexander performed well in his role since taking it on.

"He and Gina are going out to check the perimeter for any we may have missed."

Henry nodded, crossing his arms. "Good idea. I believe we've only got the one left alive?"

I looked to Luke, who nodded. "The one who attacked Gina while she was still transforming and you intervened."

"He lived?" I asked, surprised and angry, but glad Luke knew well enough to cover for what we'd all seen Spectra do. "That's a surprise." I gave Luke a stern look. Luke looked at his feet.

"I would question him, but it appears his sudden transformation to being human again left him with amnesia." Henry cocked a brow. "I didn't know it was possible to cleanse a beast without killing it."

I shook my head. "Admittedly, that wasn't what I was aiming to do. I actually don't know how that happened. Maybe he was a new convert?"

Alexander assessed me. "I'll look into it. I'd love to know how you did that." He looked around and nodded to one of the men standing at the front door in coveralls. They started filing in with body bags.

"Luke, can you escort two of the men to the pool and retrieve the sorcerer down there?" I asked politely. Luke nodded and indicated the men should follow him.

"Who was it?" Henry asked.

"Falon Lore."

"The weakest of them," Alexander considered, "but it looks like the rumor has worked. I will leak a memo at work that tonight's attack resulted in one of the attackers being exposed and successfully cured of the beast."

Henry nodded. "I will follow that up with a notice that the antidote has been moved to a more secure location. That should prevent this happening at your home again."

"Let's leak several memos. One to each sector indicating different times and places. That should narrow the field for identifying the breach." Alexander suggested. "Too long the Essence has gained access to information that should never have breached the NSIO walls."

Henry nodded. "I think I'm done here. Hopefully, you'll have your home back within the hour."

"There is one dead which will stay," I informed quietly. "Calin will bury his wife here."

Henry closed his eyes, the first bit of emotion I'd seen in him all night. "Which wife?"

"Margaret."

"She was a good woman. Give him my condolences." Henry met my eyes. "Truly good women are hard to come by these days. They shouldn't be harmed." I nodded, agreeing with every word he said. Henry looked intently at me before looking away, and I knew he was aware of my interest in Spectra.

Alexander's eyes were angry. "Identify Margaret, so the cleaners know who to leave." I nodded. Alexander Williams dropped his shield and stepped into the ether.

Henry waited a moment after his son left. "He was willing to put aside his hate for your kind to make this work, Bay, but if you try to take her from him, he will turn on you and years of planning will be destroyed."

"I seek only a taste, Henry. You know better than any that my eternity is not something I would offer the girl. Besides, we both know Alexander cannot offer her anything permanent either. She is much better off with the boyfriend she already has. That they have an open relationship works in my favor as much as Alexander's."

Henry looked at me curiously, and I resisted clarifying about Mercury, remembering that Alexander might not know about him.

Henry blew out a breath. "I adore that girl. She has a will of iron when it comes to living. She wasn't hurt tonight, was she?" My eyes widened in shock as Henry reached out and removed a long black hair from the shoulder of my jacket, holding it up with a knowing look before dropping it to the ground. I shook my head. "It was her choice this time, wasn't it?" I nodded. Henry shook his head. "He will kill you when he finds out, so keep whatever happens behind closed doors, Bay." Henry took two steps towards the door, where he preferred to vanish out of sight.

"Do you know what she is, Henry?"

Henry looked back over his shoulder at me, his eyes as dark and dangerous as if I'd just threatened his wife's life. "Leave it alone, Bay. Have your fun then let her go."

Spectra

I ran into the darkness, not having any idea where I was running or how long I'd been running. Despite the freezing cold ground and the light covering of snow, I kept running. Through the open land and then into the even darker forest, winding through the trees, catching myself and pushing on whenever my body felt like it would fail. Then an angel appeared in front of me.

I dropped to my knees in surprise before I recognized it was a statue. I knelt there panting, eyes traveling down the statue till I could just make out an inscription at the base. A grave. I was kneeling on a grave. As I scanned the area around me, I realized it wasn't the only grave in this clearing. I couldn't help thinking of the irony. I'd run from kneeling before the newly dead, just to kneel before the long dead.

I cuddled up to the base of the stone angel, shivering as my body temp cooled rapidly, but it was worth it for the peace that started seeping into me. Consecrated ground. I dropped my head to my knees and closed my eyes, wishing I could just step back into my bedroom at the convent, or maybe even into Mercury's arms. He'd be at the hospital, working hard to save those he could, praying for those he couldn't, or wouldn't. The weighing of souls. Would mine weigh a little heavier after what I'd done tonight?

Movement through the undergrowth caught my attention, and I raised my head to see a lion watching me from several meters away. I smiled. "I'm glad you're okay." My eyes lifted over Gina's head as the blond man, Calin, jogged behind her, slowing to a stride as he approached.

He ran a hand along Gina's back and whispered something in her ear then stepped cautiously towards me. He stopped a meter away and squatted to look at me. His eyes flicked to the statue and back. "Are you cold?" I nodded. He stood, slipping out of his jacket, stepping forward lightly as if I was a child that might spook and run.

I unfolded my legs, and he stopped walking. Both he and Gina watched me stand, as if they were surprised that I could. I met his eyes, and he inhaled a sharp breath. He didn't say anything, just held his jacket for me. I pulled it on, wrapping it tight around me as I started walking in the direction they came from. Gina spun around and took off in a run. I raised a brow at Calin.

"She's gone ahead to organize a bath and some clean clothes for you."

"A shower will do."

Calin shook his head. "You've run for kilometers. Your muscles will soon tell you about it. You need a nice hot bath and maybe some simple stretches before you rest."

"Is it all over?"

Calin pursed his lips. "For tonight. If L'Ordre has done his job well, and he usually does, the place should be clean as a whistle by the time we get back."

I nodded and kept walking. Calin touched my back a few minutes later and pointed to my left, using his hand to turn me and move in that direction.

"What will you do when your secret comes out?" Calin asked casually as we walked.

"Which secret?"

"About what you are?"

"What I am now, or what I was before?" I saw Calin's head swivel to consider me in my peripheral vision. I shrugged. "It would be best if it wasn't revealed. No one wants L'Ordre as an enemy, especially one who has a contract with your signature on it."

Calin stopped walking. "Were you sent as a test, Spectra? Is that why you agreed to meet with him tonight?"

I turned to consider Calin. "Bay wants something from me, Calin, and until last night, I couldn't understand why me. After last night, I can't refuse him." I smiled quietly to myself. "Alexander always says compassion is my weakness."

Calin studied my eyes. "He's wrong. Compassion and self-sacrifice are very admirable traits."

I smirked. "Well, it's not all self-sacrifice. I am hoping to get something out of it."

Calin laughed, stepping forward, and I turned to keep walking with him. "It's been awhile, Spectra. You may need to give him a few chances to release centuries of pressure first."

We stepped out of the forest into the clear field. I pouted. "But he promised me he could bring a woman to orgasm with his face between her thighs."

Calin growled, grabbing my shoulders to face him, face serious. "Do you want to be food?" I shook my head, suddenly scared. "You are not only breaking centuries of abstinence, Spectra. For centuries before that, he hasn't been with a woman without gaining sustenance from her. He'll need to resist that instinct, so don't put him in a position that tempts it."

I swallowed. "And by that, you mean the literal physical position."

Calin's mouth pulled up slightly. "Exactly." Headlights came across the field towards us and Calin shielded his eyes. "Why do people who can see in the dark use headlights? Honestly! There goes my night vision for several minutes."

We stood still for the next few minutes while the lights

came closer. Eventually, a Jeep Wrangler pulled up beside us, the top down, Luke behind the wheel. "Gina told me Spectra was tired after her run."

I looked at Calin. "How did you know I'd run the entire way?"

He took my arm leading me to the passenger side and placed me in the passenger seat before shutting the door and jumping into the backseat. "Your tracks."

Luke shifted back into drive and started speeding back through the paddock. "The clean up's finished. The boss is making arrangements for your wife's burial."

"Have we heard about Anna?" Calin asked, his face shutting down, but emotion flitting across his eyes when I turned to look at him.

"Critical." Luke glanced at me then back to the dark path in front of us. "I'll drive you in once we've seen Miss Michaels safely back."

"We can't both go, Luke."

"Your wives are exhausted, and as much as they'd all like to go, you know only you will be let in to see her. So, let your wives rest and mourn Margaret. Nothing more will happen tonight so I will take you, that way you can be by your wife's bedside if she wakes." The way Luke phrased the word 'if' made me think it was highly unlikely.

The house came into view and silence descended over the car. It started snowing again as we approached the house. Luke looked up. "If this keeps up at this rate, we'll be snowed in come Monday." He pulled into the garage and shut off the engine as Calin jumped out of the back and opened the door for me.

Calin looked at my feet and shook his head. "Definitely a bath."

Luke came around the car. "I'll take her. You go see your women. I'll meet you back here in fifteen." Luke put his arm on the small of my back, and I remembered I was wearing Calin's jacket.

I slid it off and handed it to him. "Thank you. For the jacket and for coming to find me. I'm sorry about your wife."

Calin nodded and walked off into the house through a different door than the one Luke was leading me towards, his hand resting on the bare skin of my back. He walked me up the stairs, and as I lifted my legs to climb, I could feel the muscle soreness setting in. By the second landing, I was cringing with each step. Luke looked at me with concern, shook his head, and swept my legs out from under me, carrying me the rest of the way to the third floor and the room I escaped from not even a week ago.

In the bedroom, he put me back on my feet. "There's a hot bath waiting for you. Gina left you a nightdress on the bed. The boss still has a few things to fix up, so take your time and soak those torn muscle fibers." Luke walked back out of the room through the one door I hadn't tried last time. I caught a glimpse of a study through the door before he shut it.

Sighing, I moved to the bathroom, slipping out of my dress and into the hot water. I'd put my body through too much today. Spending the day praying in the frigid garden. Then this run through the snow. I was beyond exhausted. I felt myself starting to drift to sleep and startled awake, slopping water everywhere.

I looked at my hands and cringed. I grabbed the washcloth and started scrubbing at the dirt before attacking my feet with the same vigor. By the time I felt clean, my fingers were turning pruney. I pulled myself wearily out of the tub, dried off, and wrapped the towel around me, walking out to the bedroom to find the nightdress.

As I stepped into the room, Bay sat in one of the chairs at the other side of the room. Head in his hands, as if he too were exhausted. He looked up as I closed the bathroom door, and any sign of weariness faded as his eyes trailed over me. He stood up and walked towards me.

"You're safe?" he asked. I nodded. "You're not hurt?"

"Only self-inflicted muscle soreness."

He touched my cheek, just the slightest brush of the back of his fingers. "I'm sorry the night was ruined, Spectra. You're exhausted. I'll let you sleep, and tomorrow I'll have Luke take you home."

I frowned. "You changed your mind?"

Bay just looked at me. "If I'd changed my mind about wanting you, Spectra, I would have Luke take you home immediately. You are exhausted, and you must be scared after tonight. I will..."

Bay's eyes turned liquid as I untucked my towel and dropped it to the floor. He swallowed once, shook his head, and stepped into me, catching me up in a passionate kiss that stole my breath for a second. I unbuttoned his shirt quickly and pushed it from his shoulders, not bothering to untuck it before I started unbuckling his belt. I would lose my nerve if this didn't happen tonight, and after what I'd already been through, I was getting what I came for.

Bay's pants dropped to the floor, and he pulled me tight against him, his hardness pressing painfully against my pelvis and lower abdomen. Walking us backward to the bed, I crept onto the mattress as he climbed over the top of me, his fingers seeking out my heat and sliding into me. He stroked me enough to initiate my body's natural response before he dropped his body to mine, letting his erection find its own way, and it did, like a heat-seeking missile.

He found my opening and shoved into me, patience be damned. I'd offered it, he was taking it, before anything else tried to interfere. The moan that rumbled up his throat as he slid home and started thrusting into me was beautiful. I smiled at the sounds he was making, so animalistic, so full of need. He started throbbing inside me, and I put a hand on his shoulder, pushing him back.

Bay met my eyes, nothing but lust looking back at me. I gave him a gentle look and pushed again. He rolled onto his back but kept hold of me to stop my escape. "Give me a second," I murmured and kissed him gently. I climbed off the bed and grabbed my purse that I'd seen sitting on the chair when I first walked in. I grabbed what we needed from inside then jogged back to the bed.

Bay raised a brow at me as I straddled him, ripping open one of the condoms and throwing the rest on the bedside table. "Rule one, remember? Plus it will help with your sensitivity." He opened his mouth, but I started rolling the condom on, and the feel of my pushing the rubber down his shaft made his back bow. I followed that up by sliding him back inside me. I bent over and kissed him slowly, drawing it out, just holding him inside of me.

His hands caressed over my body, taking my breasts in his hands and caressing them, doubling his efforts when I moaned for him. Pushing back up to sitting, I started riding him, tilting my pelvis as I lifted off him again. Bay's eyes rolled back, but his hands gripped my hips. I could see how much he was trying to restrain himself, and I felt like I was torturing him.

I touched his face, ceasing my body movement so he would

meet my eyes. "What do you need, Bay? Let me in, take what it is you need right now."

Bay pulled my mouth to his, dropping his shields enough for that tropical heat wave to sweep through me. My body reacted immediately to his desire. He threw me onto my back and started a hard and fast fuck, his moans growing with each thrust, his control on his shielding slipping. I reached into myself as the heat became unbearable, finding my shield and imagining pulling it gently across my chest. This time, it moved, stretching like a balloon slowly being filled with air. It made the heat bearable.

It wasn't a large shield, but I managed to stretch it across my chest entirely before it became rigid. I focused on holding it there for as long as I could. Bay's mouth captured mine, his thrusts increasing speed, his moans filling the room. I wrapped my legs around his arse, and an entirely new sound emerged as he slid even deeper into me.

He kissed me hard and fast then threw his head back and roared as his body spasmed, the feeling of which brought me to the edge of my own climax. The sensation of nearly coming jarred my focus and the shield shrank away again, leaving me bathing in the heat of Bay's power as he stilled himself above me. I could feel his cock still pulsating inside me as his mouth captured mine again and he kissed me long and hard.

He went to pull away from me, but I stopped him and showed him the correct way to pull away and remove the condom so he didn't cause spillage. He took himself off to the bathroom, and I grabbed the nightdress Gina left on the end of the bed, pulling it on before climbing into Bay's bed. I heard the shower start, but that was about all.

Several hours later, I stirred as I felt Bay slip into the bed, rolling me onto my back and climbing between my thighs. He kissed me, waiting for me to react fully to his kisses before he let his mouth wander to my exposed breast. He took my hand and placed it around his rock-hard erection, letting me feel the fresh condom already in place.

"Can I?" he murmured before his mouth closed over my nipple and drew my own moans into the room.

"Yes!"

He pushed into me, the same need riding him as earlier, but I could feel he held a little more control this time. He kept his shield in place, which I was grateful for. I didn't want him to fall back to that each time. His lips pinched my throat as his moans rose to the crescendo. I turned my head, forcing his face away from my neck in time before he lost control, and he bit into the pillow above my shoulder.

He swept a hand through my hair as his body settled and kissed me gently before pulling away, not needing any help this time. I rolled over and went back to sleep, only to repeat it all again as the light in the room lightened, lasting longer each time. All I could think of as I fell asleep in his arms after the third time was how we needed to have a serious talk about foreplay. It wasn't my legs I was worried about being sore in the morning.

Bay

I wanted her again, but she needed to rest more. As the clock ticked over to midday, I slipped from the bed, pulled on my tracksuit pants and t-shirt, and went out for a run. Luke was in the kitchen along with Selena when I came back in and went to fix myself some breakfast.

"Oh my God, I love that smell," Selena purred getting up from the breakfast bar and pouring a fresh glass of milk.

"Sweaty male?" Luke smiled, a spark in his eye because we both knew what smell she was talking about.

"Sex. Lots and lots of just-had-sex smell. Did you let the girl have any rest, boss?" Selena smirked as she grabbed a bottle of water from the fridge.

"Did you want me to take her home now or are you keeping her?" Luke teased.

"How is Anna?"

Both of them sobered. "Still critical. Calin called while you were out to give us an update." Luke stood straight.

I nodded. "You should both shower before anyone else wakes. Calin won't handle infidelity right now." Both of them went rigid, and I gave them my usual version of a smile. "I'm not the only one smelling of sex this morning."

Selena swallowed, handing both the milk and water to me. "She'll need one or both of these."

I winked at her and took them with me as I climbed the stairs. It didn't bother me that Luke and Selena took the stress and grief of last night out on each other, but I didn't want it creating in-house problems with Calin. He was grieving right now, which made him much more likely to overreact to something, like his newest wife finding comfort in another man's arms.

I expected Spectra to still be in bed asleep, but instead she stood at the window looking out at the snow-covered grounds. The little nightdress Gina had lent Spectra was too big for her, so one of the straps hung down her left arm, just making the entire sight of her even sexier. My body reacted instantly to the sight of her. Collecting myself, I shut the bedroom door, not bothering to be quiet, which startled her into turning around.

The fallen strap was exposing all but the nipple of her left breast. I remembered finding that nipple exposed last night and the feel of its tiny hard nib between my lips as I sucked it, and the way she moaned. Spectra's eyes watched me with caution, but when I kept staring at her, she looked over herself and pulled the strap back up to cover as much as the night-dress allowed.

I cleared my throat and stepped towards her. "I brought you a drink. I wasn't sure which one you'd prefer."

She smiled shyly, taking the milk and turning back to the window. "That's a lot of snow cover. It must have snowed through the night."

"The roads are still passable." I placed the bottle of water on the small table between the windows.

Spectra's shoulders tensed. She finished her milk and turned to face me, placing the glass on the table. "I'll gather my stuff and get out of your way."

She stepped forward and I took her hand, stopping her. "Or..." I pulled her across in front of me and caressed her slender neck. "You could stay another night with me."

Her eyes fluttered closed as I gripped her hip through the

flimsy nightdress. "What about Calin's wife? Shouldn't you be mourning her?"

"While his other wife is fighting for her life, they will focus on her chance to live, so the grieving will wait." I slid the straps of the nightdress from her shoulders, watching it pool around her hips.

"And work?" she murmured as I cupped her firm breast in my hand and kissed over her neck.

"I'm declaring a snow day, which I intend to spend in bed, with you."

I kissed her hard, pushing her back against the window frame so I could pin her with my body. Her hands ran up my torso, and I could feel the electricity in their wake as she lifted my shirt over my head. She kissed across my chest, her fingers scooping the drawstring for my pants out and undoing it. I loved the feel of her pressed against me, how smooth her pale back was under my hands.

Her luscious mouth closed over my nipple, and I threaded my hand into her hair, holding her close, trying to resist just taking her. Because that's what I wanted, to press her against the window jamb and thrust into her until the aching throb in my pants was sated. Her fingers slid down to my hips, pushing my pants down as she lowered herself to her knees in front of me. Just the sight of her on her knees before me, eyes glassy with desire, mouth slightly open as she took my erection in her hand, massaging my balls with her other, made me nearly lose my control.

My eyes went wide as she pulled my cock parallel and put the tip of it to her lips. She licked over the head, and I felt my balls tighten in response. As she slid me into her mouth, my knees went weak and I caught myself heavily on the wall, my other hand tangling in her beautiful black locks. I started to thrust into her mouth, but Spectra caught my hips and held them, moving herself slowly, every damned flick of her tongue controlled and done with the intention to drive me to my breaking point.

The first time I pulsed in her mouth, she gave me another teasing lick and kissed her way back to standing. When she was standing before me, we stood looking at each other for a moment and then she walked away. I blinked, confused, and then turned to see what happened. Spectra walked to the bed, shimmied her hips so the nightdress fell to the floor, and climbed back beneath the covers. I stood there, unsure what to do. After a moment, I heard Spectra sigh in frustration. She threw the blanket back far enough on one side in invitation while keeping herself covered.

I think I would have blushed at my stupidity if it were possible. I was in the bed within a heartbeat, pulling her naked flesh against mine, electricity buzzing beneath my skin wherever she touched me. I ran my hands over her body, feeling every inch of her as our bodies melded to each other. Neither of us were rushing it this time, we had what was left of the day and night to come, and so for the next hour, I kissed my way over her entire body.

I loved the way she reacted when I sucked her breasts, and then when I slid two fingers inside her, intending to do it long enough just to get her ready for me. I found a spot that made her stretch her body out beneath me and thrust her breast up into my sucking mouth. Her response made me curious. I started stroking that one spot over and over. Spectra squirmed beneath me, her hands alternatively clutching at the bed head and threading through my hair.

Spectra was struggling to breathe, her moans music to my ears. I was becoming so much more aroused seeing her come undone at my hands. After several minutes, Spectra slid her hand down to join mine, took my thumb, and placed it in a particular spot, circling it around. I took the hint and continued to stroke her while massaging this spot. Spectra's moans grew louder; her body grew tight around my fingers. I lowered my mouth again and assailed her nipple. She cried out, throwing her head back, her body shuddering as her orgasm rode her.

While her body relaxed, I withdrew my fingers and pulled her mouth to mine. I climbed between her thighs. As I sheathed myself inside her and started building to my own climax, I cursed myself. I knew what Alexander warned was true. I wasn't going to be able to walk away from her. I felt Spectra's body react again as I neared climax. She grew tighter around me, her nails scraping across my back. I pulsed inside her and she threw her head back, biting her lip as she came again. I gritted my teeth to resist tasting her pleasure and went with her, through the doors of heaven, knowing I was dragging her into hell.

I held her to me longer this time, not wanting to break the contact between us. It was Spectra who reached between us, holding the condom in place and pulling me from her before she rolled out of bed and moved to the window. I went into the bathroom to dispose of the cautionary measure and then joined her at the window, wrapping her in my arms.

"What is it?" I asked, feeling the tension in her body.

"The other wife." Spectra's voice was filled with sadness.

"Anna?"

Spectra turned, burying her head against my chest. "Not anymore."

I didn't ask how she knew. The first thing I learned about Spectra, she wasn't what she seemed. The knock at the study connecting door a moment later only confirmed it. Spectra moved her body slightly, ensuring mine covered hers. "What is it, Luke?"

Luke opened the door, stepping in but keeping his distance. "Anna has lost the battle to live. Calin is on his way home. I know you are finding yourself again this weekend, but I believe this is a time for family only."

I started shaking my head, my arms wrapping tighter around Spectra. She placed her hand on my chest and looked up at me, eyes so much older than her face led you to believe.

"He's right, Bay. Be with your family now. You know where to find me when this has passed." She touched my cheek and lifted her face to mine. One delicate kiss was all she allowed me. "Take me home, please?"

I didn't want to. I never wanted to let her go. I sighed heavily and looked over my shoulder to Luke. He stood serenely, but there was a look of respect on his face for Spectra. "I'll be back in a few minutes." I dropped my shields and felt Spectra's nails grasp my arms in pain as I stepped into the ether and emerged into her attic room in the convent. She whimpered, and I realized what I'd done. Her knees gave out from under her, and she clung to me as I snapped my shields back into place.

I looked down at her, worried, her eyes filled with pain, tears streaming down her cheeks. "Spectra, I'm so sorry. I'd seen Alexander do it with you and thought you must have been able to handle it."

She swallowed, and I could see her struggling for her voice. "I can," she rasped, then her eyes rolled back in her head and she fell to the floor, unconscious.

"Spectra!" I knelt next to her, checking her pulse. It was rapid, but as I held my hand to her skin, it stuttered and started to slow. Her breathing eased and evened out again. That's when I realized she'd hyperventilated.

I picked her up and placed her on her bed, covering her so she wouldn't be cold. I kissed her goodbye and stepped back to my bedroom. Luke was waiting, shock on his face when I looked at him.

"Is she still alive?" His voice cracked, as if he was trying not to yell at me.

"She is. Unconscious, but alive."

"When I suggested taking her home, I meant I'd drive her. Not to try and get rid of her permanently. You could have killed her exposing her to that much power."

"I had to, Luke."

"Why?" Luke asked, exasperated.

"Because there is no way I could watch her hop in a car and drive away from me."

CHAPTER 11

Spectra

I saw the feet come into my peripheral vision, basic black shoes that made my boots look fancy. Not that I was wearing any shoes currently. Just one of Alexander's old heavy metal shirts and my stained black leggings. Perfect cleaning garb. I knelt back, using my forearm to push the loose strands of hair from my face before meeting the elderly nun's eyes.

"Spectra, there's a man at the front door asking for you," Sister Patricia whispered as if she was scandalized.

"Thanks, Sister," I sighed, throwing the scrubbing brush back in the bucket, wiping my hands dry on a towel before grabbing my black shawl and leaving the upstairs bathroom. I wasn't expecting any clients. Mercury would be at work, and I never heard from Alexander during the week unless he was desperate. It was Wednesday morning. Early Wednesday morning at that. Nothing exciting happened on Wednesdays. I made my way down the two floors to the front door. I opened it and found Luke, his dark suit a stark contrast to the snow-covered grounds behind him. I stepped onto the doormat, hoping it would stop me getting too cold.

Luke looked me over and cocked a brow. "Ah, now I get it. You're Cinderella." Fog puffed out his mouth in the cold.

"It's called chores and penance, asshole. What do you want?" I grumbled, not in the mood. I could feel one of my migraines coming on. I pressed my hand to my head and applied pressure. "Sorry, I didn't mean to be..."

"How long has the headache been there?" Luke asked, concerned.

"I get migraines occasionally, I'll be fine. What are you doing here other than causing controversy?" I pointedly looked to the window where three of the sisters were peering out.

Luke smiled and winked at them. Some of them, old enough to be his mother, blushed and smiled shyly. I rolled my eyes. "You left this behind the other night." Luke held out a bulky garment bag. "The boss had your dress dry-cleaned for you or I would have bought it back yesterday. You'll find every-thing in there: jacket, shoes, purse, phone."

I took the bag, "Thank you. How's Calin and his wives?"

Luke blinked, as if surprised I'd asked. "Grateful for what you did for Gina."

"That's not what I meant."

"But it's important." Luke watched me for a minute. "He wants to see you again." I nodded, figuring that was coming. "It's just, as much as he'd love to take you out in public and spoil you, there is a certain man in your life who will cause trouble about it."

I grimaced, rubbing my temple. "Well, there are plenty of places in this city Alexander wouldn't be caught dead in. Tell Bay to meet me Friday night at the usual place, and make sure he leaves the suit behind."

Luke looked at me, concerned, gave a half bow, straightened, gave the peering nuns another wink, and sauntered off into the crisp early morning. I wondered if Bay was in the car waiting for him.

I walked back upstairs and dumped the garment bag on my bed before finishing my chores. By lunchtime, my migraine was kicking into overdrive. I made my way over to the church. Usually, a well-focused session of prayer helped. But, an hour later, I folded myself on the floor of the lady's chapel and started crying with the pain.

"Spectra?" Father Mathew pulled me into his arms, his cold hands feeling wonderful, especially the one across my forehead to hold my head.

"Migraine," I sobbed.

"Worse than normal?" he asked tenderly. I whimpered. "Let's go." He picked me up in his arms and carried me easily from the church. "Robert, can you drive us to the hospital please?"

I started to freak out. Father Mathew held me effortlessly. He looked to be in his late forties, and his clothes covered his physique well, but his face belied his true age and his strength was typical of a celestial half-breed. Father Mathew slid into the passenger seat of Robert Mulley's pick-up truck, keeping me restrained.

"Please, Father?" I begged. I hated hospitals with a passion.

"Shh, Spectra. You're burning up, and Mercury is on duty. I won't let anyone take you out of my sight."

To the morgue. That's what he meant. He wouldn't let me wake up agonizingly in a morgue again.

"She really hates hospitals, doesn't she?" Robert asked quietly. I felt Mathew nod and just hold me tighter.

The car stopped, and Mathew opened the door and slid out. "Thanks, Robert. Don't wait, it could be awhile."

Mathew carried me into emergency and to the front desk. "We need to see Dr. Raphangelis when he's free for a minute please?"

"This is not a medical center, Father. You'll see who you see," the nurse snapped.

"No," I whimpered and tried slipping away from Mathew's arms, managing one step before I collapsed and puked over the sterile floor.

"Spectra, really?" Mathew picked me back up, no sympathy for the nurse who would have to clean it up. "This girl is terrified of hospitals and doctors. Dr. Raphangelis is the only medical practitioner she'll let near her. And when you tell him Spectra Michaels is in the waiting room for him, he'll come, because he knows what it means for her to be here."

Without waiting, he carried me over to a seat in the nearly empty waiting room and continued to hold me while I whimpered and cried in his arms. Several people came and went before us, making it obvious the nurse hadn't bothered to tell anyone we were here. Mathew put his hand to my forehead. "Do you want to vomit some more on her floor?"

I just moaned at him. Mathew frowned and turned to the man next to him. "Excuse me. Could I borrow your mobile for a moment? The nurse at the desk is refusing to get this girl help, and I want to go over her head."

The man mumbled through the ice pack he was holding to his bloody nose. "Sure. That nurse is a proper bitch."

Mathew dialed. "Merc, it's Mathew. I know you check your voice mail. I've got Spectra in the waiting room with me. We've been waiting three hours, but the nurse won't tell you we are here. She's bad, Merc. Worse than normal." He hung up and handed the man back his phone. "Thank you."

It took another fifteen minutes or so before I heard the doors fly open and hurried footsteps. "Spec." Mercury put his hand to my forehead. "Shit! Follow me." Mathew stood up carrying me.

"Doctor, that woman isn't next on the list." The nurse stood, outraged.

Mercury turned to her, furious. "When a priest shows up asking for me from now on, you don't ignore them. Ever!" Mercury threw open the doors. I was lost to the flashing overhead lights. The smell of the hospital became stronger, and I clung to Mathew, sobbing. "In here."

Mathew tried to lay me down on the examination table, but despite the pain in my head, I clung to him, trying to prevent lying on that bed. "Spec, come on." Mercury took hold of me, pulling me away from Mathew, but I held on for dear life. "Jesus, Spec!"

"Mercury Raphangelis!" Mathew chastised.

"Oh please! You're going to have a go that I take the Lord's name in vain? Have you heard her when she comes?"

"Yes, actually. Why do you think she's been doing penance for a week after you get time off?" Mathew stopped trying to lay me down. I relaxed.

As soon as I did, Mathew dropped me and then pinned me to the table. I screamed. The sound aggravated my migraine, reverberating through my head, which already felt like someone had raked sharp claws through my brain. Mercury put his mouth to mine, trying to smother the sound or kiss me into silence, I wasn't sure. It wasn't going to work.

"Let her up, Mathew." Mercury replaced his mouth with his hand.

Mathew stepped back, and I clambered off the table and into the corner of the room, holding my head and crying even harder.

"Can you watch the door and make sure no one comes in? Stay on this side of it though."

"She'll be okay?" Mathew sounded panicked.

"I'll take care of her, Mathew. Just don't let anyone through the door." Mercury squatted down next to me. "Are you ready to let me help you yet, Spec?" He rubbed my back gently, then moving his hand to the opposite shoulder blade, he pulled me to him. He wrapped me in his arms, and that soothing nature of his settled over me.

Mercury waited till my fear calmed to tilt my face to his. "Show me your eyes, Spec." I shook my head, unable to stand the light in the room, even with my eyes closed. "Mathew, can you turn off the lights please?" A moment later, the brightness disappeared. His thumb caressed along my jaw. "Show me, Spec."

I opened my eyes slowly, blinking tears out of the way, and looked up into Mercury's lapis blue eyes. His pupils dilated. "Shit," he murmured softly. He pressed his mouth to mine, and I closed my eyes to anything but his healing kiss. I felt a tugging sensation and tried to pull away. Mercury put his hand to the back of my head and held it firmly in place. The tugging turned to a pull and then to a draining sensation, like my brain was being sucked into my throat and then out of my mouth into his.

I tried to pull away from the kiss, but Mercury held me in such a way that I was defenseless. I tried to scream, to get away as I felt like my mind was being dragged out of me through my mouth. It was suffocating, I couldn't inhale, but for some reason, I wasn't fading out of his hold. I clawed at Mercury, trying to get away, but despite me feeling his skin give way beneath my nails and his blood welling around them, he held me. I focused on that feeling, on Mercury's blood and flesh beneath my nails.

It seemed to drag on forever, drag being the appropriate word. Eventually, when I'd started to convince myself I'd died and been dragged into hell, Mercury pulled away and released me. I fell into the corner gasping for breath. Mercury ran to the sink and vomited, repeatedly, for several minutes.

By the time I was breathing enough to cry again, my migraine was gone. Mercury just broke my trust, and I didn't even know why. I knew he was trying to help me, but he took something from me, and that wasn't what he normally did. Normally he gave of himself.

Mercury cleaned himself up, and when he squatted down in front of me, his eyes told me he hated what he just did to me. "I'm sorry Spec, but you're not handling your power. It's not your fault. Your father should have stuck around and trained you as you grew."

I shook my head. "A balance doesn't have power."

"They do, and you are of a higher order than most balances walking this world."

I stared open mouthed at Mercury. "You know who my father is?"

Mercury dropped his eyes to the ground. "Every angel, or Angelis, no matter their rank, would be able to recognize your bloodline immediately. That's not the point right now."

"Who?" I blurted. "Who is he?"

"What happened this weekend?" Mercury countered. "You've done something to protect someone, which required more of your power than usual. What happened?"

I pushed back into the corner under Mercury's gaze. "What makes you think I was protecting someone?" Mercury tipped his head and raised a brow at me as if to say, 'how long have we known each other?' I sighed. "I protected a woman from a predator."

"How?" Mercury pressed. When I stared at the floor, Mercury sighed. "I know it was a changeling, Spectra. I could taste it. I also know your latest admirer was involved because I could taste his power running through you like a bad perfume."

Mathew turned to face us finally, confusion and worry on his face. "What new admirer?"

"Not now, Mathew," Mercury warned before turning his eyes back to mine. "I'm not angry you gave yourself to him, Spectra. I expected that to happen after I saw you together. But, I need to understand what you did this weekend that nearly made you convert."

"She what?" Mathew glared angrily.

Mercury growled, frustrated, and stood to face Mathew. "You should have contacted me sooner. It was nearly too late. Next time, check her eyes and call me straightaway. I'll come to her." Mercury looked back to me. He sighed and came to me, taking my face in his hands. "Whatever you did, don't ever do it again. Promise me." I nodded. "Promise me, Spectra."

I opened my mouth, intending to make that promise, but I couldn't. "I'd do it again to save a life, Merc."

"Find another way to save someone. Now promise me."

I hesitated, but Mercury wasn't going to let this one drop. "I promise."

Mercury kissed me, passionate and emotional, but I felt the tingle on my lips where he bound me to my word. I would never be able to save someone like that ever again.

❦

Friday came as always. And I bounced down the steps into Ténèbres, slightly anxious about the excursion I'd planned for Bay. I wanted to talk to him and work out what it was he wanted now that he'd had his one night. I slid into a spot at the bar. Tommy smiled and placed my usual bottle of water in front of me. "How's the master forger tonight?"

"Off duty." I slid the money for the drink over the bar and broke the seal, handing the lid to Tommy.

Tommy held up two silver tokens in front of me. "We are agreed on the cost?"

"I'm hoping you'll be decent and give me a freebie so I can sort out what he's after."

Tommy laughed at me. "Oh Angel, we all know what he's after, and after last week, I'm pretty sure you're going to give it up. So, are we agreed?"

I rolled my eyes and held out my hand. "Fine!" Tommy laughed and put the silver tokens in my hand along with a silver key.

Cassie slid onto the stool next to me, her hair shock-pink this week. She slid her credit card across the bar to Tommy. "The usual please, Tommy."

"How are you doing, Cass?" I asked carefully. She was moody at the best of times. To say she wasn't quite within the realm of right would be an understatement.

She looked at me with her bloodshot eyes. "What's it like to die?"

"Cassie!" Tommy hissed in warning.

"No really, I want to know. You died, right? You have that look about you, like it's not dying you fear, but living." She threw back the shot Tommy poured her and put it out for another one.

I swallowed and looked at my bottle of water. "Dying is easy. Living... living is hard work."

"I'm dying."

"I know," I whispered. She looked at me. "It's in your eyes."

"It sucks you know. You died and walk around full of life. I'm living, but I may as well be dead already." She threw back another shot. I picked up my water and took a long drink, knowing where this conversation was heading. "I want it to be over already."

"Suicide is a mortal sin."

Tommy watched from the end of the bar, eyes tight with worry as he served the crowd slowly filling the place.

Cassie grasped my wrist with desperation. "Will I go to hell for the life I've led?"

I sighed, patting her hand. She released it. "Get out of here. Go see a priest and ask for absolution. Do your penance and then clean your life up, Cass. Face death with dignity and clarity of thought. Not from the bottom of a bottle."

Cassie sucked in a deep breath. "What's it like on the other side?"

And there it was, the question she really wanted to ask, what everyone always wanted to know when they were looking down the barrel of the gun. I closed my eyes, remembering because I recalled it clear as day even after all this time. I felt the smile light up my face even as the tears started to fall.

"Home." I sighed. "There's no other word for it. It's...

home." I lowered my head and wiped the tears away. I turned and faced her, taking her hand in mine. "You won't be alone, Cass. You'll think you are cause you won't ever see him, but if you feel for it..." I smiled at the tear that ran down her face and wiped it away with my thumb before squeezing her hand. "...he'll have your hand the entire time and walk with you to the afterlife."

I kissed her forehead as her tears started to flow, gave her hand one last squeeze, and slid out of my seat to face Bay who stood there, watching. I took his hand and walked his sad eyes out of the nightclub. Bay didn't question what he'd overheard, but I could see the sympathy in his eyes.

I huddled into my jacket against the cold. The snow stopped falling on Wednesday, but the wind through the city was still like ice. Bay took my hand, and I felt the slightest tendril of heat leak into me. I smiled up at him as we walked the two blocks to our destination.

Bay stopped outside the door to Reins de Tombées and raised his brows at me. "The Fallen's Loins. I've never heard of this place, and I know nearly every Nachtwelt haunt in this and several other cities."

I smirked. "Like Alexander, you keep your noses in high society. You're about to enter a whole other realm of Nachtwelt." I looked over his outfit. The black slacks, black button down, and black ankle length military jacket was perfect for our destination tonight. I hesitated at the top of the stairs. "You should know, I tend to get stared at a little in here."

Bay considered me. "Because they know what you are?"

"We are probably going to cause quite a stir. I've only ever been here with Mercury. This is his turf, but it's the only place in this city that I know we can talk without it getting back to Alexander."

Bay nodded, placed his hand in the center of my back, and led us down into the nightclub with an attached restaurant. It started at the bouncer. I slipped out of my jacket and handed it to the attendant. Bay glanced over my Gingham Gothic Lolita Dress appreciatively before removing his own coat. The bouncer leered like I was dessert, but he let us pass with barely a raised brow at Bay.

As we passed through the tight press of male half-breeds and human female bodies on the main floor, the not-so-hushed whispers of exclamation started.

"It's the Michaels girl."

"Oh my god she's a Michaels!"

"She's not with Raphael's son, does that mean she's available?"

"Holy shit! That's Bay Ryder. What the hell is she doing with him?"

Bay put his mouth to my ear as we passed through. "You may have understated people's interest in you?"

I kept my eyes straight ahead. We made our way to the stairs that led up to the dining room hanging over the dance floor, the window seats able to watch the bodies grinding against each other. Buchanan, the concierge, smiled. "Miss Michaels, how lovely to see you again. Mr. Ryder, welcome. As it's your first visit, I will explain that you have restricted access here, and no powers may be used of your blood or your condition."

"Neutral territory?" Bay queried. Buchanan nodded. "I understand."

The concierge pulled back the black rope and led us up the stairs. "Would you prefer a window seat or booth?"

"Booth please," I answered before Bay could. I didn't want us to be on display.

The concierge led us to the back wall of the restaurant and handed us our menus before we slid into the curved leather upholstered seating. "Your waiter will be along with wine and tea shortly." I placed the two silver tokens on the edge of the table. Buchanan smiled and collected them.

"This place looks rather fancy," Bay observed casually.

I smirked. "It's got good food, all Asian though." I tapped the chopsticks on the table.

"What's with the tokens?"

"You have to be a celestial yourself or a direct descendant to get a table here. Usually, I'm with Merc, so it's not an issue. You're the first sorcerer allowed access. They consider your line too distant to let your kind in. It's why Alexander and yourself are ignorant of this place. When I called for the booking and asked to bring you for a business meeting, Buchanan put a charge on the request. Tommy came through for me."

"Why do I feel like there is a catch to him helping us out?" Bay studied me before taking my hand, which I'd been flexing, in his and placed it on the seat between us so he wasn't openly holding my hand.

I sighed. "I hate that your touch settles me. Your kind used to revolt me."

"Stop avoiding the question." Bay gave me a stern look, catching on to what I was attempting.

I blew out a breath. "He wants to watch us fuck."

"Vulgar."

"He's a watcher. I've found most of them to be sexual voyeurs."

"I meant that word on your tongue. I already knew Tommy wanted to watch us together."

"Fucking is what you wanted me for."

"I would like to think there is a little more to us, but either way, while I don't mind the use of the word, in general, I don't like hearing you say it. It doesn't seem right, considering I've seen you on your knees..." I raised a brow. "In prayer," Bay finished pointedly.

I smirked. "How would you refer to what we did last weekend?"

"Sex..." Bay started but stopped as the waiter stopped in front of us, placing down a pot of Chinese tea and a bottle of red wine with raised brows.

I smiled. "We are debating the use of the word fuck to represent sex. Would you care to weigh in?"

"Banging," the low-level Nephilim winked at me. "Or in your case, corrupting."

"High aspirations?" I raised a brow, unfazed. I'd been propositioned many times here.

"We've all got to dream. What can I get for you?"

"Chicken chow mein, soft noodles, no vegetables please." I pushed my unopened menu back across the table.

"Vegetable spring rolls as an entree and Singapore noodles for main please." The waiter pressed corresponding buttons into his tablet and left with the menus. Bay poured us a glass each of the wine. "As I was saying, sex would be what last weekend was. I'm hoping going forward it could be more."

"More what?" I asked cautiously.

"Well, we seem to be dating if you consider dinner before sex."

"I have a boyfriend."

"That you hide."

"Not at all. Everyone who wants to know about Merc does. Alexander is too self-absorbed to care who's in my bed."

"I believe you are very mistaken about that." Bay gave me a gentle look.

"The point is. We aren't dating. Merc is my boyfriend. Going forward, if we kept seeing each other, we would be fucking, and only when my boyfriend isn't around."

Bay opened his mouth but shut it promptly as a high order Nephilim slid into the booth beside me. "Hey there, Spectra."

I gripped Bay's hand hard and fought not to grimace. "Hi Lucas."

"So I hear you finally gave Raphangelis the flick. Ready to trade up?"

I raised my eyes to the ceiling, praying for patience. "Wrong on two counts, Lucas. Going from an Angelis to a Nephilim is not considered trading up, and I'm still with Mercury."

"The Archs didn't even exist when my grandfather was the apple of the All Father's eye."

"No, but it was the Archs who kicked your grandfather's apple out of heaven when his pride instigated the fall."

Lucas looked at Bay. "Still better than hooking up with one of the condemned."

"Who's hooking up with a condemned?" Mercury sauntered up to our table, a brow quirked over his lapis blues. "Lucas, are you hitting on Mr. Ryder? You should know you're not his type."

Lucas scowled, standing up. "Just keeping your seat warm, Merc." He moved back to the table he shared with another Nephilim.

Mercury slid into the seat next to me and took my face in

his hands. "Any PDOA?" I shook my head. "Good girl." Mercury kissed me languidly, making a show of it.

Bay's hand squeezed mine where they were still clasped. I pulled out of the kiss slowly and sat back in my seat. Mercury turned to Bay and held his hand out. "We haven't met formally. Mercury Raphangelis."

"Bay Ryder. PDOA?" They shook hands.

"Public displays of affection." Mercury put his arm around my shoulders, lowering his voice. "Really, Spec? On my turf?"

I untangled my hand from Bay's to pour some of the tea. "I needed somewhere out of the public eye that I wasn't likely to run into Alexander."

"I've heard Bay has a lovely remote mansion that's well guarded." Mercury smiled pointedly at Bay, aware of the others in the restaurant stealing glances.

"We were actually just determining the definition of our relationship." Bay's eyes glinted in the light.

"One night of sex is not a relationship." I sighed. "Could this conversation become more awkward?"

"I could ask Alexander to join us?" Mercury teased. I glared at him. Mercury sat back patiently. "Sex doesn't require dinner beforehand, or after, or at all, Spec. If that's all that's happening between you two, then just go to his place when it's to happen and leave it at that. Don't overcomplicate things."

"You're not jealous?" Bay observed.

Mercury settled a hard gaze on Bay. "She's my girlfriend, not my possession. We have a relaxed relationship. Mind you, that's only ever allowed for Alexander before this, but time changes everything."

"It's killing me to have your arm around her," Bay admitted.

Mercury sighed. "Then what's happening here is more

than sex for you and you need to make a decision. Can you let that possessive nature go to enjoy Spectra's body? Her heart and soul are not available to you, so it's her body or nothing."

"The rest belongs to you?"

Mercury shook his head sadly. "I only wish."

Bay looked between us then sat back, contemplating. "You're still waiting for Alexander. Despite knowing you'd need to be a direct descendant of an arch to be even close to powerful enough to be with him." Bay shook his head. "And he will let you hope if it means he can keep you on tap."

"It's not like that," Mercury warned, his hand reaching quickly to grab mine as I went to strike Bay. "You have half the picture, Mr. Ryder."

"Then fill the other half in for me."

"He's hoping she'll make it," Mercury admitted.

"Merc!" I slapped his shoulder.

Merc took my face in his hands. "You can't expose your-self, Spec, but everyone else in this place knows who your father is except the two of you. It's time that changed, and Bay deserves the right to challenge Alexander if he wants it."

"I won't be doing that," Bay grumbled.

"She's a balance." Merc kept his eyes connected with mine.

Bay became deathly still in my peripheral vision. "That may well be, but that means nothing for..."

"She's Michael's daughter."

Bay stopped and stared. "You're joking?"

"Michael who?" I demanded, trying to finally discover that missing piece of my life.

"*The* Michael, Spec. You are the daughter of the Archangel Michael. The first female Angelis to walk this planet and since you died, you have been balancing a fine line between Angelis and celestial." Mercury informed quietly.

"Wednesday?" I breathed.

Mercury closed his eyes in regret. "As you unlock more of your powers, you push the envelope further. "

"That's how she can become incorporeal." Bay was still staring, murmuring in awe. "And how she was able to rip the beast from the predator."

Mercury's eyes went wide, then he shook his head and released me. "Jesus, Spec!"

"I reacted on instinct." I sank back into the chair, trying to comprehend who my father was. "My mother was seduced by an archangel who pretends to show no interest in humans."

"Very few." Mercury took my tea and drank it as our entree arrived at the table. "I'll have the satay chicken please." Mercury gave his order to the waiter and waited for privacy to continue. "Only one other Michangelis is walking this planet, so if Michael has been bedding women, he's played it safe to only ever get two pregnant," Mercury smirked. "Considering how fertile those bastards are."

I frowned. "Mathew knew? He's the one who suggested Michaels for my new surname."

Mercury nodded. "Mathew knew about you because your mother met Michael in his church." He chuckled. "Apparently, you were conceived on the altar, how's that for sacrilegious?" When Bay just sat blinking at him, Mercury gave up and turned back to me. "Mathew ensured your mother got a good job and arranged with Henry Williams to take care of you."

"Sounds like an arranged marriage." Bay finally broke free of his shock.

Mercury shrugged. "The Williams didn't know who her father was or they would have trained Spec up at a young age. I think that she turned out to be a balance surprised them, but they still don't know she's higher order or she'd be married already."

"I have to pass the test first," I whispered.

Mercury looked at me and brushed his fingers down the side of my face. "The marriage is the test, Spec. You pass, or you die." Mercury relaxed, watching Bay. "Still not going to challenge?"

Bay met his eyes, and there was anger there, but a moment later it cleared. "No. I will enjoy her, but I will not start a war for her."

Mercury gave a half smile. "Good."

Bay looked confused. "You approve?"

"Of course I do. You've created a suspension. She will be pulled between the two of you now, which means Alexander will lose even more of his grip on her. That keeps her with me, with her own kind, and that I approve of." Mercury took a spring roll. "Now, should we discuss this arrangement?"

CHAPTER 12

Bay

As we approached Ténèbres, I spotted a familiar car parked on the street. I came to a stop and blew out the annoyance I felt. First Mercury crashed our dinner and discussion. Granted, he was rather pleasant and supportive of my interest in Spectra, but the bombshell he dropped about her father not only impacted Spectra but myself. Spectra was still shell-shocked, and her eyes were slightly wider than normal, pupils unfocused for the rest of dinner.

Mercury and I negotiated ground rules with barely any input from Spectra at all, and I held the distinct impression I would need to explain what Mercury and I decided on when she returned to the present.

Spectra paused and looked at me, confused. "What's wrong?"

"Alexander is parked up the road, so I expect he's at the club looking for you."

Spectra looked up the road, and when she spotted the car, her shoulders sagged. "Tonight is going to be one of those nights, isn't it?" Spectra pulled a silver key out of her pocket and held it up for me to see. "This was meant to be us tonight. It's the key to the back room at Tommy's."

I raised a brow. "You're actually willing to let him watch us?"

"No. I'm uncomfortable as all hell with the idea, but a bargain was struck."

I took the key, taking her hand and pulling her to me at the same time, tucking her body against mine. "I can delay Tommy. What do you need tonight, Spectra? Do you need to go home and have time to yourself? Do you want Alexander? You gave me what I needed last weekend. I'll do the same for you."

Spectra looked up the street. "Alexander probably wants to know how my interview went today. I really don't want to discuss it with him," she sighed. "Take me home?"

I kissed her hand and turned the corner so that we wouldn't accidentally run into Alexander leaving the club. When we circled our way back to the car, Spectra was biting her lip. I waited till we were in the car and the engine started to turn and look at her.

"Did you want to talk to me about the interview?"

Spectra looked at me, sat back in the seat, and gave me a weak smile. "It's a long drive to your place, I guess it would fill the silence."

I blinked when I realized she'd meant my home, that she still wanted to come home with me. I put the car into drive and started winding my way to the freeway.

"I'm not interviewing with the NSIO till after I graduate, but I was offered two positions from the private sector upon completion. I met the first company this morning, and I'll interview with the second next Wednesday. Alexander wasn't happy I went. He thinks I should just come work with him."

I suspected the benefits of having Spectra working in the same building was his focus and not her finding a job. "So how did the interview go?"

Spectra ghosted a smile. "Good. The company is excited to bring me on. They showed me where I would be working and introduced me to the team I'd be working with. The pay is reasonable for entry-level, and it's only a fifteen-minute train ride."

"You don't want the job they are offering you, though." Spectra shook her head. "So why don't you want to tell Alexander that?"

"Because I still want to consider it and don't want to be talked out of it yet."

"That's fair enough. Can I ask which companies are head-hunting you?"

"Baulkims was today, and Pendant Security is next week."

I felt my eyes widen slightly as the name of my company passed her lips. "Have you researched these companies and looked at your options and who they would usually hire?"

"Baulkims I know everything about, it's your typical software company. Pendant was a little harder to get information on. They aren't an IT company, the IT is a component of the private security firm by the looks of it. I suspect it will be the same kind of work as the NSIO. Checking people's credentials, fixing operating systems, the usual sort of stuff."

I was drumming my fingers on the steering wheel. What the hell was HR thinking approaching a human, because they would have thought she was, to bring into the company?

"Is something wrong?" Spectra asked, watching my fingers.

"Just remembered I need to discuss something with Luke when I get home."

Spectra pouted. "Oh! Straight away again?"

I tried to restrain the smile at knowing she didn't want to wait to be with me again.

"It's not urgent."

She smiled and looked back out the window. "How's Calin and his family doing?"

My fingers stopped drumming. "They are holding it together. The funeral for both women was yesterday." I looked across at her. "Luke said you were unwell Wednesday when he saw you. You mentioned something about Wednesday to Mercury?"

I watched Spectra swallow and look out the window. "I get migraines on occasion, usually after I extend my abilities. The one on Wednesday saw me rushed to hospital so Mercury could help me."

"Because you pulled the beast from that man to save Gina?" She nodded slowly, and I could see she was angry. "How bad, Spectra?"

"Mercury had to do something he hated, and I hated that he did it. Even though I know he only did it to save me, I felt violated by it. He's made me promise never to do it again."

I swallowed my concern. I wanted to know how she did what she did. I wanted to know if it could be replicated, but at the same time, I'd spent the week trying to work out how to ask her never to do it again. If the Essence found out she could do that, they would take her and force her to be their weapon.

Knowing now that it was life threatening for her, well, that just ensured I wouldn't want her doing it ever again.

"I agree with Mercury. While I'm grateful for you saving Gina, I won't put your life at risk either."

"You seemed to get on well with Merc at dinner." The accusation in her voice made me realize she wasn't as spaced out as I'd assumed.

"It was good to lay out our interests and ground rules, Spectra. While I'd never consider you a possession, I am possessive, and males do tend to be territorial about women they are sleeping with when that woman means something to them."

She met my eyes, wariness swimming in them, and I realized what I'd just admitted. I sighed, pulling off the freeway and into the country roads that led to my estate. "If we'd just had sex that first night, I might never have thought of you again. Your actions forced me to get to know you, Spectra, and now I want you permanently in my life."

"But you accept that Alexander will be my primary?"

"I accept he is your first preference. I'm also aware he's already broken your heart, and, why you may think it's not the case, you are in love with your Angelis. If you marry Alexander, you will need to give the Angelis up, and I don't think you could do that. You marry Mercury, however, and he will still allow you the freedom of lovers. So, from a selfish point of view, I know who I am rooting for."

Spectra turned her eyes to the window. "You don't want me to yourself?"

I considered lying, but I didn't feel right doing that with Spectra. "I do." I cleared my throat. "But I work closely with Henry and his son. For Alexander to even know we are lovers would jeopardize years of work. I'm not saying you're not worth fighting for, but there are right and wrong times to wage a war, Spectra, and this is not the time to challenge for a woman who still prefers the other man."

"He broke my heart to keep me safe."

"No, he pushed you away to keep you safe. He broke your heart to live a playboy's life."

The rest of the drive was ridden out in silence, with Spectra looking out the window as if lost in the darkness. I pulled into the garage and climbed out of the car, opening her door for her. Part of me liked the fact that she allowed me to. I touched her face and started drawing her mouth to mine. I'd been dying to kiss her all week. She put her hand on my chest and pushed back.

"Not here."

I pulled back, confused why the privacy of my garage wasn't a good place to kiss. Spectra blushed and lowered her eyes shamefully, but with a glint of naughtiness showing in them. That look alone made my cock stand at attention for her, but the words that followed brought the ache of disuse back with a vengeance.

"I'm in a mood, and I know myself well enough to recognize that if I let you kiss me here, we won't make it out of this garage till at least one, or both of us, are spent."

I groaned as my cock throbbed hard, ready to lift her skirt and plow her there and then, but Spectra wasn't that sort of woman. She was old-fashioned in some ways, and there were places to fornicate, and this wasn't one of them in her eyes. I took her hand and pulled her through the house at a light jog, grateful for her practical boots instead of heels. Luke came out of the lounge as we jogged up the stairs. I didn't stop for him but acknowledged him.

"Evening, Luke. We need to talk tonight, but not right now."

Spectra blushed again but smiled as we made the second-floor landing and started the last flight of stairs. Luke gave us a quiet smile, shook his head, and went back to the lounge. I threw my door open with more force than necessary, tugged Spectra inside, and threw her up against the wall as the door rebounded and slammed shut again.

She was pulling her jacket off as my mouth found hers and I kissed her with the ferocity of my need. My shirt and jacket joined hers on the floor to encircle us in black cloth. Her fingers made light work of my belt and fly, and then her hand was gripping me. I moaned as just her hand nearly made me lost. She smiled wickedly. I heard myself growl as I turned her and pushed her against the wall roughly.

I slid the zip down on her dress, unhooked her bra, and slid my hands around under the material to mold those beautiful breasts of hers to my hands. The first brush of my fingers over her erect nipples made her gasp and throw her head back on my shoulder, exposing her elegant neck to me, her hips pushing back to rub against my groin. I closed my eyes, trying to control myself. Not my hunger, I wasn't tempted to feed from Spectra, I'd never seen her as food. Spectra Michaels was lust first, something more on an emotional level second, but she definitely wasn't food.

Spectra pulled her arms from her sleeves and then dropped her dress and bra to the floor around her feet. I kissed down her spine, my hands tracing the wonderful curves of her pale body till I was on my knees, where I pulled her panties down those long pale legs. I left the knee-high boots. I loved those boots on her. Pulling her hips back, I separated her cheeks and delved my tongue into her heat.

The sounds that came from Spectra's mouth were heaven to my ears. While I tasted her, I unzipped her boots before pulling away to remove my own. Spectra turned around, eyes glassy as she leaned against the wall breathless, waiting for me. From my position on bended knee, there was no denying she was angelic. No man could be looking up at her naked beauty from this position and not think it of her.

I stood slowly, keeping eye contact with her. I pushed my pants over my hips and watched Spectra's eyes flick down to watch as I unrolled rule one. She licked her lips and closed her eyes as if trying to control herself. I didn't want that. I stepped into her quickly, kissing her furiously, pulling her pelvis to mine. I gripped her beautiful arse in my hands and lifted her. Without hesitation she embraced me in her thighs, twining her ankles behind my back.

Spectra broke from my mouth, reached her arm between us, and maneuvered me. I lowered her enough to dip the head of me into her. I loved how it felt to enter her tight heat. I savored the moment and then walked us to the bed, sitting down, the movement forcing me deeper into her. I lay back to look up at her. I wanted to watch my angel ride me. I wanted to see every moment as she came undone for me.

Spectra untied her legs, allowing me to lie back between her ankles, and as she did, I slid even deeper into her. I saw her eyes widen as I went as deep as her body allowed, and I closed my own eyes momentarily to enjoy the feel of her. Spectra started sliding her hips back and forth, slowly at first, but as she became comfortable in that position, she rocked faster. I felt myself growing thicker and harder. This position was amazing. I knew I wasn't going to last long, but by the sounds of Spectra, that wasn't going to matter.

Her cunt was clenching around my cock, and I knew she

was already on the edge. I put my thumb to that place she showed me last Sunday and watched her head loll back as she prayed. I smiled as she took the All Father's name in vain and shattered herself upon my hardness, not even trying to be quiet, or maybe she couldn't be.

The feel of her coming was too much. I pulsed and watched Spectra's eyes fly open in surprise, and I knew I was too deep and that it hurt her, but it was too late. My entire body seized as I lost myself to her. I couldn't focus, and my shields dropped. Spectra cried out, but I was falling down the well of pleasure and couldn't pull it back in.

A moment later, my body relaxed. I pulled my power back in as quickly as possible, but not so fast I'd give her whiplash. I sat up, concerned for her. She sat there breathing heavily, face to her chest, hair covering her face, skin gleaming in sweat. "Spectra, I'm sorry. Are you okay?"

She nodded but kept her face hidden. I swiped her hair aside and touched her face gently, lifting her closed eyes to mine.

She slowly opened her pale blue eyes. "Don't you dare have sex with any other person until you can control that."

I nodded, understanding I'd kill a human if I lost control like that with them. But I'd already spent the week testing myself. I knew it was only Spectra with whom I lost control. After one night with Spectra, I could fuck and feed myself for the first time in centuries. It wasn't a human I was worried about right now.

She smiled lightly. "Please do that to me again before we go to sleep tonight?"

She kissed me, wrapping her arms around my neck. I wrapped her in my arms and kissed her thoroughly, twisting to put her on her back before pulling out of her. She gasped as I did and I wanted to thrust straight back into her, and I would, very soon.

I rolled to the side and watched her slowly calm her breathing. "Are you hungry? We could raid the kitchen."

Spectra rolled on her side to face me. "I could go for a drink, but I need a quick shower first. You really made me sweat."

I smiled, took her hand, and led her into the bathroom with me. Watching her hands wash over her wet skin was enough to bring me back to life. As I pressed her face-first against the bathroom wall and slid into her, she moaned. I felt her tense and dropped my shields to drown her in my desire. I knew what I was doing, as I drove her to orgasm again, could ruin what we had. Using her weakness like this to take her pleasure was underhanded, but as soon as her body shuddered around me and relaxed again, I slid my shields back into place and withdrew from her body.

I felt her tense, ready to scold me. "Wait." I breathed heavily in her ear as I took myself in hand and, pressing against her wet nakedness, brought myself to an end, remembering what happened in the bedroom just now. When I turned her to face me, I expected anger in her eyes. Instead, she held my face and kissed me passionately before rinsing off and stepping out of the shower.

I kept my promise and after some time out, chilling in the lounge room and watching a movie with Luke and Selena, I took Spectra back to my room and made her pray in a way not appropriate for church. Spectra was asleep in my bed by the time I finished my shower. I pulled on my tracksuit pants and walked into my study. Luke sat there reading over reports.

"Is this a work or relationship matter?" Luke queried.

"Actually, it's both." I sat down in my armchair opposite him. "Spectra has a meeting with our human resources office next Wednesday."

Luke's eyes widened. "Does she know?"

"No. I can't even mention the name of my company to anyone. She was headhunted straight from college before I'd even met her."

Luke's brows furrowed. "The recruiter would have thought her human like we did. There is no way they would have contacted her."

"But they did."

Luke shook his head. "That doesn't make sense. I'll contact Alfred. We'll cancel her interview, and I'll have a good talk with the recruiter."

"Yes, you will call Alfred and make him aware the recruiter bought in a human. No, you won't cancel her interview. Yes, you will definitely speak to the recruiter and find out what the hell they were thinking."

"You're going to let her take the job?" Luke's eyes were full of concern. "Is that wise?"

"The NSIO want her and so do Baulkims. She must be very good at what she does, Luke."

Luke leaned forward onto his knees. "You don't think this is pushing the limit? You can keep that you are screwing her behind closed doors, but you can't keep her working for you from Alexander. He will think you set it up. Not to mention when she finds out you are her boss. What that will do to this arrangement you have?"

I shook my head. "We would rarely see each other at work."

Luke stood up. "You are going to put her in a building full of predators, boss. Think about that for just a moment. She hates our kind, and from what you told me, it's a thoroughly justified and possibly understated emotion. She can spot our kind a mile away, and you are going to let her walk into a city building full of nearly every predator known. I doubt she's going to be impressed by the fact you managed to bring species that normally loathe each other into a peaceful work environment. She is going to flip out and possibly have a panic attack."

I sighed, leaning on my knees. "She knew the recruiter was a predator and she is still coming in for the meet."

"Which brings us back to why they would even offer her the job." Luke walked to my laptop at the desk and started tapping away at the mouse, his eyes fixated on the screen.

"What are you doing?"

"We profile everyone before approaching them. I want to see what they have on Spectra Michaels and how she got a green tick."

I frowned, walking over to watch over Luke's shoulder as he found the profile on Spectra.

"My God! We've been watching her for two years." Luke read on, astounded, and I could understand why. The recruiter had targeted Spectra when she was still a college junior and followed her progress. Her transcripts were on file as well as a full security workup. There were red flags on her file. Like the fact she didn't exist until seven years ago despite a validated birth certificate and school transcript.

Luke tapped the screen at a name on the profile. "Who is

Miranda Jackson? I know everyone in HR, and there isn't anyone named Miranda Jackson."

"Look her up."

Luke started clicking again as he made his way through the personnel profiles. "Here we go. Miranda Jackson. Profiler for the Intergovernmental NSIO, transferred to us as liaison three months ago." Luke flicked through her data. "She must have bought Spectra's file with her because she's been watching her for years before she joined us."

"Stop," I called as he scrolled through the data. "Go back up a little." Luke scrolled up, and I pointed at a note related to her background training. "Shit!"

Luke looked at the screen, disbelieving. "Who the hell let this woman into our company?"

"She's using my company to pull Spectra away from working for the NSIO. She'll bring her in, recruit her, and then disappear with her." I stood straight and sighed. Luke sat back, waiting as I walked back around the desk to look out the window. "Okay. Keep Spectra's recruitment active. Let Henry know about this predator, put a copy of both of those files on a memory stick for me, then send a team to bring Miranda Jackson in."

I started walking to my room as Luke jumped into action. "What are you going to do?"

"I'm taking this to Alexander." I moved quietly into my room and dressed in my typical suit and button down. I didn't bother with the tie, it was already past midnight. Spectra stirred in her sleep. I swept a strand of hair back from her face and kissed her cheek. She smiled in her sleep and snuggled deeper under the covers.

Moving back into my study, Luke handed me the memory drive. "If she wakes up?"

"Why would you be in my room for it to matter?" I raised a brow.

Luke's eyes widened in shock. "I wouldn't be, but she may come in here looking for you. That girl has an appetite."

I smiled quietly, thinking he really had no idea how great an appetite. "That's actually normal of their kind. Possibly because their fathers spend so much time resisting the temptations of the flesh that it's where they find their greatest pleasure."

Luke blinked. "You found out what she is? When?"

"Tonight. She's a balance, but we're not going to be mentioning that outside of this room." I pocketed the memory drive and put my phone in the opposite pocket.

Luke looked ready to have a heart attack. "Did you seduce L'Ordre's future wife?" I shrugged, and Luke went red with rage. "What the hell are you still doing with her? You are risking our livelihood. Everything you've spent centuries building will disintegrate in our hands, Bay."

I stood by Luke and put my hands on his shoulders. "Spectra and I will not be seen together outside of this house unless we accidentally run into each other at a city event, in which case, while we will acknowledge knowing each other, that will be all we will do. We will not tell anyone what she is, because she is valuable to Essence as a weapon."

"Because of what she did to the beast." Luke nodded with understanding.

"Which will never be mentioned ever again. Doing that nearly killed her." I sighed and dropped my shields. "I should be back by morning."

I stepped onto the street outside Caprica's Bar, a regular upmarket bar that I knew Alexander visited, mainly because I quite often ran into him here. I went in and was shown to a private bar that only their best patrons could access. Alexander wasn't here, but he'd usually moved on with whatever sex-on-legs item he picked up by now. I pulled out my phone and called him.

"Hello?"

"We need to talk."

"I'm kind of in the middle of something," Alexander grumbled, and I could hear a woman's giggle in the background.

"Mr. Williams, do you think I would be calling you on a Friday night to chitchat?"

Alexander sighed, frustrated. "Back off," he mumbled to someone with him, and the girl's giggle cut off. "I've told you to stay away from her."

"I'm not your problem tonight, Mr. Williams. I'm at Caprica's. I'll stay for one drink. If you are not here by the time I've finished, I will take it that you are no longer in love with the girl and leave her to be taken." I hung up the phone as the waiter put my scotch on the table. I knew that last word would work.

Alexander was shown into the private bar ten minutes later, anger radiating off him like a walking furnace. He sat opposite me and waited for his drink to arrive before speaking. "You intend to take her now?"

"Never." I slid the memory stick across the table. "Fantôme do. One of them infiltrated my company to recruit Spectra. It was very nice of them to upload all their research to our personnel database, but then they had to to pull of the recruitment. We profile every prospective employee."

Alexander took the memory drive and looked at it. He closed his eyes tight. "What is the name of the recruiter?"

"Miranda Jackson."

"And you found out about this how? You just happened to be surfing through your employee database and spotted Spectra's name?"

"She's human. That sort of rings alarm bells within human resources in my company."

Alexander smirked. "You really should consider changing what HR stands for in your company, don't you think? Maybe Hell's Residents?" Alexander took a mouthful of his drink. "You will cancel Spectra's interview."

"No. That will remain." I finished my drink and stood. "Don't glare, Alexander. How likely is it that Spectra would want to work surrounded by predators?"

"She won't last five minutes in the building." Alexander blew out a breath in relief.

"Exactly." I sobered. "I saw the dossier Miranda worked up. Spectra is very talented, and I suspect she was proud to be headhunted before graduation. There is no need to take that away from her."

Alexander frowned. "Did you seduce her yet?"

I sniffed the air. "You've smelt like the same woman for the last three weekends running, Alexander. Does Spectra know you've found a balance yet?"

Alexander stood instantly. "She doesn't need to know that. That would only hurt her deeper than you could imagine."

I shook my head. "I would never. But if you suspect this female Nephilim is strong enough to become your wife, it would be a kindness on your part to let Spectra go."

"So you can taint her?" Alexander scowled.

"No, Alexander. So you don't break her." I walked away from the table as Alexander slumped back into it. The Nephilim would need to be high order to even stand a chance with Alexander. Outside, I dropped my shields and stepped back into my study. Luke was there with Selena.

"Shit!" Selena cried and gathered her dress from the floor, covering herself before fleeing from the room.

I gave Luke a hard look, and he had the decency to cower. "End it, Luke. She is married to your brother and is his newest bride at that."

Luke looked away. "The problem is I don't care. I want her." Luke met my eyes again and defied me to demand him to let her go, which, of course, I couldn't. I'd wanted Spectra, and despite the danger she presented in other areas of my life, I'd gone after her till I got her, and now, I couldn't put her aside.

I shook my head. "Then Calin should know. If he finds out by accident, there will be hell to pay."

Luke gave one firm nod. "Not right now. He needs time to grieve. He's lost two wives already."

And right there, Luke just told me his intentions about Selena. He meant her to be his.

CHAPTER 13

Spectra

I WOKE TO THE SOUND OF THE DOOR CLOSING and realized Bay wasn't with me. Moments later, I felt the faint flare of power and knew Bay was gone. I sat up in the bed looking at the clock, wondering what took him out so late on a Friday. I picked up the bottle of water I'd brought back up from the kitchen with me and finished it. Noise in the study drew my attention. I tiptoed to the door and heard a female's voice, followed by Luke's. I didn't need to guess who it was. I'd seen the way they looked at each other while they watched the movie tonight.

Grabbing my phone, I opened it to check my email and remembered there was no reception in Bay's room. Pulling on the black button-down Bay wore out this evening, I trudged down the stairs to the kitchen, hoping to find a signal. Moving to the back window, I finally got enough reception to check my emails.

Already Baulkims sent a follow-up email outlining the details of the job offer and asking me to come in for a formal interview the following Friday. Along with that were another two emails from other companies asking me to visit.

I sighed, closing my phone. Many of my fellow graduates would be polishing their resumes and sending them out in the hopes of finding a decent job. I hadn't even written my resume yet. Perhaps that said something about my willingness to actually let my business go.

The fridge opening behind me startled me. I turned to see Calin, dressed just in jeans, feet dirty as if he'd just come back in from a run, pulling a beer out of the fridge. I instantly tugged Bay's shirt down despite the fact it came to mid-thigh on me. Calin smirked, but his eyes were dark with suppressed rage.

"Evening, Calin." I wanted to ask how he was, but I'd hated that question after Danika and Mom died. 'How the fuck do you think I am?' was always on the tip of my tongue for the month following. "Been out running?"

"So the boss brought you back?" Calin growled. "You reignited his appetites, and now he'll fuck what doesn't belong to him?" I swallowed, stepping back from Calin's anger. Calin looked me over. "If you're here, why is he fucking my wife?"

"I..." I stared in shock that Calin thought Bay would screw me and then Selena immediately afterward.

Calin stepped around the big stone kitchen bench and moved so swiftly I felt the movement rather than saw it. He swept me up with an arm around my waist and sat me hard on the island bench. "Would it be fair that while he's up there fucking my wife, I'm down here fucking you?"

"Wait, what? No!" I pushed him away as he tried to move between my thighs. "It's not Bay!" I yelled at him.

Calin glared at me. "I saw her sneak up to his study just now. Why else would she go up there?"

"It's not for Bay!" I yelped as he grabbed my wrists to stop me pushing him away. "He's not even here! He left over half an hour ago."

Calin stopped and stared at me, eyes calculating my words to my body's truth. He stepped back, confused. "If not for the boss, then why is she there?"

"I don't know her. I can't answer that question for you." Over his shoulder, I saw movement in the hallway and recognized Gina staying in the shadows, watching. Her body language told me she'd been ready to step in and help me, but now she was standing back to see what happened next.

Calin shook his head. "No. Not him. Not Luke?" His body shivered with rage, and he turned to walk around to the other door. I jumped off the bench and ran to stand in front of the door, blocking his path. "Get out of my way. This doesn't involve you."

"A minute ago you made it involve me when you decided I could be your pound of flesh."

Calin assessed me. "My brother is upstairs fucking my wife. I couldn't attack the boss. My brother is another matter."

"Does the fact they are in love make any difference?" I begged. "I'm sure they didn't mean for this to happen. Maybe on her nights off they spent time together and a friendship formed, and it evolved to more. Maybe it was love at first sight. It doesn't matter. What does matter is they haven't done this to hurt you. Sometimes our hearts make decisions without asking for our opinions first."

Calin stroked his fingers along my jaw. "So much compassion." I heard the insult. He said it the way Alexander always did. He moved closer to me and lowered his mouth to an inch from mine. "Would you pity-fuck me to stop me going up those stairs and killing my adulterous wife?"

"No." I looked away. Calin grabbed my jaw and forced my face up to his. "If you try, you'll be doing it as a human." I flicked my eyes up to his and put all the threat behind my words into my glare because he didn't know I'd promised never to do it again.

Calin smiled, and his rage seeped out of his eyes as my anger grew. "I understood the boss's attraction to your beauty and your compassion. Now I see what was the cinch for him."

Gina stepped into the room and carefully touched her husband's shoulder, "You have plenty of wives, and Luke has been alone for a long time. Could you not love them both enough to let them love each other?"

Calin stepped back from me. "When did you get so romantic?"

Gina smiled shyly, "It's logic, not romance. Something men seem to lack when it comes to affairs of the heart." She tugged his hand. "Now take some of my logic. Apologize to Spectra and then take me to bed. I've missed you."

Calin smiled at her. He kissed my cheek. "I'm sorry I scared you."

Gina led her husband out of the kitchen, and I took three deep breaths to steady myself. My phone rang, and I nearly jumped out of my skin. I walked to the window to make sure I kept the reception.

"Alexander, what's up?"

"I want to see you. Can I come by?" He sounded frazzled.

"I'm not home. I've been spending time out of the city on the weekends."

"Yeah, Tommy said you were out of town. What's happening?"

I bit my lip. "Tonight? I'm helping a woman not get murdered by her angry husband."

"Oh, work as usual then?" Alexander sighed. "I thought you were letting the business go?"

"Until I have a job, I can't afford to do that just yet."

"Well, can I see you tomorrow night?"

"I probably won't be back until Monday. With college finished, I'm sort of taking time out and enjoying getting away for a while."

Alexander huffed frustrated. "Dinner on Monday then. No excuses. I'll take you to Margareta's."

"I'd rather not. Can we just do Italian down the harbor?"

Alexander was silent for a moment. "Margareta's is your favorite."

"Was my favorite. Right up until I walked in on you fucking the maitre d' and you started taking your new girlfriend there. I'll meet you at the bottom of the stairs by the harbor at seven on Monday." I hung up the phone. I'd seen him with the Nephilim last weekend and recognized Raquel from the club. Female offspring of celestials were kind of rare enough that if we ran across each other, we took notice.

Taking a deep breath, I grabbed a fresh bottle of water and trekked back up to Bay's bedroom. He was just walking out onto the landing as I reached the top of the stairs.

"Everything okay?" he asked, concerned.

I gave him a quiet smile, knowing he could read me perfectly well, and held up the bottle of water. "Thirsty." I stepped into him and went on tiptoe to kiss his lips. "Ready for round three?"

Bay wrapped me in his arms. "I was ready for sleep, but seeing you in my shirt changed my mind."

❧

"So how's business?" Alexander asked as the waiter took our menus away.

"Still there."

"Have you heard from Ryder?"

I shrugged. "I ran into him at a party the other week."

"He didn't try anything?"

"He tried to get me alone, but it didn't work."

"And you haven't heard from him otherwise?" Alexander studied me.

I kept watching the crowd walking past the harborfront restaurant. "A couple of times, but he's been quite the gentleman and when I told him to leave, he has." I turned my eyes to Alexander. "Are you going to marry Raquel?"

Alexander sat back. "How did you know about her?"

I looked at him. "Female offspring are rare, Alexander. We tend to know each other, and I saw you going into Margareta's with her last Saturday. With the way you were touching each other, I'd say you've been seeing each other for a few months now. Were you ever going to tell me?"

"She can shield. She was raised by her father and trained at a young age." Alexander kept his eyes downcast.

I swallowed over the lump growing inside my throat, a ball of hurt sinking to my stomach. "You must be happy to have found someone worthy of you, Alexander."

Alexander's dark eyes lifted to mine. "She's not you, Spec."

I sighed. "No, Alexander, she isn't." I put my napkin on the table and stood up. Alexander's eyes went wide with fear, and I knew this was what he'd always feared. "Good luck, Alexander."

He stood, grabbing my hand. "Don't walk Spec. She's a Fallen's get. She may not be strong enough."

"The fact that you've told me about her tells me you think she is, Alex. At the very least, you're sure she's stronger than me." I kissed his cheek, holding my tears at bay while I walked away from the table.

I wanted to go straight home and cry my heart out, but at the same time, I didn't want to be by myself. I pulled out my phone as I neared the grounds of Saint Benedict's.

"Hey, everything okay?" Mercury sounded worried. There was lots of noise in the background, so I knew he wasn't at work.

"Can I see you tonight?"

Mercury hesitated. "I'll be home in thirty minutes."

I hung up the phone and walked straight to the caretaker's cottage. Robert answered the door. He opened his mouth to tell me Mercury wasn't there, but the tears started falling, and he swallowed those words, opening the door wide enough for me to come in.

"Does Mercury know you're here?" I nodded my head. Robert nodded and shut the door, walking back to his television show.

I made my way back to Mercury's room, throwing my jacket in the corner along with my boots before sitting cross-legged on his bed and cuddling myself. Mercury came in twenty minutes later. He saw that I was physically unharmed and relaxed a little. He sat next to me on the bed and put an arm around me, waiting for me to be ready to talk.

"I thought it would hurt more..." I sobbed. "If he ever found a balance worthy of him. I thought it would be like dying all over again. It's not. It hurts, and I feel like I left a part of me back there with him, but it's not killing me."

Mercury blew out a breath, and I got the feeling he'd known for a long time about Raquel and Alexander. I looked at his jeans and shirt and sighed. "Are you off for tonight?"

"Yes."

"You were with another woman, weren't you?"

"Yes."

"Jesus! I'm sorry, Merc."

"Is it over with Alexander?"

"Yes."

"Then don't be sorry." Mercury pulled me into his lap so I sat facing him. "I will always choose you over any other woman."

I gave him a weak smile. He made me happy. He made my heart beat harder, and as I looked into his worried lapis blues, I knew Bay was right. I'd fallen in love with Mercury years ago and never even realized it because I'd been so focused on becoming the woman Alexander needed. Mercury just needed me to be me.

I pushed his jacket from his shoulders, and I watched Mercury's eyes grow heated. I lifted his shirt over his head and ran my hands over the strength of those shoulders and arms, my fingers tracing over the tattoo where it ended at his neck. I traced the wing down across the pectorals to his side where the wing joined to the warrior angel, brandishing a sword in one hand, the rod of Asclepius in the other.

Mercury touched my face, bringing me back to him. "Nothing happens tonight, Spectra. You're heartbroken. You can't make decisions in this state of mind."

"I wasn't..."

"You were. I can see it all over your face. You've just realized what I mean to you, and you're terrified you'll lose me too if you don't give me a reason to stay. You won't, Spectra. I've been yours since the first time we kissed. What you need to realize is that you and Alexander have been over for twelve months or more. You'd faded into nothing more than friends with the occasional roll in the sheets. You love each other so you couldn't admit it was over, but it was. Tonight isn't going to change anything except you'll avoid him more than you already do."

The pain in my chest yawned open, and while I knew Mercury was right, it hurt even more that he was. Mercury pulled my face to his neck as I started crying again. He held me tight, and as my tears ran dry, he laid us down on his bed and continued to hold me till we both fell asleep, still wrapped in each other's arms.

I woke in the morning by myself. Mercury's jacket and boots were gone, so I knew he'd left for work already. Collecting my stuff, I made my way back to the church grounds to the convent and my attic bedroom. I showered and changed before grabbing my stuff and heading to the library to finally fix up my resume and send it off to the two new companies asking to meet me.

By the time the library was closing and I was packing up to head home, I'd already received a call arranging a meeting on Thursday with Galaxy Systems. Their head office was out of town in one of the business industrial parks. I decided to get something to eat and then look up how I could actually get there.

As I walked into the convent two hours after dark, a woman was sitting in the waiting area. She stood when I came in, which drew my attention. "Phillipa. What are you doing in the city this late?"

"Henry is working so we will get dinner after." She looked upset, and I could only gather she'd spoken with Alexander. "I'm sorry, Spectra. I shouldn't have given you hope when you visited last time. I knew about Raquel then. I just... I wanted it to be you because I know it's you he loves."

I looked at the floor, unable to meet her eyes. "He will be happy with her, Phillipa. She's trained, and she'll make the perfect wife for L'Ordre. She wears all the right clothes and will fit in with his high society life."

"You were raised high society, Spectra, and dressed the part till..." Phillipa choked, unable to say what changed me. She stepped forward, taking my hand. "They aren't married yet, Spectra. Don't give up. I know you have the potential to be a strong balance. He's a powerful sorcerer; she may not be worthy."

I took my hand back. "He thinks she is, Phillipa. He gave up on me years ago. It's time I gave up on him too."

I turned and walked up the stairs. I couldn't say goodbye to Phillipa. I couldn't lose that too this week. Alexander tried ringing me a few times today, but I'd decided, when I woke up, that the best thing I could do was sever all ties with him. I'd called the NSIO before lunch and canceled my meeting that was set for after graduation. I'd never wanted to work there, so I didn't see the point in going through with the meet.

My phone buzzed as I closed the door to my room, and I opened the message from Mercury.

Bad night. Won't be making it home at all. Will you be okay?

I typed back I would be, and his reply was almost instant.

Good luck with the interview tomorrow.

Immediately afterward, an email came through.

I can't stop thinking about you. B.

I sighed, sitting on my bed, considering the timing of both those messages. I looked around my room and typed my response without looking at the screen. The truth was I didn't want to be alone.

Then come and get me.

I went to my wardrobe and picked out what I would wear to the interview tomorrow. My phone pinged with another email.

Calin will pick you up in thirty minutes. Bring what you need for the night.

I smiled and zipped the bag I'd already packed. My phone started ringing. I looked at the caller ID, saw it was Alexander, and silenced it. A moment later, my room flared like a flash firestorm. It lasted a blink, but it was enough to make my shield activate. Just two weekends with Bay and I'd stretched it to encompass my entire torso.

I blinked through the tears from the impact of that power to find Alexander standing in my room, still in his work suit. He looked angry. "You're ignoring my calls."

"We're over, Alexander. It's best for both of us if it just stops."

"No, it's not!" He ran his hand through his hair. His power was still there, he wasn't shielding me like he normally did, and so his anger whipped out and lashed me with that power. I cringed, but my shield took the brunt of it, stretching to cover my thighs. Alexander's eyes softened as he pulled my mouth to his. He kissed me passionately, and for a moment I fell into his kiss, his passion.

"Stop." I whimpered as his hands started pulling my skirt up. I felt his emotions as if they were mine. Lust, love, fear, anger. I pulled at his anger, taking it from him and making it mine. "Stop!" I shoved him away from me. "I'm not yours anymore. That stopped four years ago when you pushed me out."

Alexander looked at me, shocked. "I did that to protect you…"

"You did it to have the freedom to screw around, to be able to seek out a woman worthy of you. You decided four years ago I was never going to make the cut, but you didn't want to give me up either, so you gave me the hope to keep me under your spell. And I believed it. I believed it right up until I saw your mother a few weeks ago. Do you know what she told me?"

Alexander shook his head, his anger starting to build again. As his power burnt around me, the shield spread to my ankles. Growing my shield was becoming easier with each exposure.

"She said I needed constant exposure to learn, that pushing me away, shielding me constantly from your power, would never train me."

"What are you saying?" His anger was becoming danger-ous. I could see the power swirling around him now. My shield spread to my elbows and I couldn't help thinking that if I stayed in this room another ten minutes with Alexander angry, I might finally make my shield complete.

I dropped my voice, softened it, so I didn't come off threat-ening. "I'm saying you never wanted me to make it, Alexander. You knew I needed to be exposed. You knew, and you didn't do it. And, now I know it too."

I stepped forward, collecting my bag from my bed. Alexander grabbed the bag from me and held it up. "What's this?" The shield stretched, only my hands, feet, and head exposed to the fire now.

"I'm leaving."

Alexander's face dropped, his anger fading suddenly as his fear came to the surface. I realized what I'd said and what he'd heard were two different things, or maybe they weren't. As we stood there looking at each other, I acknowledged to myself that both the jobs I'd applied for today took me away from the city. Subconsciously, I'd already decided I was leaving for good.

Alexander placed my bag carefully on my bed. "What about your job interviews, your business?"

"I'll still see out the interviews this week. The business is transportable."

Alexander met my eyes, the pain, and sadness in them a crushing, clawing weight on my chest. "I can't give you up, Spec."

I hesitated, stepped towards him, and gave him the gentlest kiss. My heart felt like it was being ripped open and I was bleeding everywhere. I pulled back from the kiss, keeping my eyes closed against my own tears, knowing the moisture I felt on my face were Alexander's tears. "I'm not giving you a choice, Alexander."

I collected my bag and walked out of the room. Mother Superior was standing in the walkway outside my room as I came out and shut the door. She waited till I came close to speak and kept her voice to a whisper. I knew sound traveled around this space. I held no delusion that she didn't hear everything.

"There is a man downstairs saying he was sent to pick you up."

I nodded, looking back over my shoulder at the sound of Alexander's crying.

Mother Superior touched my shoulder in comfort as my tears started to fall. "Go. I'll make sure he's okay." She gave me a gentle push towards the stairs.

Downstairs, Calin took one look at me and put his arm around me as he walked me to Luke's Wrangler. We drove in silence, just the occasional tear escaping. As we pulled into the garage, Calin's phone vibrated. I climbed out of the car while he read the message.

"The boss is just finishing up dinner. He shouldn't be too long."

"If you don't mind. I'll wait in his room."

Calin nodded. I took my bag and walked into the house, making my own way.

CHAPTER 14

Bay

"I THINK that's the fastest we've ever made the drive back from the city," Luke scowled as we pulled into the garage.

I rolled my eyes, climbing out of the car. "Spectra is here."

Luke slammed the car door. "So we've gone from weekends to weekdays as well. Soon she'll be moving in."

I slapped him on the shoulder as I walked past. "What a great idea. I'll get the place sanctified so she feels comfortable and she can move in next week."

Luke stiffened, his feet coming to a halt. I kept walking, smirking to myself at his growl as I walked into the house.

"...tell the boss. Something bad might have happened." Gina's voice came from the library as I walked in.

"It's her business, Gina," Calin replied calmly.

"The boss is using her for sex. That's not the person she's going to confide in," Cynthia chimed in. "You made friends with her, Gina, she saved your life. You should be the one to go talk to her."

"Jesus! Would you both stay out of it," Calin sighed, frustrated.

I stepped into the library, leaning against the doorjamb. Gina sat at her normal desk, her blonde hair half pulled up in a bun with a pencil stuck through to hold it. Calin sat on the desk next to her looking a little stressed. Cynthia stood naked, arms crossed as she stared Calin down.

"What are we staying out of?" I queried, and all three jumped. "Cyn, I thought you were on duty tonight?"

Cynthia met my eyes. "I am, but I heard something, and it worried me, so I came to report to Calin. I'll get back out there now, boss."

"What worried you?" I asked before she could leave. I knew from the conversation I'd overheard that it related to Spectra.

Cynthia swallowed and looked back at Calin. Calin gave a small shake of his head.

Gina groaned in annoyance. "For fuck's sake, Cal!" She stood up to face me. "Spectra's crying her heart out up there. She was pulling so hard into herself when she arrived that she actually became insubstantial and walked right through me on the stairs."

Calin glared at Gina. "Which I was just explaining is none of our business."

"It's his business!" Gina pointed at me. "That makes it our business."

I started to turn. "Your wife is right, Calin. It is my business." I found Luke standing outside the door listening, concern all over his face. Annoyed as he pretended to be at Spectra's presence, he liked the girl.

I moved up the stairs and opened my bedroom door, expecting to find a broken heap on the floor. Instead, she stood by my reading chair laying a black pantsuit out so it wouldn't crease. She looked up, startled by my sudden entrance, then smiled as if she didn't have a care in the world. Everything about her lied, telling me she was perfectly fine and happy. Everything but her eyes. Her eyes were darker than I'd ever seen them, a deep ocean blue.

I closed the door, using the action to turn my back for a moment and compose myself. I could smell Alexander Williams all over her even from this distance, but it wasn't sex, just close contact.

"How was dinner?" she asked cheerily. I turned back to her and raised a brow. Spectra's eyes went wide when she realized what she'd just asked.

"Satisfying." I stepped towards her. "But not what I was craving."

I kissed her before she fell apart again. I wanted her to tell me what happened, but I understood she didn't want to talk about it. So I kissed her. It took several minutes of kissing before her tension leeched out enough to relax her body to mine. I kissed her slowly, letting my hands hold her. My thumb brushed the zip on her long skirt, so I slowly lowered the zip and let the skirt fall to the ground. As my hands pulled back up, I lifted her top over her head, forcing us to break from our kiss.

I kept her eyes locked with mine, watching them slowly lighten, moving my hands around her waist and up her back to unhook her bra. As it fell away revealing her beautiful breasts, I nearly broke eye contact to look at them but stayed with her as I dropped into a squat and slowly inched her panties down her long, slender legs. Her eyes were nearly midnight blue now as I rose to standing and I slipped my jacket from my shoulders.

"You don't ever have to hide from me, Spectra." I stroked the side of her face. "You don't know how irresistible I find the naked beauty of your soul."

For a moment she closed her eyes, and I thought she would let me see her pain. Instead, she rubbed her cheek against my hand, and when her eyes opened, they held danger. "You hide from me, Bay. You shield your power; you hide what you are about, your true intentions. Even naked, you wear a suit of armor."

I swallowed as she started to undress me. "Pick one. The most important of those three. Pick one, and I will reveal it to you now."

She pushed my shirt from my body and kissed me across my chest. My fingers tangled in her hair out of reflex as her mouth descended south, her hands pushing my pants down in unison. She dropped to kneeling, taking my firmness in her hand. Her eyes flicked up to mine. "Shield."

My fingers gripped her head, stopping her mouth's descent. "Are you sure? It could kill you, Spectra. At the very least, it would be very painful."

"Give me this, Bay, and I will give you what I've never given any other."

Her choice told me her state of mind. It was her life she was putting on the line by asking me to show her my true power. The reward she offered informed me that Alexander finally told her about the Nephilim bitch and Spectra finished whatever version of a relationship they'd been having. Her tongue flicked the tip of my cock before twirling around the smooth head. I loosened my grip on her hair, and she descended until her nose touched my abdomen. Her body rebelled the depth of my penetration, but she held herself for two breaths before pulling back.

I used her hair to stop her descent as I knelt in front of her, confusion clouding her features. I fisted her hair and kissed her hard, using my weight to force her to fold back to lie on the floor. She spread her thighs automatically, bidding me welcome as I lay between them and nudged my erection between her labia till I found her opening. She wasn't ready for me, but I wasn't going to wait in case she changed her mind.

Kissing her deeply, I pressed into her tightness. She gasped, her body resisted me, but I drew back a little and pushed forward again. She turned her head to the side, biting her lip. Her body resisted again, but I gained ground. Two more times I pulled back and thrust a little deeper. By the time her body surrendered, Spectra's nails were scraping down my arms, her back bowed, head hanging back.

Once I was buried deep within her, I dropped my shields enough to drown her in my desire for her. She moaned and pulled my mouth to hers, kissing me intensely as her legs wrapped around my hips. I started moving within her, pulling nearly all the way out of her slowly before thrusting deep into her as fast as I could. I let my shields drop even further. She gasped, but her body kept pressing up to meet my thrusts eagerly.

Lowering my shield, I watched her grimace, the pads of her fingers gripping my arms. Her body kept our rhythm, and after several minutes, any discomfort with my power burning around us was forgotten. I held my shield there a little longer, waiting until her moans rose in volume and her body started tightening around mine. I could barely move inside of her now.

"Are you sure?" I murmured before thrusting hard into her.

Spectra cried out with every thrust, her voice growing even louder as her body found the edge of pleasure. "Yes," she gasped.

I moved my arms so I could take all my weight in the one hand. I caressed my free hand from her knee, over her hip, up her slender waist to encompass her pale breast. Her back arched, presenting her breasts to me, and I felt myself swell even larger inside her, my desire rising to meet her body's response. I moved my mouth to her ear as my free hand caressed up her neck.

"Please be strong enough." I dropped my shield entirely.

Spectra's back bowed higher, and she screamed, my hand quickly covering her mouth to muffle her. Her fingernails dug into my back as her body bucked beneath mine. I gritted my teeth, counting in my head. Thirty seconds. That's all I'd give her. If she was still screaming, I'd pull my shield back together and try and save her. As I reached fifteen, her scream changed to a sob. As my count hit twenty-five, I could move my hand away from her mouth. She let out small little whimpers.

I watched her eyes blink open, tears streaming free of them. She blinked a few more times, and then her beautiful eyes, once again their natural pale blue, focused on me. She gave me a weak smile, waited a moment longer till her breathing wasn't so labored, and then she wiggled her hips.

I kissed her hard, holding her hip with my free hand. I thrust hard and fast into her. Her head fell back, and she moaned so beautifully I felt it deep within me. I throbbed and went inside her. Spectra's eyes grew wide with surprise. She mouthed that vulgar word I'd scolded her for using, and then she came with me. My magic swirled around us and tingled down my spine. It was so subtle I doubt she even felt it.

As we lay there, recovering, our bodies still connected as lovers, I smiled quietly to myself, my mouth hidden against her neck. She was mine now. I knew she wouldn't deny Mercury the same privilege eventually and he'd get her pregnant shortly after. But I was the first she'd let own her body completely.

Spectra started laughing. I pulled back to look at her.

"What?" I asked gently.

"I get it now. Why it's worth risking. That was so amazing!"

I smiled down at her. "Are you talking about me coming inside of you or risking death from my power?"

"Both." She deflated and went limp underneath me. A smile played across her lips, her voice barely audible as her eyes started to shutter. "I was strong enough."

I smiled gently. "More than."

I removed myself from her, kneeling back to admire her sprawled and drifting on the edge of sleep. My eyes traveled down to her heat, and I ran my thumb between her labia, admiring the cream of my pleasure seeping out of her. "You're mine now, Spectra."

"I know," she sighed. "I think I always was."

I cocked my head to the side, wondering if she truly did understand, but I decided she didn't. I doubt Alexander or his father would have warned her in the hope that she would bind herself to Alexander in her naiveté. I smiled, standing up and going to the shower, leaving her there to fall the rest of the way to sleep.

When I came out, she was rolled on her side, breathing deeply. I picked her up and carried her to the bed, tucking her in so she'd be warm. I stood back watching her sleep in my bed and thought how nice it'd be to have her there every night. I rubbed my hands over my face, frustrated that she'd come into my life at this point, and moved to my study.

An hour of reading reports later, Luke came in and sat down in his usual seat. "Is she okay?"

I looked up at him and sat back. "Alexander and her are over."

"That doesn't change anything with you two."

"Not outside of that room, it doesn't." I frowned, hating I would have to keep her a secret just as much as he had.

Luke gave me a sympathetic look. "You're in love with her, aren't you?"

"It doesn't matter, Luke. She's better off with the Angelis."

"But you will take her to your bed when she avails herself to you?"

"Of course." I frowned. "She succeeded in her purpose in my life. My desires are reawakened, and I'm able to procure my own food without asking Calin to do my dirty work. Whatever I've come to feel for her is irrelevant."

Luke blew out a breath, shaking his head as he stood and moved to the door.

"Where are you off to with that look?"

"To find out how hard it's going to be to get a priest to bless this house so your angel wants to live here." Luke opened the door and looked back at me. "If the Angelis is going to live here too, then we should clear out the guest rooms on the second level. That way she can be in his bed when he's home, and your bed when he's not."

"Her living here is not an option, Luke." I wished it were possible though. "It would still put her in danger, and Alexander would find out eventually."

Luke gave me a leveling look. "Fantôme wants to recruit her. Essence will take her if they even hear a whisper of her ability, and who knows who else will want her? Can you really think of a safer place for the girl?"

"That's not going to sell it to Alexander."

"Then sell it to Henry, and he will order Alexander to accept it." Luke took a step back into the office. "If either of those two groups gets their hands on her, she will be taken, brought into an eternity of preying on those she once protected. She detests our kind, Bay. She is looking past that for you because you call to her on a level above your condemnation, but while she tries to be amicable, her loathing is very obvious every time she looks at me. Could you imagine being forced to become what you hate more than anything else? What do you think that would do to her?"

I rested my forehead in my hands, knowing the answer already. "She'd beg L'Ordre and L'Paix to end her. And, if they refused, she'd commit a crime so heinous she would force their hands."

"Exactly," Luke smiled. "You love her. It's worth risking everything else to have her, isn't it?"

I sighed. "I'll discuss it with the Angelis and we'll go from there."

CHAPTER 15

Spectra

THE CAR RIDE BACK TO THE CITY WEDNESDAY morning was silent. I sat in the back with Bay, Luke up front with Calin, who was driving. Bay woke me early to take his pleasure again, taking mine right along with it. He didn't even bother shielding with me, and he didn't need to now. Last night's exposure finally stretched and sealed my shield to encompass me entirely now. When that seal formed last night, I felt something within me shift.

This morning, every one of my senses was more alive. Every little touch of Bay's fingers on my skin was intense in the way my receptors responded. As I watched the world pass by outside the windows, colors were richer, textures sharper. Breakfast was like an orgasm in my mouth as the taste of the bacon and eggs were taken to a whole new level. I felt like I'd been living in a bundle of cotton wool until this morning.

Bay's thumb rubbed against mine where he held my hand as we entered the city streets. "Are you nervous about your meeting?"

"No."

"What was the recruiter like when you met them?"

"She kept talking up the company, telling me how there would be lots of room for advancement for someone with my skills." I noticed Luke listening intently; his head was turned towards Calin, so he heard every word. I frowned, looking to Bay, who was watching me with the same intensity. "Is there something you two know about this meeting you want to tell me?"

Bay patted my hand. "There's nothing I can tell you yet. You said you have another interview tomorrow?"

"At Galaxy. I still have to figure out how I'm going to get out to Stokes. There isn't much in the way of public transport. And then I've got my formal interview at Baulkims on Friday."

"Can you drive?" Calin asked.

"Of course," I smirked. "I grew up in suburbia with an absentee mother. I was driving her car to the shops for food before I was even licensed."

Calin nodded. "Stokes Business Park isn't even twenty minutes from the estate. Why don't you stay tonight at our place and borrow one of the cars in the morning?"

I looked to Bay, unsure how to word why I couldn't. "I am..."

"Meant to see your boyfriend tonight?" Bay finished for me. I swallowed and nodded. Bay's eyes drifted to Luke, who gave the slightest nod. "We'll bring him to you. Luke will arrange the guest room for your use."

I narrowed my eyes and assessed all three of them. "Why?"

Bay raised a brow.

"Why would you be willing to allow me to sleep under your roof with my boyfriend and not you?"

Bay gave the tiniest smirk. "You chose shield, not intentions, Spectra. The offer gets you out of a bind; that's all that should matter for now."

I couldn't trust there wasn't an ulterior motive. I turned my eyes to the back of Calin's head. "Thank you for the offer, but no. I'll find my own way. If I took the job, I'd have to make arrangements to get there anyway."

Luke's smile disappeared, and he turned his face fully back to the front of the car. Bay just watched me, and I could see what he was thinking in his eyes.

I smiled. "You're only just working out how stubborn I can be?"

Bay's left eye squinted like he was concentrating. "You don't have any intention of taking this job today, do you?"

"No," I answered straightforward.

"Why?"

"I've been aiming for Galaxy for two years. That was my goal."

"Then why go in for the meeting at all?" Bay was highly suspicious of me now. His shoulders were tense, his body posture guarded.

"Galaxy isn't guaranteed. They are very particular about who they hire."

"How are they different from the other companies?"

I looked around the car and noticed the other two were the same. "What am I walking into here, Bay?"

"Answer my question."

"Look... I might be interested in the job at Pendant once I've seen the place, but if it's going to be like the NSIO, I'm not interested." I met Bay's eyes.

He relaxed a little. "The recruiters at this place are trained profilers, they'll throw you out on your ear if they think for even a second you're not serious about being there."

I nodded, and Calin pulled the car up to the curb outside a beautiful historic office building. "Good luck, Spectra," Calin called. "Call me after you're finished, and we'll have lunch so you can get your bag back." Calin's eyes drifted to the bag with my clothes at my feet. Bay's and Luke's eyes were on Calin, and surprise didn't even cover the look on their faces. It was a mix of surprise, disgust, possibly distrust. Whatever it was, it was hostile.

"Thanks, Calin. Text me so I have your number and I'll call you when I'm finished." He handed me his phone, and I typed my phone number in. Bay's eyebrows shot up as he watched me hand the phone back, but he didn't say anything.

I leaned over to kiss him goodbye, and Luke coughed loudly, "Lipstick."

I laughed, remembering that I was, in fact, wearing a rosy lip gloss just to give my lips some color. "I'll see you next week sometime."

Bay caught my wrist. "This weekend."

I shook my head. "I'm with Mercury until Sunday evening. He starts night shift again Sunday night. We need to work some stuff out between us, so we need this time."

Bay frowned. "I'll contact you Sunday night to arrange to see you again."

I nodded, opened the door, and stepped out of the car. I walked towards the front door of the building and looked back as I stepped into the revolving door. Bay's car was already gone. On the other side of the door, I instantly wanted to get back outside. Everyone I could see was a predator. I stood there scanning over the entry foyer. The security guards, the ladies at reception, the people coming and going, making their way to the elevators.

I stood there trying to remember to breathe. "Miss?" The security guard on this side of the door stepped forward, giving me a quizzical look. "Are you lost?"

I was certainly starting to feel that way. I focused on the guard in front of me, blocking out my surroundings. "Is this Pendant Security?"

"Yes, Miss." The guard looked confused. I'm guessing they didn't get many humans walking through their door. "Do you have an appointment?" I nodded. The guard's brows nearly jumped off his face. "Tracey at the desk will fix you up with a pass."

I nodded, took a deep breath, and made my way to the desk. The look on Tracey's face when I stopped in front of her was just as shocked as the security guards. Okay, they never got humans in here. "Good morning, I'm meeting with Miranda Jackson from recruiting this morning. My name is Spectra Michaels."

Tracey typed into her computer and pressed a button, adjusting her headset. "Miss Michaels is in the foyer. Yes, sir." Tracey disconnected the call. "If I could see your ID please, Miss Michaels?" I pulled out my license and handed it to her. She put it on a scanner and scanned it before handing it back to me. "Please look at the camera on the wall behind me."

I looked at the camera, and then Tracey was typing again. She pulled a lanyard out of a drawer and the machine spat out a visitor's pass. Tracey swiped the card through a device and pointed to a black pad mounted above what looked to be an optometrist's device on the counter. "If you could place your hand on the pad, your chin in the strap, and your forehead in the brace please and look straight ahead."

I swallowed, becoming slightly nervous about this level of security, but did as requested. A red light shined over my eye at the same time I felt a tingling in my hand. "Thank you, Miss Michaels." I stood straight, and Tracey handed me my pass. "You have limited access." I nodded, slipping the lanyard over my head.

"Miss Michaels." The man who now stood beside me held out his hand. I turned to look at the thirty-something de Sang and felt my heart rate pick up. He could have been Calin's brother. Since I knew Luke and Calin were brothers, I guess that made him Luke's possible brother as well.

"Son actually."

"I'm sorry?"

"My name is Alfred Abernathy. I'm head of recruitment here at Pendant. I'm Luke's son from before he was taken and before you ask, no, my father did not take me. I got myself into the same sort of trouble some years later." Alfred smiled a generous smile at me as he held out his hand.

"I actually asked that out loud?" I queried cautiously as I shook his hand.

'Not at all, Miss Michaels,' Alfred smiled as his voice came into my head.

'Fuck!'

Alfred looked me over with a very naughty smile. "I'd love to, but maybe later."

"What?" I asked cautiously, not sure which of my thoughts he'd just heard.

Alfred smirked and directed me to the elevators. "Shall we get started? Our recruitment process is quite rigorous. We'll start with a lengthy interview, then I will give you a series of tests to see where your skill set would be most valuable to us. If you pass that, I will give you a quick tour of the area I think you would be best placed..."

"Wait." I put my hand up as we stepped into an elevator alone and Alfred pressed the button for the first floor. "I'm sorry. I thought I was meeting Miranda, and she never mentioned anything about this process. I haven't had the opportunity to study for any test, and why is there is no other human in this building?"

Alfred's smile dropped, and he hit the stop button on the elevator as concern smothered his features. "Miss Michaels, you need to breathe. I'm not going to hurt you, but you are about to fail straight out if you can't control your panic response."

Oh my god, it was just like that first time Bay dragged me into an elevator alone with him. Alfred watched me for a moment, turned quickly, and hit the start button. He waited for the doors to open, stepped out, and put his arm out to keep the doors open for me. I closed my eyes, took a deep breath, and took one step forward, followed by the other until I was standing in the open space of the lift foyer on the first level.

Alfred let the elevator doors go and watched me with curiosity. "Miss Michaels, are you aware you're claustrophobic?"

I swallowed and glared at Alfred. "Only when it comes to enclosed spaces and predators."

Alfred grabbed my upper arm and dragged me off to the side where no one could overhear. "You were attacked as a child. That doesn't explain to me how you can tell there is not one other human in this building. Considering I can smell you had sex with a particular predator this morning, I can tell your fear of enclosed spaces is not restricted to a predator being in it with you."

I met his eyes. "Just because you can see my thoughts does not mean you know me. I can tell there are no humans in this building because of the way the security guard and the receptionist reacted to my presence here, not on any Nachtwelt ability. Who I'm having sex with is none of your business, but let me assure you, it took a lot for him to convince me to see past what he is. He and his staff are the only predators I would trust in an enclosed space with me, and I only trust your father because he fears his boss. Now where is Miranda?"

Alfred glared at me for a moment. "Miranda is no longer with this company." Alfred walked over to a set of glass double doors, swiped his staff card, and pulled one open. "Would you like to continue with your interview, Miss Michaels? Or would you prefer to give up now?"

Bay

"…WILL NEED TO BE READY TO GO ACTIVE in two weeks." Luke read calculations from his worksheet.

"We can do that," Calin responded.

"Is that everything?" I asked, watching my inbox fill up out of the corner of my eye.

"Yes," Luke sorted his reports, ready to leave.

Calin smirked. "How did Spectra go with her interview?"

"I haven't seen Alfred to ask yet," Luke answered factually.

"How was she at lunch?" I asked as I opened an email I'd been waiting on.

"Pissed off would be putting it mildly. She wasn't happy to be interviewed by a telepath. Said she was glad she canceled her interview at the NSIO if she was going to go through a similar situation there."

I felt my brows lift with curiosity. "She's canceled her interview with NSIO? When?"

Calin shrugged. "Not sure. Anyway, she doesn't expect she'll get an offer to work here." Calin stood. "I'll get back to my work so we can meet these deadlines."

"Why did you ask her to lunch?" Luke queried on my behalf. "She's not your type."

"She's feminine, strong, beautiful, intelligent, and dangerous. What about her isn't my type?"

"She's not blonde," Luke grumbled.

"She's also not available to you," I added.

"I just wanted to make sure she was okay after she got out of here. She's a nice girl, but I know which bed she belongs in. However, I did manage to get her phone number for you." Calin smiled, taking a piece of paper from his pocket and holding it up. "Should make contacting her a little easier, don't you think?" Calin put the piece of paper on my desk and walked out.

Luke walked over to my desk and picked up the phone. "Alfred. Come up to Mr. Ryder's office please." He hung up.

I looked at him through my brows. "I have another meeting in twenty minutes and still a lot of stuff to get through. Couldn't it wait?"

"No." Luke sat back down. "You want to know how she went more than any of us. More so, you want to know if he worked out what she was."

I didn't argue with him. I read my emails, replying where needed while Luke scribbled notes in the margins of reports and typed other notes into his tablet. A few minutes later, Alfred knocked at the door and came in. He wasn't his usual smiling self, which said there was a problem straight off. The next giveaway was the look he gave me. He knew about my involvement with Spectra and wasn't happy about it.

Luke took one look at his son and sighed. "She passed, didn't she?"

Alfred handed a sheet to his father. "With flying colors. One of the best results we've ever seen, so it's particularly impressive for a human. I can see why the boss seduced her."

"Let's keep that out of her file," Luke grumbled.

"Easily done." Alfred looked at me as he sank into the spare seat at the table. "I only know about you because I recognized your smell on her. Otherwise, I would never have gotten that out of her. She hid you quite well."

Luke frowned. "You tested her fear response? That's not standard for professional staff."

Alfred winced. "That was accidental. She is claustrophobic. Started having a panic attack in the elevator before I even got her to the interview room. It took me a minute to understand why she was freaking out, and I made it worse by stopping the elevator. Once I saw the connection to her childhood..." Alfred shook his head. "That girl will never hide in a wardrobe again, that's for sure." Alfred shivered, and part of me wanted to know what he'd seen. "Anyway, I got the elevator going again and got out, holding the doors to watch if she recovered."

"Which she did," Luke affirmed, reading the report.

"Yes. This is not a good place for a survivor to work."

"But?" I queried because there was a 'but.'

"But, Evan would die to have her in his department. You don't get many with her skill level."

"You got her to hack the Nachtwelt Security and Intelligence Office?" Luke damn near choked, reading through her test sheet.

Alfred smiled. "I didn't specify a place. I just asked her to access a secure database. She seemed pretty interested in the information she pulled on a..." Alfred looked at the file he was holding. "Raquel Nephilezza. A female Nephilim who's working at the NSIO as a personal assistant to L'Ordre. She then further impressed Evan by using the wireless on the laptop I'd given her to hack our network and email something from that girl's file to someone else. Though she did it so quickly, I actually missed she'd done it till Evan checked the laptop after she left."

I frowned. "What did she email to who?"

Alfred's brow raised in interest. "You're obviously behind on your emails today, boss. She used my access and sent it to your private account, so look for an email from me."

I changed accounts and scrolled through my emails until I found one time stamped just after ten.

Thought you might find this interesting. I think I'll be leaving town for a while.

I opened the attachment and found a thread of emails. I pressed print. "Luke, call Henry and tell him he needed to meet me an hour ago. Then call Calin. Tell him to find my ghost and get her underground, so deeply hidden that even I don't know where she is, but don't use her name cause it's likely your phone is cloned."

I looked to Alfred. "I want your appointment with Spectra deleted instantly, so it never happened. Actually, just change the name to some other person we were looking at recruiting but failed."

Alfred pulled out his tablet and started tapping frantically. "You think they'll try to find out who hacked that information?"

I looked at Luke speaking hurriedly in the corner. "It's what we would do."

My door opened and Claire, my assistant, walked in on her ridiculous heels, placing what I just printed on the end of my desk. "Claire, I need to consult a physician about one of our staff. Could you call Saint Benedict's Hospital and put it through when you have the directory please?"

Claire nodded and walked out. She was a de Viande. I wouldn't let a de Sang near my office I didn't personally trust. It's why I had Alfred take Spectra's interview rather than one of his staff. Alfred was on his phone asking Evan to delete Spectra's digital trail from today. Luke was telling the front desk to bring L'Paix straight up as soon as he arrived.

My phone rang, and I picked it up. "I have Saint Bene-dict's Hospital for you." Claire hung up.

"Hello sir, how can I help?"

"I need to contact one of your doctors on duty. His wife

has gone into labor, and there were complications. She is being rushed to our local hospital and asked me to call him. His name is Dr. Mercury Raphangelis."

"Please hold, and I'll find him for you."

I sat, drumming my fingers impatiently as the directory assistant tracked down the doctor. Luke hung up and came over to the desk, reading the email. His eyes widened. "Are we bringing Alexander in on this?"

"No. We're going to use him."

"Who is this?" Mercury's voice came on the phone, hostile.

"Mr. Raphangelis. I'm Mr. Ryder. Your wife works for me. She's gone into early labor, and I've been informed her current situation is perilous. Your wife needs you. I'm sending one of my staff to collect her hospital bag from your home. If you can meet him there, he will take you to your wife."

I heard Mercury wanting to ask me straight out what was happening, but I counted on him being smart enough to know better. "Damn it. She's not ready for this. I'll be at the house in twenty minutes. Thank you for calling me, Mr. Ryder." Mercury hung up.

I looked at Luke. "Mercury will meet Calin in twenty minutes at their house." Luke nodded and was on his phone again.

Evan came through the door, his eyes fixed on his tablet screen. "We've got an internal hack. I found it while tracing the candidate's activities while here. It's why the girl could hack Alfred's account. Someone already opened the door for her. Damn, she was good though. Any chance we're bringing her on?"

"She could probably solve this faster than you," Alfred teased.

Evan waved the tablet at him. "She already did. She tagged it for me."

"In English, French, or even Gaelic please?" I grumbled.

"Think of it like a leaking pipe. To find where the hole is, you run blue dye into the pipes and see where things start turning blue." Evan tapped his tablet screen and put it in front of me. "They're monitoring your activity, boss, and this is where all your internal communications are leaking out too."

Luke looked over my shoulder. "A witch. Makes sense."

"Not to me." I looked at the profile. "I thought older witches were technophobes?"

"This one definitely," Evan agreed. "She sits down in archives so it's unlikely anyone would see if she were up to anything. I would say someone set it up for her and she just passed on any information that might be valuable. Security is already collecting her and her system so we can analyze the activity." Evan picked up his tablet and walked to the door, opening it. "I want that girl on my team come Monday."

"You know why that can't happen, Evan," I groaned.

Evan gave me a mischievous look. Alfred shook his head in warning, but Evan didn't get it. "I can make it happen."

"She is protected," Luke warned.

"She is human. Who the hell would protect her?" Evan looked at everyone, confused.

"That would be me!" Henry Williams's voice boomed into the room. Evan stepped back to let a very unhappy Henry walk into the room. "That is, I assume you are talking about Spectra?"

Evan blew out a frustrated breath. "Damn it. She found this in under two minutes in our system. She is really good, boss."

"That is why she is coming to work for the NSIO." Henry smiled at an unhappy Evan.

"Not anymore she's not," Luke murmured, and Henry turned his angry dark eyes on him.

"We might move to another office while this one gets checked over a bit more thoroughly." I stood, grabbing the emails Spectra forwarded to me. "Sorry to drag you out, Henry, but we found one of the leaks at your office."

I walked down the corridor and into the ladies' bathroom. Henry followed with a slight smirk as I shooed the one de Sang touching up her lipstick out. "I love what you've done with your meeting room, Bay."

"Would you bother bugging this room?" I asked. Henry shook his head. "Spectra came in for her interview today..."

"I gathered that."

"To prove her skills, she hacked your office." Henry's eyes bulged a little. "Since she's recently been heartbroken by your son..."

Henry frowned. "What have I missed?"

I looked at him, astounded. "You know he's taken up with the Nephilim, correct?"

"Yes, that's old news. How does that affect his relationship with Spectra?"

Luke and I looked at each other. "He's marrying the Nephilim."

"Not a chance in hell, that bitch isn't strong enough for him, and she certainly isn't decent enough for my family." Henry crossed his arms, determined. I raised my brows at him. Henry ground his teeth. "He didn't tell Spectra?" I nodded. Henry's power exploded through the room. "He can't be serious! Why would he give Spectra up for that... that... I can't even find a decent word to use."

"Um, for the potential to marry a woman and have children?"

Henry raised his brows at Luke's condescending tone. "We will see about that." Henry looked back at me. "What does all of that have to do with Spectra hacking the NSIO, which I'll speak to her about later?"

"Well, since Spectra believes Alexander is going to marry the Nephilim girl, she thought she'd check her out while she was there. Interesting that Raquel entered your son's life by becoming his personal assistant, or did he get her the job after he started seeing her?" Henry ground his teeth, and I continued. "Either way, Spectra pulled these emails from your future daughter-in-law's account."

Henry took the papers from me and read through it. I could tell when he read the description. "You said you pulled the beast out of the man. It was Spectra?" Henry looked to me for confirmation.

I met his eyes unflinchingly. "How on earth would a human girl be able to do that, Henry?"

Henry scoffed at me. "You know very well she's not human, Bay, don't give me that. You're not stupid. I dare say you know exactly what she is by now."

I let one eyebrow lift. "Enlighten me, Henry."

Henry huffed. "She's a balance. Nephilim of the third generation most likely. Not powerful enough to marry even the weakest of our kind... unless this is true?"

I relaxed back against the sink and shook my head. "She can't do what is claimed here. She got scared and just happened to run the same instant this happened." It was an easy lie. Spectra couldn't do it again, so there was no point admitting she ever did it in the first place. "That's not going to stop them coming after her though."

Luke's phone rang. He stepped outside the bathroom to answer it.

Henry stood straighter. "I'll have Alexander pick her up."

"No, you won't!" I growled. "You may as well put a neon sign pointing to her if Alexander makes any move to protect her. I've already arranged for her and her boyfriend to leave town for a while. What you need to do is use your son's bride-to-be as a way to misinform our enemies."

Henry read through the emails again. "I don't even understand how she got this information. He's feigned amnesia since the event each time we've questioned the man."

"Possibly he's only spoken to those he knew were of Essence. Like Alexander's girlfriend." I tapped the papers he held. "We can use her and when we're done with her..." I shrugged. "Let Alexander marry her."

Henry glared at me. "She's not strong enough. For me, yes maybe, but not for him."

I smiled. "Oh, I'm very sure of that."

"You would let Alexander kill the woman he loves?" Henry's eyes went dark, his power swirling to a focal point.

"God no! Spectra is far too good to deserve that. The one he intends to be his wife? Yes."

The side of Henry's mouth lifted slightly. "Spectra is his, Bay. Even if she separates herself from him, he owns her heart and soul."

I leaned forward slightly. "But not body."

Henry's brow dropped in confusion. "They've been sleeping together for nearly eight years, Bay."

"Spectra is paranoid about getting pregnant out of wedlock, Henry. She's never let her lovers claim her, and that includes your son." Luke came back into the room. He looked pale and worried. I stood straight immediately. "Where is she?"

Luke shook his head. "They must have gotten her name before we could stop them. They had three hours on us. They killed a nun when they took her. The Angelis is going nuts. It looks like she tried to make a run for it, but they got her. They found her bag stuffed with clothes and her laptop halfway across the grounds. Calin is trying to track where they took her. He's called some of his students to help and added it as extra credit."

I was heading for the door. "Henry, you need to head this off at your end. Make sure the Nephilim finds out I have a ghost, but it was just coincidence that she passed through the beast the same moment Gina hit him with the antidote. Maybe, if we're lucky, she'll pass it on quickly that it was misinformation and they will release Spectra."

"If we're unlucky?" Henry grumbled, following me back to my office.

"Your future daughter-in-law is taking out the competition while she can, and we find Spectra dead by morning." I walked into my office, opened a Word document, and started typing furiously.

"What are you doing?" Luke queried.

"Writing a statement that Henry is going to leave with the Nephilim bitch for Alexander to read." I finished typing a plausible explanation for what the beast saw. "It might be good to make a scene with Alexander, too."

"What about?" Henry was tapping into his phone.

"As far as everyone is concerned, Spectra got married to her Angelis boyfriend of four years last night, and they were leaving on their honeymoon this afternoon."

Henry stopped. "Did she marry an Angelis last night?"

"Not your priority concern right now, Henry." I pressed print and stood up, grabbing my jacket.

"Did she marry last night?" Henry pressed angrily.

I met his eyes. "Yes." Henry stepped back like I'd punched him. I wasn't going to explain that it wasn't a legal marriage and it wasn't the Angelis, but last night Spectra had naively married her body to mine. That was close enough to the truth to cause the stir I needed right now. Spectra would marry Mercury now anyway, so if the rumor made its way back to them before it happened, so be it.

"I have contacts to run down if we're going to save her, Henry. You do your bit, I'll bring her back safe." I stormed towards the door as Claire came in. I grabbed the document and held it up against the door as I signed it. "Copy that for me and give the original to Henry, Claire."

"Yes, boss." Claire ran, well the equivalent of it in her heels, off to the photocopier.

"Luke, let's go." I walked out of the office, slipping into my jacket as I made my way to the elevator.

When the doors closed, Luke looked at me. "You didn't tell me you married her last night."

I kept my eyes straight ahead. "She doesn't know what she gave up last night, Luke. They kept her ignorant in the hope Alexander could manipulate her every step of the way. They weren't going to give her a choice if she proved strong enough."

Luke met my eyes in the reflection of the elevator door. "Which she is, isn't she? You would have killed her last night if she wasn't."

I watched the numbers count down to the ground floor. "She was using me to build her resistance so she would be strong enough for him. He'd given up on her because they didn't know who she is. Until last night, she'd wanted to prove herself worthy of him."

Luke bowed his head. "And she is."

"No." The elevator counted down to P. "She's too good for him."

CHAPTER 16

Spectra

I RAN UP THE STAIRS TO MY BEDROOM and started throwing clothes in my bag along with a few other items I was going to need. I stripped out of the suit I was wearing and pulled on my favorite lace and velvet long sleeved dress. I folded the suit neatly and placed it on top of the bag along with my laptop and heels.

I was just zipping up my faux lace up knee-highs when someone knocked at my bedroom door. I pulled on my jacket as I considered the two shadows under the door. The nuns rarely ever trudged up to the third floor. "Who is it?"

"Spectra, it's Penelope. There's a phone call for you downstairs." Penelope was one of the newer nuns. Still young at only twenty.

I hesitated. I couldn't remember any one time I'd ever

been called on the convent phone. Nope, not one. "I'm just getting changed. I'll come down in a second." I pulled my bag across my body and moved to the window. Pushing it open, I climbed out onto the roof and gently closed the window again, then slid to the parapet. I moved quickly across the roof to the other end of the building.

At the far end, I prayed my clothes would shield my laptop and dropped my bag over the edge. I heard it hit and winced. The one downside to becoming insubstantial, I couldn't carry anything with me except the clothes I was wearing or what was in them. I breathed out to become incorporeal and stepped through the stone parapet, floating down to the ground.

I felt when I hit. It wasn't the same as falling whole-bodied, but you still felt the impact. Breathing in, I collected my bag and started running across the grounds. I wasn't going to exit via a gate, they might be at either of them. Instead, I went for the caretaker's cottage. There was a wood pile stacked against the six-foot stone fence.

Halfway across the grounds, a man stepped in front of me from out of nowhere. I felt his power wrapping around him like a ball of fire. Stupid sorcerers and their ability to travel through the ether. I came to a halt as he looked me over.

"Do you know who I am?" I shook my head, taking a step back. "I am Paul Samus. And you..." he smiled at me, fresh blood still clotting in his mouth. I thought I was going to puke. "...are the ghost who can cure the beasts. I thought I was being sent to collect a talented hacker till I saw you jump off that roof. Turns out it's a two-for-one deal." I shook my head. His smile dropped away. "You should be proud of your gift."

"No, really. I can't do what you say. The ghost bit, okay, but I can't cure anyone." My heart was thudding in my chest. I was oath bound. They could torture me and even if I wanted to, I could never do that again.

"But you were there when it happened?" he asked. I swallowed then nodded. "Did you see it happen?"

"I saw a panther change back to human in mid-attack. I was scared and ran. That's all I saw, I swear it."

I heard a snarl and turned my head in time to see a wolf beast racing for me. My eyes went wide as I realized it meant to attack me. I breathed out, becoming incorporeal as it sprang for me. The bag I was carrying dropped through my incorporeal body to the ground. The beast flew through me and landed with a growl on the other side. It turned back and watched me through its animal eyes.

Paul Samus chuckled. "Well, look at that, he's still a beast. So you aren't the cure. Sadly, I expect he intends to kill you, just to make sure you can't cure him. I do hate when a good pet turns feral."

I started moving to the fence again, the beast's eyes tracking me. The sorcerer flung out his hand toward me, releasing some sort of magic, and hit me with enough force that I sucked in air as I fell to the ground, becoming corporeal. The Changeur sprang but the sorcerer flung out his other hand, and the wolf burst into a ball of howling flames. I watched, wide-eyed, pain in my chest at whatever I'd been hit with forcing me to breathe.

The sorcerer strode towards me. "A hacker of your skill will be of great value to us." He swung his hand and pain impacted the side of my head, stars shooting across my vision, then darkness closed around me as I fell to the ground. The cold press of the ground on my cheek the last thing I felt.

I woke on a bed with white Egyptian cotton linens. I touched my hand to my head and winced. Whatever he hit me with left a bump and bruise. I pushed up to sitting and realized I was naked. I grabbed the sheets to cover me while I looked around the room to find my clothes. Long curtains were drawn across the windows so I couldn't see out. Among the few plush furnishings of the room, I couldn't see anything that resembled my clothing.

A cat sat on the settee at the end of the bed, watching me with interest. "Wouldn't happen to know where my clothes are by any chance?" The cat's head turned to the only door in the room. I doubted it was telling me that was the wardrobe.

The door opened, and the sorcerer stepped into the room with a tray containing a teapot and two teacups. "You're conscious."

Well, at least he didn't try and pretend I'd fallen asleep happily. "I'm naked."

He smiled, placing the tray on the settee before shooing the cat and taking its place. "Yes, you are. I wanted to see if you were food."

"No!"

His eyes creased with humor. "Yes, the lack of scarring on your body told me that. You only have the one bite, but that was a very long time ago, over a decade I'd say. Is that what killed you?"

I sat, staring at him. "I'd prefer to be dressed for any conversation."

"Are you always clothed when you talk with the distinguished Mr. Ryder?" I continued glaring. Paul smiled. "You don't like my kind, do you?" I gave a slight shake of my head. "Understandable. You were a child when you were attacked.

That sort of thing leaves a bad taste in your mouth." He poured two cups of tea. "Milk and sugar."

"I don't drink tea."

"How very un-English of you."

"My mother was French."

"And your father?"

"A one-night stand, so I really have no idea."

Paul simpered and lifted his teacup to his lips. "Why were you at Bay Ryder's house when Falon Lore attacked?"

"Who's Falon Lore?"

"The sorcerer who led that attack. He died. Tripped and fell, hitting his head before falling into the pool. I guess compared to the Changeur de Corps he took with him, it was a pleasant enough way to die."

"He was mortal?" I wrapped my arms around my bent legs and engaged in the conversation.

"Yes. We hadn't felt the need to take him yet. He wasn't really powerful enough to bother." Paul took another sip of tea. "Bay Ryder is a different matter. Sadly, he stands opposed to our cause. What is your connection to him?"

"What cause?" I asked. "You are both the same. Condemned sorcerers. What could you really oppose each other about? A preference for blood types maybe?"

Paul quirked a brow. "Have you never heard of Essence?"

"Of course, I have. It is a philosophical term for what invariably makes up the nature of a thing or entity."

Paul's smile died as he assessed me. "Hmmm." I guess that wasn't the answer he was after. He put down his tea. "You're not food, it's well known Bay Ryder does not partake in the physical pleasures, and you are not involved in his Nachtwelt business. However, you were at his company today, and you did use his network to hack the NSIO and steal emails from L'Ordre's assistant's computer."

"Wait. Ryder owns Pendant Security?"

Paul's brows shot up. "You didn't know?"

"No. I've just graduated. A recruiter offered me a job. I was there to interview, and they asked me to access a database. It seemed an obvious choice. I used the activity to highlight a weakness in their security."

"You sent the email to Ryder?"

"Yes, but to his personal email account. He was a client of mine..." I stopped and swallowed.

Paul stalked forward. "Ryder hires you to hack other secure databases?"

"No."

"But you are a hacker?"

"I did that today to satisfy my own curiosity. I didn't expect to find anything of interest, but when I found that stuff about the attack, I forwarded it on."

Paul sat at my feet on the bed. "So, what work does Mr. Ryder normally require of you?" I glared at him. He laughed. "Are you really going to claim client confidentiality?" I gave the slightest nod. Paul sighed. He watched me, almost analyzing me. "Did it involve the antidote?"

I had no idea what this guy was on about. He sighed, reading my reaction, and stood up, walking back to collect his tea tray. "Well, it appears you really are just a hacker. However, Mr. Ryder obviously finds your skill valuable and may be willing to exchange something for you. After all, it's not every day you find a wraith."

My blood ran cold, being identified for what I am now. There was a knock on the door and then a piece of paper was slid underneath.

Paul put the tray back down and collected the piece of paper, reading it. His eyebrows shot up, and he looked back to me. Paul waved the letter. "Everything this says I'd already determined. But I'd like to ask one last time. What were you doing at Bay Ryder's estate the night Falon Lore attacked?"

"Delivering what Bay Ryder wanted from me."

"And I bet that something required your wraith skills. Right?"

I blinked. "Can I get my clothes now, please?"

Paul picked up the tray and walked to the door. "I promise you will have them when it's time to leave here."

"Will I be alive when that happens?"

Paul smiled at me and gave the door a tap with his foot. It opened, but I couldn't see who was in the hallway. Paul looked up to the corner of the ceiling, and I followed his gaze. Hidden there was an infrared camera. They'd be able to see me even if I was incorporeal. Paul laughed. "Your eyes could freeze boiling water, my dear. I guess I've really pissed you off now."

As soon as the door shut, I tugged the flat sheet from the bed and turned it into a makeshift dress. I made my way to the windows and threw back the curtains to find a blank wall. "Oh god!" I stepped away as I turned to look at the door. "Don't focus on that, Spectra. You could still be above ground. You're not buried. You can move around."

I walked to the blank wall beside the bed and studied it. Eventually, I saw the seam, and I pressed on the opposite side. A hidden door opened to reveal a bathroom, also with no windows and its own infrared camera. "Well, that's just rude."

Moving back into the bedroom, I lay down on the bed and practiced the meditation Alexander taught me when we were growing up. I focused on my breathing and my heart rate, slowly blocking every other noise out till my breath and heartbeat were all I could hear. I felt myself growing lighter with every breath until I felt like I was floating above the bed.

I opened my eyes to look at the ceiling and watched it coming closer. Turning, I saw myself still lying on the bed as if asleep. I smiled and closed my eyes, concentrating on Mercury. I felt the pull easily. As I started to move, I opened my eyes and caught a glimpse of the outside of the building before I sped across the rooftops and came to a stop in a cafe. I looked around and saw Mercury sitting a few tables away, playing with his food, while Calin and some other predators inhaled their meals.

I went to the table and waved my hands at Mercury. One of the predators decked out in a SWAT team outfit said something as he turned pale. Mercury and Calin looked up instantly. Mercury stood and looked me over, his mouth moving too fast for me to catch a single thing he was saying.

"Slow down, I can't hear you," I tried saying, and then realized if I couldn't hear him, he possibly couldn't hear me. "Shit!"

Mercury stopped. Apparently, he'd caught that word. Calin was saying something to him. I looked around, trying to find a way to communicate to him, but it felt hopeless. Mercury stood there, staring at me like a small child, and finally, he spoke slow enough for me to read his lips.

Please don't be dead.

I shook my head. "Not yet." Mercury blew out a breath and said something to Calin, who pulled out his phone. I closed my eyes and focused on Bay. If Mercury was with Calin, then Bay was helping look for me.

Bay

I stood at my office window watching the city lights two hours after sunset. I received some credible leads from my sources, especially after the body of the Changeur was identified, but so far, nothing panned out. Mercury was with Calin and his group, still trying to track Spectra. In case she was injured, Mercury wanted to be on hand.

Calin called over an hour ago to say they couldn't find her. I'd tried tracking her drift, but whoever took her circled through the city several times and used the one intersection every time, so eventually I lost that too.

"Are you staying here all night?" Luke appeared at the open door to my office, concern evident in his face.

"I'll stay till we receive word."

"What about dinner?"

"I'm not hungry."

Luke nodded as if he expected that answer. "Calin will be back soon. They've driven around a few more times to see if they can pick up her scent."

The phone on the desk started ringing. Luke picked it up. "Mr. Ryder's office. May I ask who's calling? I'll just see if he is available." Luke stopped breathing. I heard him physically stop. I turned to look at him and watched the blood drain from his face as he pressed the mute button and held out the phone to me. "It's the call you've been waiting for."

I crossed the room in two steps, took a deep breath, unmuted it, and put the phone to my ear.

"Hello?"

"Bay Ryder?"

"And you are?"

"That's not important. What does matter is how much Spectra Michaels is worth to you?"

"Put her on the line."

"No."

"Then you don't have her."

"Check your email. I can wait."

I took a restraining breath and moved to the computer, pulling up an unknown email. There was nothing written, just a photo. I opened it. Spectra lay unconscious on a bed, the sheets arranged just the right way so while she was covered, I could see she was naked.

"You have my attention."

"Good. I want the antidote, and I will send her back to you unharmed."

I laughed, and I could tell whoever this man was, he hadn't expected that response. "You greatly overestimate Miss Michaels worth to me. Not to mention, I no longer have access to the antidote. You will need to negotiate with L'Ordre for that."

The man on the other end of the line cleared his throat. "So she means nothing to you?"

"I like Miss Michaels, she is a very resourceful young lady. While I would hate to see her harmed unnecessarily, she is not worth the antidote. If you were asking for a simple ransom of a certain amount of cash, I would gladly pay that to keep her skills available to me. Would you like to reassess your request?"

"No. If the girl can't get me what I want, I will take what I can from her and leave it at that."

"I'm sorry to hear that. I understand her husband loves her very much. If you could let me know where to find her body when you are finished, it would be a kindness to let her husband bury her." I hung up.

Luke stared at me. "Did you have to let that happen?"

I blew out a breath. "If I showed I cared at all, they'd kill her for certain. She must have convinced them she can't cure the beasts or we would never have received that call. So we at least have that." I picked up the phone. "Evan, did you get a location on that call? Okay, pass those details on to Calin. They sent me an email. See if you can backtrack that as well." I hung up the phone and went back to the window.

"Did we get a location?"

"No. But we know the call came from the east side of the city. Calin will take his team and wait in that area until we get something new or they see something that gives them a lead."

"How do we know she's even still alive?" Luke stood by my computer, looking at the photo I'd left open on the screen. "She might even be dead in this picture."

"Could you kill her?"

"I know her."

I watched over the city in the direction of the east side. "I could never have harmed a hair on her head from the moment I met her."

"You're hoping whoever this is feels the same way?"

"Sorcerers spend their lives looking for their balance, Luke. If a sorcerer has her, he may not understand why, but he will find it hard to hurt her."

My mobile started ringing. I pulled it out and answered. "Henry?"

"I just intercepted a call from the kidnappers to Alexander."

"And?"

"And I denied any interest in exchanging the antidote for some girl they kidnapped off the street." Henry blew out a breath. "Alexander left for the evening with his assistant already, so he's unaware of what's happened."

"She's still alive, Henry."

"Then deal with it." Henry hung up. I sighed and put the phone back in my pocket.

"Ah, boss?" Luke called out as his phone started ringing.

"What is it, Luke?" I was losing patience at not finding Spectra. I expected her to somehow reach out to me by now. I don't know how she could, but something told me if anyone could somehow communicate from a prison cell, it would be her. I was starting to think that was an unrealistic expectation.

"You have a visitor."

I turned and found a faint version of Spectra standing opposite Luke at the desk, her finger pointing to the keyboard. Luke was scribbling on a pad as she indicated different letters.

"Finally! I expected you hours ago." I moved over to stand beside Luke as he wrote down her letters. She didn't smile. I quickly realized she couldn't hear me and she couldn't talk, so this wasn't her, it was a projection of herself.

She stopped pointing and stood to look at me. It was only then that I realized the white dress she wore was a sheet wrapped around her and tied off like a toga. I looked at the pad as Luke drew slashes to indicate spaces to form words.

"Paul Samus," I growled. I grabbed the notepad and wrote on it hurriedly. I ripped the page away and held it up for Spectra to read. Her eyes moved over the page, and then she tried to cover herself more with the sheet. She was already scared, her eyes showed me that, and I doubt anything I could tell her now would add to that fear.

She started pointing to letters again. I started writing it down.

Luke picked up the phone. "Evan, we have a name. Paul

Samus, he's a sorcerer." Luke looked up at Spectra and then to what I was writing down. "Yes, she's managed to send us a message, but she's far from safe."

Spectra's hand stopped moving mid-word and started flexing and clenching. I recognized her nervous gesture and looked up. For a moment that seemed paused in time, her eyes met mine with the most intense fear. Her head turned to the side in a way that made me think an unseen hand was moving her head for her. When Spectra's expression turned to pure terror, I understood she wasn't alone. Her neck moved back at an odd angle, an angle I'd moved women's necks into too often not to know what was happening now.

"Spectra, I'm so sorry," I murmured.

Her eyes squeezed shut, a single tear leaking down her face. Her mouth opened in a voiceless scream just as she vanished from sight.

Luke cringed and looked away, swearing beneath his breath. He took several deep breaths before he pulled the notepad across in front of him, "No, we just lost her. The only other thing we got is that she thinks she's being held underground. The room looks recently renovated."

I stood there, watching the empty space where her apparition stood only moments ago. I closed my eyes and dropped my face down, praying for the first time in too many years that we could save her.

"Let me know if it gives you anything." Luke hung up and stared at the empty space in front of the desk. "Will he kill her outright?"

I shook my head and took a breath. "It's highly likely we just saw the last moments of Spectra's mortal life. Let's go."

"Where?" Luke queried, collecting his tablet from the desk.

"You're going to dinner, you look famished. I have one

more person to see." I walked down the corridor to the elevator.

Luke caught up by the time the elevator doors opened. "Who?"

I licked my lips. "Remember when I signed the contracts with the NSIO?" Luke nodded. "Alexander warned me that Spectra was protected by people more powerful than him." Luke looked at me, eyes narrowed. "Who could be more powerful than L'Ordre, Luke?"

Luke shook his head. "His father?"

The doors opened, and we stepped into the elevator. "That's what I thought at the time."

Luke's eyes went wide. "You think there is someone else?"

"Yes, I do." The lift opened on the ground floor. "Go eat. I'll meet you back here in an hour."

Luke nodded and left. He knew I didn't involve him for a reason. I waited for the doors to close, swiped my staff card through the security lock, and pushed a coded sequence in the lift numbers. The lift started its descent below ground to the crypt.

When the lift arrived, I stepped out into the glass foyer and walked up to the reinforced glass doors. The three security guards sitting behind two different sectioned off areas watched carefully as I approached the security check, placed my palm on the print pad, and put my eye at the right level for the retina scan.

The first set of glass doors opened, and I repeated the process at the second set of doors. Once through them, a fourth guard smiled up at me from his desk. "Evening, Mr. Ryder. We weren't expecting anyone tonight. Can I have your code phrase please?"

"My first basic belief is that you first need to realize the usefulness of compassion." I quoted the Dalai Lama. The voice scanner recognized my voice and matched it to the copy of me saying that phrase on file.

The guard nodded. "How can we help you this evening, boss?"

"I'm here to see Miss Miranda Jackson. She was brought in on the weekend. I'll need a hood. Miss Jackson might be vital to a case we are working tonight."

The guard stood up, and his handprint let us through the crypt doors, leading us down to the interrogation rooms. We didn't keep prisoners here long. Normally, just until their guilt or innocence was determined, and then they were dealt with. At the interrogation room that held Miranda Jackson, the guard swiped his card and put his palm on the scanner, opening the door for me.

I stepped inside to find Miranda squatting in the corner, still wearing the cocktail dress she'd been wearing when she was picked up. She severely injured five guards when they captured her. Her strawberry blonde hair was straggly, and the dark sunken hollows under her emerald eyes showed me she wasn't being fed. She gave me a haughty smile. "I should feel honored, I guess. The great Bay Ryder has come to deliver me to the executioner personally."

"That all depends on the next few minutes, and I warn you not to delay. We are on a fragile time frame, if it isn't already too late."

Miranda's eyes turned dark. "The NSIO took her, didn't they?"

I tilted my head listening. "Now why would L'Ordre take Spectra?"

"The Williams are high up in the office, yes, but in the end, they don't make all the calls. There are some decisions made higher up, by people you really shouldn't trust."

"You were watching Spectra for years. Did we remove Spectra's protection when we captured you, Miss Jackson?"

"Did you really think I would take her? After everything that girl has been through? She would be the first one to hand herself in for destruction."

"Who sent you to watch her?"

Miranda leered at me. "Did you really think you were the first predator to want her?" She scrunched her freckled nose. "You were just the first we let have her."

"Why?"

"Do we have time for this, Mr. Ryder?" Miranda tucked her long lean legs beneath her and stood gracefully. "Or would you like me to retrieve the woman you love?"

I eyed her. "You couldn't know about us."

She laughed. "I didn't need to, Mr. Ryder. That you are here personally told me what I needed to know." Miranda cocked her head and gave me a naughty look. "She must be a good fuck to bring you back from the dead. When was she taken?"

"Just after lunch." I pulled the information we had out of my pocket and handed it to her. "A member of Essence has taken her. They thought she could cure the Changeur de Corps, but when they discovered their information was wrong, they sought to use her as collateral. When that failed..."

"You didn't negotiate for her freedom?" Miranda asked matter-of-factly, flicking through the reports I'd handed her.

"Paul Samus is only interested in one thing, and I couldn't give him that."

Miranda froze. "Paul Samus took her and held her for..." she looked at her bare wrist and then scowled. "How long?"

"We believe he's held her for nine hours."

Miranda flicked to the photo I was sent and swore. "Let's go. We're out of time. He'll take her soon."

"He's already started the process. I managed to warn her, and I'm hoping she will be able to delay him."

Miranda didn't ask how I warned her. She walked up to the door and held out her arm for me to escort her out. "She can do it, or she'll die trying."

I pressed the buzzer next to the door. The tray opened and I removed the cuffs, placing them around Miss Jackson's slender wrists. "You sound sure."

"My predecessor taught Spectra how to defend herself from attack." Miranda met my eyes as I prepared the hood to cover her head. "If she is taken, the person who sent me here will kill anyone thought to have led to Spectra's demise."

I nodded and slipped the hood over her pretty face. I took her upper arm and pressed the buzzer twice in succession. The guard opened the door and walked behind us as we moved back to the elevator. At the desk, I signed Miranda out, no one talking through the exchange. When we stepped into the elevator, I pressed the return sequence and took us to the car park. I sat Miranda in the car, walked around to the driver's side, and made for the east side of the city.

"Do you know where to find Samus?" I asked reaching across to pull the hood from her head.

"Essence has several safe houses in this city. Your guy said east side, which only leaves one choice."

"I have a team ready, they'll go in with you."

"No. I'll call you when it's done, and your team can go in and bring her out."

I pulled up behind one of our Range Rovers and parked it.

I unlocked Miranda's cuffs before I got out. Calin hopped out of the driver's seat, coming back to see what I wanted. "Boss?"

"Give Miss Jackson whatever she needs. She'll call us once she's secured Spectra."

Calin nodded and opened the back of the car for Miranda to take her pick of his arsenal. She looked at another member of Calin's crew. "You look my size. I need your clothes."

The guy looked at Calin. Calin nodded, and the guy stripped out of his gear right there on the sidewalk before hopping back in the car so as not to be seen. Miranda changed out of her cocktail dress and pulled on the black ensemble before selecting a minimal number of weapons and piling her hair under a black cap. I noticed a tiny tattoo of a lily on the inside of her wrist as she tucked the last strand of hair away. It pulled at something familiar in my memory, but I couldn't place it.

Miranda turned back to me. "So, it goes without saying that once this is done, I'll be reassigned." I nodded, understanding I wouldn't be seeing her again. "Someone will be sent to replace me. If you discover who that is, don't lock them up."

"I'll try my best."

Miranda smiled. "I was doing you a favor recruiting her. I never expected you two to meet, though. Even if you don't hire her, don't let her work for the NSIO." Miranda turned and walked down the street, disappearing as soon as she crossed the road.

"We're trusting a Fantôme to get Spectra out?" Calin queried quietly.

"You got a better idea?"

"No, just checking. What now?" Calin shut the back of the car.

"Where's the Angelis?"

"Inside, why?"

"I fear we're going to need him." I sat back on the bonnet of my car.

Calin turned to one of his team still dressed. "Go get Mercury." Calin assessed me quietly for a moment. "How do we know she's injured?"

"She's being fed on and possibly taken as we speak." I looked at my watch. "We lost contact with her twenty minutes ago."

"Please tell me you are not talking about Spectra?" Mercury jogged to where we stood.

"I wish I wasn't." I stood straight. "Will the priest sanctify my place so Spectra can move there?"

"Perhaps, but why would she do that?"

I unfolded my arms and shoved them in my pockets. "Because when you two get married this week, you'll both come live with me. You will have your own wing of the house, we'll even set up a nursery for you. That way Spectra is close to her work, and she just has to come upstairs to my bed in your absence."

Mercury considered me. "Has Spectra agreed to any of this?"

"I need your answer now. If it's yes, I'll collect your priest and have the place sanctified while you retrieve her. That way, you can bring her straight there and the place will be ready for you both."

Mercury looked to Calin. "Is he on the level?"

Calin shrugged. "He's in love with her but knows she needs you, and you're definitely the better choice over Williams."

Mercury lifted a brow. "Yeah, well, I won't argue with that." Mercury pulled out his phone and dialed. "Mathew, it's Merc. We think we've found her but not sure what state she'll be in. Bay Ryder is coming to get you. We need you to make his house a safe place for us." Mercury listened. "I share your concern, but it's time we moved on. Okay. And Mathew? Once this is over, you're going to marry Spectra and me." Mercury smiled at whatever Mathew said. His eyes flicked up to me, mischief in them. "Actually, Bay Ryder will give her away."

He hung up the phone and raised a daring brow at me.

"I would be honored to give you my wife in holy matrimony."

Mercury swallowed his smile but nodded. "She was ready to give herself to me whole after he broke her heart too. I held her off because I wanted to make sure she knew the choice she was making."

"I'm not that nice a guy," I answered and walked to the driver's side door. "I'll see you at home with our wife."

Spectra

To say that Bay's note freaked me out would be putting it mildly. Death I could cope with. But not this.

He collects beautiful women. He will take you. Delay him as long as you can.

I felt a weight settle over my body just before my hands started to itch, and that's when I realized I was out of time. I wasn't ready yet; I still needed to tell Bay the number on the building, but then teeth were at my throat, and my scream swept through my head like talons to my ears. I slammed back into my body like I'd fallen from a roof. My body jerked under his and I felt his lips turn up where he suckled at my neck.

I instantly started trying to get him off me, but he'd positioned himself well to fend off any defense easily. After a few seconds, I gave up and sobbed as he drained me. I moved my hands across his shirtless back and felt him tense at that electricity that always passed between a sorcerer's bare skin and mine. He lifted his face away from my neck and hovered above me.

"Look at me." Paul demanded. When my eyes stayed closed, he grabbed my jaw and shook my face gently. "Look at me!" I blinked my eyes open, fighting against the instinct to sleep. "Were you a Nephilim before you died?" I started to close my eyes. He shook my face again. "Spectra! Are you a half-cast celestial?"

"Yes," I whispered, just wanting to sleep.

"Prove it!"

I struggled but moved my hands up his shoulders to his neck and face. I concentrated and felt joy and excitement. I siphoned off some of his excitement to re-energize myself.

The adrenaline kicked in, and I was able to open my eyes and look at him. His face lit up. "Remarkable!"

"You have no idea." I smiled and then moving quickly, I hooked my thumbs into the inside of his eyes. I pushed in hard and then scooped out to the sides. I felt the squish and burst of fluids around my fingers and over my face. Paul howled and leaned away from me. I shoved him and he fell, screaming in agony. I quickly rolled to the other side of the bed and dropped to the floor.

Paul was gaining his feet. "You bitch! Do you think that will stop me? I'll heal in a matter of minutes, and then I'm still going to take you, Spectra. That way I can make you pay for that for a lot longer."

I slid under the bed while he yelled, using his noise to cover my movement. I put my hand over my mouth to muffle the sound of my breathing, because for some reason I couldn't stop breathing. Paul became still. I saw his bare feet and trouser pants on the other side of the bed. He was waiting till he healed to find me.

I felt a small puddle forming under my shoulder and moved my hand to my neck. I was still bleeding. He didn't seal the wound when he stopped drinking from me. I sobbed before I could stop myself and Paul chuckled. "I can smell your blood, Spectra. Didn't you realize I didn't heal you?" His feet turned as he took a deep breath. "My eyes are nearly fully reformed. I have all the time in the world, but you, you might bleed out before I find you. Of course, now instead of fighting you, I just have to wait. Within minutes, you are going to be too weak to fight me anymore."

I grabbed a handful of the sheet still wrapped around me and pressed it to my neck to try and slow the bleeding. I wasn't sure how long he was drinking from me before I came back to myself. I couldn't die here. He would take me, and I couldn't become one of them. I couldn't be a predator. So I pressed the sheet to my neck and willed myself to live.

"Just waiting for my vision to return now, Spectra. How are you going? Are you still conscious?"

I fought the pull into sleep, my eyes trying to close as that weight in my head became heavy, my blood pressure crashing through the floor.

"Ah, here we go. Still blurry and no color, but only a few more seconds to wait." His feet moved towards the curtains and moved one back. "Tell me. If you're insubstantial when you pass out, do you return to corporeal again like a Changeur when it dies?" I tried to focus on his feet, but they started to become blurry.

"Of course you do. Your body would automatically breathe in." Paul moved towards the base of the bed, and I lost sight of his feet. "Have you tried breathing out since you've been here?" I closed my eyes longer and forced them open with more energy than it should take. "This safe house is purpose-built. Everything in these holding rooms is controlled. The temperatures, the visibility, the oxygen levels."

My eyes closed for the last time.

"I'm very good at observing people. When the Changeur went to attack you, you exhaled all your oxygen just before he launched, and that's what made you disappear. The wolf was rather helpful in that he then tracked you for me. It proved my theory when I hit you, and you sucked in air and returned to my vision."

When Paul's voice came to me next, it wasn't muffled by the bed and I knew he'd found me. "So when I brought you here, I pushed up the oxygen levels so that you wouldn't have a choice in breathing." I heard a noise next to me, like a scraping on the floor. "Just out of my reach there, Spectra. That is the problem with such large beds, but don't fret, I'll have you out from under there in a moment."

There was a loud noise outside the door. Adrenaline kicked in again, and I was able to force my eyes open. Paul's feet were back beside the bed when the door burst open. "Who are you?"

Another loud noise roared through the room, and Paul stumbled back until he hit the wall behind him. His knees buckled and he slid down the wall to sitting before collapsing to the side. There was a bloody wound at the neck where his head used to be attached. I groaned and closed my eyes, drifting, my hand at my neck relaxing and falling away.

"Spectra?" A woman's voice called from low and close to me. "Jesus! I'll get you help, honey, just hold on a little longer." I heard buttons pressing on a phone, her voice muffled. "Two one seven Marshal Terrace. In the basement, room at the very end of the hall. Hurry! I can't help her. I haven't fed in days and her blood is too tempting."

The footsteps moved away and back to the door and down the hall in a run. I lay there in the darkness under the giant bed, happy to go now. He couldn't take me. That's all that mattered. If I died here now, I'd stay dead. Thunder sounded in the distance, and I smiled when I found myself lying in a field of wildflowers as the storm blew in.

"Where is she?" Mercury's voice yelled across the field. "Spectra?"

"Merc!" Barely a whisper

More thunder, closer above me now, and then sunlight broke through the darkness of the storm.

"Spectra, fight for me," Mercury whispered softly in my ear.

"How bad?" Calin's voice asked gently.

"She's nearly bled out," Mercury advised, and then he placed his hands on me.

The field filled with bright sunlight, chasing away the thunderstorm. Noise, smell, sight disappeared. Nothing but the brightness of the sun and the heat of Mercury's hands on my body.

"Fight for me, Spectra," Mercury demanded. "Fight, goddamn it, and I'll marry you the moment you open your eyes again."

The sunlight turned to white light. Pure, radiant light poured over me, into me, filling me up. I welcomed that light, bathed in it, lived in it. All I wanted was to be in Mercury's arms and never leave them. I heard Mercury exhale dramatically. His hand swept through my hair and pressed my forehead to his. "I love you too," he whispered before he kissed my mouth lightly.

"We're good to go." I felt Mercury lift me into his arms and start walking with me. "Sleep, Spec. It's going to be an exciting week. We've got a wedding to plan, and we're moving house. You wait till you see where we'll be living."

I pressed my face to his chest and smiled. As long as I was with Mercury, I didn't care where we lived.

CHAPTER 17

Spectra

"SPEC." Someone poked me in the side. I grumbled and rolled over. Mercury chuckled. "Come on Spec, you'll be late for your interview."

"Argh! I feel like I've been hit by a truck." I threw back the blanket and started walking towards the... I stopped and looked around the room. Bay stood at the foot of the bed in his standard suit, mild humor on his face. Mercury was still on the bed shirtless, openly laughing as I looked at them, confused. Bay pointed to one of three doors leading from the room. "Thanks."

I opened the door and turned on the hot water, stepping under it and sighing in relief. My suit was hung up in the beautiful stone and glass bathroom. The shower was next to a wall-to-ceiling window that was opaque, so it let in maximum light without exposure. After the shower, I dressed and went back into the bedroom. That's when I actually took in the size of the room and the luxurious furnishings. Mercury was still half naked, standing and talking to Bay in the large open space by the bed.

"Where are we?" I asked, buttoning the black silk blouse I'm pretty sure wasn't in my wardrobe before today. I took in my laptop on the breakfast for two table nestled in the far corner by a large round window that made it look like an adjoined tower room.

"Your new home," Mercury smirked, standing back and crossing his arms to watch me.

I looked at him, unsure. "I've missed something or a couple of somethings by the sound of it."

Mercury walked towards me, his eyes gentle. "It's not important right this minute, Spec. You need to get ready for your interview. Gina has offered to drive you over to it and back. When you get back, we can discuss the details of living here and everything else that goes with it."

I met his eyes and he sighed. "Where are we? A converted monastery or something?"

"You're at my estate," Bay butted in. "This wing has been relatively unused except for occasional guest accommodation. The rooms on this side and level are now your apartments. This is the master bedroom. You have two other bedrooms, a modest lounge room, and..." Mercury shook his head at Bay, "… another room that could be put to whatever use you desire. You will still need to share the kitchen and laundry, but my cleaners will clean your apartment for you unless you wish to do it yourself."

"This place is too peaceful to be yours, Bay."

"Father Mathew came and blessed Bay's house so we could be comfortable here." Mercury touched my arm, gently bringing my attention to him.

"We?" I asked, my voice hesitating over the word.

Mercury smiled. "As husband and wife."

I felt my heart flutter but looked at Bay before meeting Mercury's eyes. "Are you sure you want to live here?"

"Why? Because it's hideously spacious, opulent, and someone else will clean the toilet for me? Oh my lord, Spectra, you are right, what was I thinking to move into a hellhole like this?"

Bay hid his smile behind his hand. Mercury took my hand in his and pulled me closer. "The land is blessed so we will find it restful. It is guarded so that you will be safe. You will get this job at Galaxy, so it will be close to your work. I've been at Saint Benedict's too long now anyway and need to move on before the humans start asking why I haven't aged in ten years. There is a hospital twenty minutes from here that I can go work at. I've already called this morning and arranged an interview."

"But..." My eyes flicked to Bay.

"The days and nights I'm here, you're mine. When I'm working or engaging in my other interests, you are free to be with your lover." Mercury swallowed. "Though once we have children, he will probably need to come to our bed to be with you."

Mercury saw the look on my face and grabbed my elbows before I could pull away. "You do want children, don't you?"

"I don't know, Merc." I sighed and stepped into him. Mercury wrapped me in his arms, and I felt instantly more at ease. "Is that a bad thing?"

Mercury kissed my forehead. "It's absolutely your choice, Spectra. We can be careful till you think you're ready, or we can just let nature take its course." Mercury stepped back from me and dropped down on one knee. "Let's take this one step at a time. Spectra Michaels, I would be honored if you would be my wife, in this life and life ever after."

I felt butterflies take flight in my stomach and tears started falling down my face. I'd always imagined I'd marry Alexander, but I understood now, holding part of my soul didn't mean he held my heart, nor I his.

"Yes," I whispered.

Mercury stood and pulled me into the most wonderful kiss. I started rubbing my hands over his back as I pressed myself to him. Mercury sighed into my mouth then stepped back, laughing. "No. You have an interview to go to and I have a wedding to organize. Tonight when I take you to bed, you'll be my wife."

"Tonight?" I queried, shocked. "I don't have a dress."

"You will." Bay smiled. "I'll organize the dress and your dinner at my expense. My gift to the happy couple."

"You've already let us move into your place, Bay, and we aren't poor." I sighed.

"To have you close to me, Spectra, and to keep you safe, it is an easy price." Bay took a step towards us. "I've arranged for other guards to patrol the estate unseen from now on. We will never be surprised like that again."

"You don't get to touch her today," Mercury stated firmly, stopping Bay's approach. "She has to wait till we are married to get any now, just as I will."

Bay smiled broadly. "Can I at least escort Spectra downstairs so she and Gina can leave?"

Mercury gave an amused huff. "Sure." He pulled me in for one last kiss. "I'll see you at the church this afternoon."

Bay held out his arm. I put mine through it, and he led me through the apartment to the main staircase, down two levels to the main foyer and then out to the garage. "Are you happy?" Bay asked gently.

"Did last night happen?"

Bay's face became unreadable. "I don't ever want to be in the position of not knowing if you are safe ever again."

"If you guard me like I'm precious, Essence will use me against you, just like they tried last night."

Bay turned and gave me a hard look. "Paul would not have told you about them. How do you know, Spectra?"

I met Bay's eyes and let the hidden knowledge shine in my eyes. I noted Bay's hesitation, but I took no pleasure in it. "While the men in my life seem to prefer me naive, there are those who want to keep me safe and therefore also keep me informed. I know Essence is the reason Alexander hid me initially, but then he grew to like the life he lived, and I became secondary to it. It took meeting you to realize, if he truly loved me, he would have managed it differently."

Bay cleared his throat. "Do you understand our connection?"

I smiled, understanding what he was asking, and started walking to the garage. "I was already paranoid about unprotected sex. My friend warned me what it would mean to let Alexander have me entirely, and while I don't understand the entire concept, I understand our bodies are wedded."

"You did it to punish him for the way he treated you?" Bay queried.

"No, Bay. I did it because we are connected somehow, because it felt right for me to be tied to you in a way I wasn't to anyone else." I turned to face him and lowered my voice as I saw Gina crossing the foyer to come to the garage. "I love Mercury, and he has my heart. He will be the father of my children when we choose to go there. My soul is intertwined with Alexander's, and because of that, separation over long periods is hard on us. I've been working at staying away from him as long as I can." I touched his face tenderly. "I'm still working out exactly why I need to be near you, Bay, but it is a need."

"Ready to go?" Gina bounced past. She didn't stop. Just gave me a smile and kept on to the garage.

Bay waited for Gina to enter the garage. "You are my wife now. When you marry Mercury tonight, you will take two husbands. Mercury and I have already talked, and we hope to make this work for all three of us. When Alexander finds out about this, he will try to have both Mercury and I killed."

I smiled. "I guess you're lucky then." I stepped towards him and put my mouth to his ear. "That the people he'd hire to kill you love me more than him." I kissed his cheek and turned, walking into the garage and climbing into the Wrangler next to Gina.

Bay stood at the door, hands in his pocket, a mix of worry and surprise on his face as we drove out. I grabbed onto the dash bar as Gina sped up the driveway and swerved onto the road with barely a look for traffic.

"How are you feeling this morning?" Gina asked.

"I was fine till we left the garage," I answered, a little wide-eyed with panic.

"Relax, I've been driving these roads for years now." Gina sped down the road, and I did as suggested and relaxed. "Are you hoping to get this job today?"

"I am. Though I'm still a little nervous about moving into Bay's."

Gina nodded. "I'm sort of glad though, it'll make my job a little easier." Gina tucked her hair behind her ear, flashing her tattoo purposefully this time before she turned to meet my eyes and we smiled at each other. "Miranda asked me to say goodbye."

The End

GLOSSARY

ANGELIS - Children of Angels. The offspring of a celestial and a human woman. They possess the powers of their fathers and, though ageless, live for centuries. They do, suffer mortal wounds and deaths just like their mothers. On dying, an Angelis will convert to become a celestial.

BALANCE - A female of the celestial bloodline. When trained, a balance can syphon the emotions of another and turn it into something that person needs. They are also able to shield themselves from the powers of the Nachtwelt. They can identify creatures of the Nachtwelt by their forces because each power runs on a different frequency. For this reason, balances make excellent trackers.

CELESTIAL - are different species to humans. They possess the powers of the divine and can cross the veils between realms. They are created, not born. They are all male and physical perfection personified. The celestials rank within triads. The ones humans know most about are the first triad, the most powerful and the closest to god. The archangels rarely involve themselves with a human, and so it is rare to meet the offspring of an arch. But there are many more in the second and third triads who entertain the company of human women frequently.

CHANGEUR DE CORPS'S - Shapeshifters (also referred to as De Viand).

ELEMENTALS (Witches, and illusionists.) - People who embody the power of nature.

EMPATHS (Clairvoyants/telepaths) - those who can share another person's emotions, and thoughts. Some may be powerful enough to breach the barrier between the living and the dead and able to divine with spirits.

NACHTWELT - the supernatural world (Nocturnal world)

Nephilim - Grandchildren of Angels. While celestials are extremely virile, they only produce male offspring. Therefore, for the Angelis to reproduce, they must also take human women as their lovers.

PREDATORS - those who prey on others to live or for pleasure. They may hunt humans, animals, or other Nachtwelt. It is the hunt that makes them a predator, not the type of prey.

PREDATOR DE SANG - Predators of blood

PREDATOR DE VIAND - predators of flesh. These are the predators who hunt to eat the meat of their prey. While most shapeshifters can also be referred to by this term, not all De Viand are shapeshifters.

SORCERER - the offspring of two Nephilim or a sorcerer and a balance. Sorcerers will carry some powers of their great-grandparents. Their power usually burns across many frequencies, and they must learn to shield others at a young age to prevent harming innocents around them. For a sorcerer to reproduce, he must find a balance strong enough to withstand his power, or their child would kill the mother before it could be born. For this reason, every sorcerer spends their lives searching for their balance.

SYPHONS - feed off people's emotions or energy (syphons who feed on lust are Succubi and Incubi).

THE TOLERANT - those with power, Devine or otherwise. They are tolerant because they are willing to tolerate the existence of others or behaviours with which they disagree. Classification as a tolerant species does not in any way insinuate they are peaceable.

OF SHADOW AND LIGHT

Messina Doe was just looking for a warm place to spend the night. What she discovers is a place the human race had long ago buried and forgotten.

The dark Fey haven't forgotten humans. The throne room of the Unseelie court is the hottest underground nightclub around, but if you step through the wrong door, there is no going back.

No one ever escapes. Never.

Once, someone did.

SINK

❖

"Stop chewing on that," Lisa snapped yanking my finger out of my mouth.

"I can't help it. I'm freezing and starving," I murmured trying to keep the shiver out of my voice. Stepping to the side, I looked at the line to get into the club. It was too long tonight; there was no way we were getting inside.

Lisa went back to fidgeting with her blond curls. "Would you relax. Tirades will open soon. Half of those inside will leave, and we'll get in. Just chill. You will never survive the streets if you whine all the time."

"Chilling isn't a problem." Since the music was audible outside, I started dancing on the spot to keep warm.

Lisa had been on the streets for six months now. When we met a few weeks ago, she made it sound so much more appealing than my home situation, so I'd packed the measly belongings I owned and joined her. We spent the nights clubbing so we were inside and warm, and the days at the university, sleeping in the library or stealing people's scraps in the cafeteria between classes - Easier done than you would think. You just carried a dishcloth, wiped a table as you collected a tray, and walked off.

Lisa's big brown eyes latched onto my hand as I lifted it to my mouth again. With a huff, she started playing with my dark hair. "We'll be fine, Mess. Stop fretting, okay?" Nodding, I forced myself to relax.

"Ladies." A man materialized out of the darkness next to us. Truthfully, he'd probably been leaning on the lamp post there, and I just hadn't paid attention to him until he spoke to us. Lisa's eyes widened, her shoulders rolled back so that her small breasts were the focal point in their push up bra. Knowing that move already, I lifted my eyes to see just how good looking this man was.

If I were to describe him, it would be in one word. Shadowed. The man was good looking, but to me, he seemed to surrounded by shadows which made him blurry and stopped me from really describing his features in detail. Dark hair, but no specific color, dark eyes that I wouldn't say were brown, and an average complexion. The man wore all black, so in the pale streetlight, the only color on him was his mouth. Red, as if he'd just finished eating pomegranates.

"You look like girls out for a night of fun. I'm heading to an underground nightclub that stays open till dawn. I wouldn't mind a beautiful entourage."

"What's the entry cost?" Lisa flirted while she sussed it out.

"Free," he advised, typing something into his phone. "There's food too. In fact, it's the owners birthday tonight, so he's catering."

He had Lisa's interest now. "Where's this club?"

"Just outside of town. I'm heading there now if you want to join me?"

Lifting her pale brow in challenge, Lisa scoffed. "Cause I'm stupid enough to go off with a strange man."

The man smirked. "There's a bus. It picks up other patrons, so no one drinks and drives. The owner is very big on the safety of his patrons." He pointed up the street where a bus was approaching. It was painted black with purple neon lights along the sides. "I'm Gus, by the way." Stepping to the curb, Gus waved down the bus.

"Come on." Lisa took my hand.

"Are you sure?" Didn't she just mention not being stupid and going off with a strange man? The bus pulled up where a girl and three guys who were already waiting stepped inside. Laughter and music blasting out into the cold night from inside, offering warmth and safety. Gus put his foot on the first step and raised an eyebrow at us.

"I'm sure." Squeezing my hand, Lisa strode towards the bus.

Gus's smile was closed lipped, his eyes reflecting the neon purple side lights as he led the way on board. Lisa followed dragging me after her. As I reached the top of the steps, the heavily tinted doors slammed behind us. For a moment, my pulse thrummed in the side of my neck, making it feel like someone was tapping my carotid artery.

The scene before me was a busload of relatively young people having a great time on a party bus. My lungs exhaled with relief as skimpily clad girls danced, some trying to use the poles, guys cheered and laughed as they drank their beer, the atmosphere relaxed and not unlike any bar on campus.

Releasing a squeal of joy, Lisa shrugged out of her jacket as she headed for the seat Gus was saving for us. Taking a deep breath, my head spun under the onslaught of men's cologne and women's perfume filling the bus. Blinking rapidly, I shook my head till it cleared, dark shadows racing across my vision as I followed Lisa. My hand still captive with hers until we took our seats.

"Do you want a drink?" Signaling the man behind the bar, Gus noted Lisa's hesitation. "My shout."

"I'll have a beer. Thanks."

Nodding, Gus looked at me. "I'm fine for now, thanks. Drinking and moving isn't a good combination for me."

"Motion sickness?" When I nodded, Gus patted my leg in reassurance as he stood to go to the bar. His touch left a chill on the bare skin of my thigh causing me to rub it to warm it up.

Watching me, Lisa put her mouth to my ear. "Are you still cold?"

The bus was fairly warm by the layers all the other occupants were removed, but I always took forever to warm up. Poor circulation or some such. "What are you doing?"

"One drink won't hurt."

"We're underage. I don't want to get thrown out for drinking alcohol as a minor. We're just here for warmth and food, remember?"

"Shh! Like anyone could tell that looking at us." At only nineteen, Lisa was hot and could easily pass for twenty-one. When she graduated high school last year, her step-father kicked her out because she refused to earn her keep by letting him charge his associates to screw her. Lisa's attitude was if men were paying to have sex with her, she'd be the one making money, not her scum-sucking step-father. I admired her for that.

Everyone was partying and having a great time as the bus moved to the next stop and picked up more people. Busy watching Lisa flirt with Gus, it took me a while to notice we hadn't stopped in some time. Peering out the heavily tinted windows, I cupped my hands around my face to block the inside light from my vision. Trees.

"Something wrong?" A woman asked sitting down next to me. Jumping back from the window at her sudden appearance, I looked her over. She was beautiful, but like Gus, she had that shadowed sensation which stopped me making out any exact details. In fact, the harder I looked, the less detail I could see. Her eyes appraised me hungrily, lingering on my jugular.

Licking my lips, I created a little more distance between us. "We're not in the city anymore." The woman raised an eyebrow, eyes jumping to mine, narrow in focus. "Gus said the club was just outside the city, but I can't see anything but trees."

The woman smiled, her shoulders easing back a little. "It is. There are a lot of people arriving for the banquet, so they've asked the bus to drive around an extra thirty minutes, so they can stagger the entry and avoid a large queue."

"Oh." As inexperienced in clubbing or these sort of underground clubs as I was, I decided to accept the excuse. However, the nagging sensation everything wasn't as it seems kept grating at my nerves.

The woman exchanged a judgemental look with Gus. "This one has eyes of light."

"I realized that after she was on the bus."

Standing up, the woman shook her head as she moved away. "Watch her hands when the fun starts."

Tilting her head "What language are you speaking? It sounds cool when you speak it."

"How many bears have you had?"

Shrugging me off, Lisa ignored my whispered question and

returned to batting her eyelids at the handsome enabler beside her.

"Eirnish." Looking past Lisa, Gus noticed my frown at his answer. Smiling at me, he reached out to tug at my jacket collar. "Are you cold?"

Unhappy to have lost Gus's attention, Lisa turned her shoulder to try and block me out. "Mess takes a while to warm up."

Tall enough to lean forward a little more and maintain eye contact, Gus waited out my answer. "Poor circulation."

Tilting his head in interest, Gus appraised me again. "Huh, me too."

The bus hit a bump the same time a loud mechanical noise started outside. Gus smiled as the bus came to a halt. "We're here!"

We let the others go first, then Gus put an arm around Lisa and me, and walked us off the bus last. We alighted into an underground car park filled with expensive sports cars. My eyes went wide. Whoever came to this club had money.

Turning my head towards the mechanical noise, I watched as the carpark gate closed and locked. Instantly, I started searching for an emergency exit, but other than the door we were walking towards, I couldn't see another way out.

Holding my tongue, I shivered in fear with a very uneasy feeling crawling up my spine like a venomous spider. The same feeling I had when my adoptive mother married Chris when I was six. She met him, married him, then died, all in twelve months. The turnaround left me with a stepfather who felt burdened with me, and a year later, a stepmother who detested me.

"Still cold?"

Shaking my head at Gus, I kept my mouth shut. The truth

was, I was too anxious to feel the cold now. We stopped in line at the door where a big man was stamping everyone's wrist and scanning everyone's license. He physically placed everyone's license on a scanner and copied them. They were keeping an electronic database of everyone who attended the club.

Waiting patiently, Gus grinned at us. "When he asks, you want a red stamp." Giving him a lascivious smile Lisa batted her eyelashes.

Listening as the bouncer asked the drunk guys in front of us if they wanted red or blue, I frowned at the lack of explanation. "What's the difference?"

Gus, yet again, studied me. "You know, no one has ever asked that question." Still failing to answer it, Gus stepped us forward letting Lisa hand over her license.

"Red," Lisa purred when asked. The bouncer winked at Gus and stamped a big red bat on Lisa's delicate wrist.

"Red or Blue?" The bouncer asked taking my license to scan.

"What if I don't like either color?"

The bouncer raised a brow at me. He, like Gus, tilted his head to study me. "She's different."

Side-eying me, Gus nodded. "I've noticed."

"Hmmm." The bouncer considered me. He took my wrist in his hand and turned up the delicate side to look at it. Brushing his thumb over my birthmark, his brow furrowed as he peered at my pale flesh and the purple mark that looked like intertwined hearts. "Looks like purple is your color." With another glance at my face, the bouncer opened a drawer and took out a different ink pad and stamp.

"A present for the birthday boy then." With a smirk, he stamped a black cursive **W** on my wrist while Gus chuckled.

"I'm sorry, what?" Glaring at them, I snatched my wrist back.

Both Gus and the bouncer stared at me. "You understood that?" Gus asked.

"Of course I did. I'm not stupid!"

"Mess?" Lisa looked confused. "When did you learn another language?"

Frowning at all of them, my eyes went back to Lisa. "You only had the one beer, right?"

Gus laughed, but it was a nervous laugh as he rounded us both up and headed inside. Exchanging a nervous look with the bouncer, Gus sobered as the bouncer picked up his phone while we walked inside. The heavy door slammed shut behind us, the noise reverberating through my body as if I was hollow and the sound of doom echoed inside me. It took everything in me not to turn around and run back out into the carpark looking for an exit.

Passing down a small dark passageway, we entered a large cavernous space. The roof was three stories high and consisted of gothic style arches that seemed carved into a natural rock ceiling. There were open areas for balconies on the upper levels, arching around the walls like the viewing booths at the old style theatres. All of them with their black curtains closed tonight.

Ignoring the music playing, I stood in awe of the room itself. It wasn't massive, possibly the size of my school gymnasium for floor space. One half of the room contained the dance floor and DJ. The other half held the bar, the long table of food, and some lounges and armchairs, on which, people were already getting tongue tied to each other.

Stopping at the edge of the dance floor, Gus smiled at us both. "Shall we dance?"

"You two go ahead. I'll get some food." Indicating the table, I stepped out of Gus's arm. Lisa mouthed thank you as Gus led her into the grinding throng of bodies. Slowly meandering my way to the food table, I took the path closest to the wall to avoid the crowds. Reaching out, I touched the stone look walls only to find they were stone. No one would bother duplicating the grit of touching earth for decoration, nor would you want to.

Above touch was the sense of earth. Taking a breath to stabilize as a pulse of balance flowed into my fingertips. With that one touch, I knew we were underground. Interestingly, the stone work soothed me a little. This was a place that had stood for a long time, that was used regularly, and that they intended to keep using. It's not the sort of work you do just to burn the place down to hide the mass genocide that took place inside like maybe a shed.

A sheer curtain hung behind the buffet table creating a semi-covered hallway between the table and the wall. A slight breeze stirred the curtains as a door opened behind them, a short woman emerging into the veiled corridor carrying a large platter of fruit. It was much too big for the small woman, and she nearly stumbled with it.

Catching the tray with one arm and her with the other, I helped her stand before I placed the fruit on the table. The woman looked at me with large black eyes, much too big for her face.

"Are you okay?"

She looked old enough to be my mother but only came up to my chest. Gazing around the room hesitantly, she then back to me. "Only the fruit is safe," she hissed, then dashed back through the door.

Frowning, I tucked my dark hair back behind my ear. "Okay...." Talk about weird encounters.

Looking over the table, I browsed the selections of cupcakes, various cheesecakes, fresh fruit, and cream at one end. At the other was steaming hot food that looked direct from a Yum Cha restaurant. Various dumplings, pork buns, and other steamed foods. It smelled and looked delicious. Watching others walk up to grab food, I eagerly waited for them to make a selection. Starving, my stomach vocalized how much it needed sustenance. Licking my lips, I was already making my selection in my mind, watching the others step to the side with their plates full. Finally my turn, I placed a pork bun on my plate.

"Yum, this is so good," murmured the guy who had gone before me. Looking his way, I froze. He was smiling and happy, but as he ate, the food in his hand changed to look rotten. Maggots squirmed over the meat inside, blood dripped down his wrist, and the smell was rotten eggs. Peering at the man's face, I realized I was wrong, he was a boy. He looked to be a year younger than my eighteen, and by the looks of his unwashed jeans and shirt, also homeless. Blood dribbled down his chin as meat juices would, and I watched a maggot squirm free of his lips on the blood.

Vomiting in my mouth, I dropped my plate on the table and ran to the bathroom just past the buffet table. Just making it into a stall, I puked bile. I hadn't eaten in twenty-four hours, so there was no food to vomit, but my body was going to try.

"Are you okay?"

Peering over my shoulder, I saw a stunning woman, shadows swirling around her. "Yeah, just reacted to a bad smell." I was going nuts, surely.

With a smug smile growing on her face, the woman walked forward grabbing my wrist. "Red or blue?"

"Black!" Snatching my wrist back, the woman frowned, her shadows howled around her, and for a moment, the beauty faded to expose gaunt, red-eyed paleness, like she was covered in talc with purple markings like tribal tattoos up her arms.

'Glamor is free.'

When I blinked, she was beautiful again. Examing the mark on my wrist, the woman snarled and stormed away from me. Flopping over the toilet bowl momentarily, I waited for the energy to hoist myself up. The needed to get out of here got me to my feet. Washing my face at the basin, I stared back at my turquoise eyes. My stepmother used to call them unholy demonic eyes, but then again, she considered me a slut's offspring or a fatherless bitch.

Stripping off my jacket, I looked myself over. Unable to ever get a tan, my skin was too pale. With how easily you could see my veins, I was basically translucent. My breasts were a bit more than a handful, then again, I had small hands, so maybe they were the average person's handful. My legs were long and gangly. The short dress I was wearing made them look even longer. The dress was Lisa's, I only owned two pairs of jeans, a couple of shirts, and a jumper.

My step-mother didn't believe in spending money on me for anything but the necesseties. Hell, she'd only bought me a bra because the school I'd been at complained that it was improper for a girl of fourteen not to own one. So I got one and had to wash it by hand every night. The underwear I was currently wearing was a five finger discount, the heels were left behind after a university party. At least my childhood prepared me for living in the university boiler room.

There were rich men here tonight. Lisa planned to try and

get herself a sugar daddy, that was always her plan to get her life back on track. Maybe I should consider it. Assessing my reflection, I shook my head. "Not a chance. You're a mess, and no one wants you."

Nothing about me was going to score me a sugar daddy, not when there were natural beauties like Lisa out there. Scowling at myself for even considering it, I grabbed my jacket and went back out to the nightclub. Still hungry, I remembered the lady saying only the fruit was safe, so I decided to give it a try. If it sprouted maggots and blood, I was out of here.

Grabbing a clean plate from the Buffett, I went for the fruit that everyone was avoiding. After piling my plate high, I retreated behind the sheer curtain and held up the wall while I ate. Nothing gross happened with the fruit, though, I deliberately avoided watching other people eat, focusing entirely on the food I was holding. When my plate was empty and my stomach satisfied, I focused on the dance floor.

Lisa and Gus were dancing like they were in the bedroom. Their hands and mouths all over each other. If it weren't for the clothes, it would be porn. Sighing, I hoped she found her sugar daddy. She'd been through worse than me and had more strength then I could ever possess. She deserved happiness.

"Happy Birthday, Ty!"

My focus shifted back to the buffet table to a group nearby. My breath caught in my throat. The man called Ty that everyone was congratulating was gorgeous. Truly gorgeous. No shadows were swirling around him to stop me seeing the detail. This man with his pale skin, tall, slender build and his sharp bone structure, was appealing in a way no other man had been for me before.

Appearing to be late-twenties, he was dressed all in black.

Black shiny slacks, black shiny collard shirt, a black jacquard jacket and matching tie. He walked with a black walking cane, though, he didn't use it for support, and he walked like he owned the place.

"Nice party you've thrown," the man he'd just murmured something too praised. The owner. That's what Gus had said. It was the owner's birthday. This man, Ty, was the owner.

My wrist itched. Looking down, a small purple glow was emitting from the black ink stamped on my wrist. Confused, I looked up to watch Ty prowl the buffet, but not even considering the food. He was focused on the faces of the females filling their plates and stomachs. By the looks of them, they were homeless too.

My wrist burned as Ty came parallel with me, only the curtain and buffet separating us. Ty glanced at me. His deep-set dark eyes made darker by the shadow of his brow. The overhead light threw a shadow on his high cheekbones, making him look positively gorgeous and dangerous all at once.

He observed me between one step and the next. My wrist pulsed with the purple light from the ink burning into my flesh. Grimacing from the pain, I closed my eyes and bit my lip to stop from crying out. Suddenly, the pain was gone. Looking up, so was the owner.

'A present for the birthday boy then.'

Fear pounded in my heart. The cursive ***W*** was no longer a stamp on my wrist, but a black and purple tattoo, etched permanently into my flesh.

Read Of Shadow and Light

ABOUT THE AUTHOR

Ebony lives in Sydney, Australia, with her husband, daughter, and six cats. She loves to read fantasy, thrillers, and paranormal romance, spending most of her free time with her nose in a book or writing.

Having always possessed an over-active imagination she spent her younger years regaling friends with fantastic stories, holding her audience captive with the passion and suspense of her characters plights.

Now in adulthood she has numerous published works and shows no signs of stopping her imagination from spreading across as many pages as it can find.

If you'd like to follow Ebony or simply say hi you can find her here:
Website: http://ebonyolson.com/

facebook.com/EbonyOlson.Author

twitter.com/Ebony_Olson

instagram.com/ebony_olson

amazon.com/author/ebonyolson

bookbub.com/authors/Ebony_Olson

goodreads.com/Ebony_Olson